# A HOME FOR CHRISTMAS

## An Angel Ridge Novel

## Deborah Grace Staley

# CHIVERS

British Library Cataloguing in Publication Data available

This Large Print edition published by AudioGO Ltd, Bath, 2012.
Published by arrangement with Belle Books Inc.

U.K. Hardcover    ISBN   978 1 4084 7784 7
U.K. Softcover    ISBN   978 1 4084 7785 4

Printed and bound in Great Britain by
MPG Books Group Limited

For my husband, Fred Staley,
whose love has given my heart a home.

# ACKNOWLEDGMENTS

To my girlfriends who keep me sane and grounded: Charis Wolfe, Janene Satterfield, Kim Thompson, Beth Catchot, Beth Eason, Patty Harrison, and Teressa Gregory. I don't know what I'd do without you! For Susan Sipal. Your vision and focus make the stories so much stronger. You're the best! For Ruth and Keith Law, my thanks for allowing Blake to live in your house. Last, but certainly not least, for the readers who have embraced this series, your enthusiasm keeps me writing.

# WELCOME

Hi, y'all. Excuse me a sec, would ya?

"Hey, boys. Come on in and have a seat. I'll be right with you."

"No hurry, Dix. Take your time."

Sorry about that. Lunchtime's busy around here, but I've always got time for you newcomers, and you return visitors, too. Welcome to Angel Ridge! Dixie Ferguson's the name. As you can see, I run Ferguson's Diner. You won't find better food or service in any fancy-schmancy restaurant you'd care to compare us with. I hear tell folks pay good money for insects, toads, and crawdads in some of them places. Crazy. Anyway, let me tell you a bit about the place I've called home for most of my life.

Angel Ridge. Population three hundred forty-three — soon to be three hundred forty-*four* seein' as how Sally Crawford's expectin' any day now. Yeah, Angel Ridge is

9

a fine place to put down roots and raise a family.

It was established along the Little Tennessee River in 1785. In the early days, its first families — the McKays, the Wallaces, the Houstons, the Jonses, and the Craigs — built plantations along the river. Well, all except for the Craigs. They were traders and craftsmen. Men of commerce, if you will. Meanwhile, the town developed above the river on a high ridge.

In the early 1970s, the Flood Control Board bought up all the property along the river so they could put in a dam. Some folks say they was forced out of their homes, and I guess they were. So those rich folks down in the valley moved up to the ridge with everyone else. Course they built elaborate Victorian mansions such as this quaint little town had never seen. Stick out like a sore thumb if you ask me, but I digress.

Most of the families I mentioned earlier are still around. You'll recognize their names on the businesses along Main Street. These folks are hardy people. Why, in all the time they've lived here, they've endured Indian attacks, floods, divided loyalties in the Civil War, and yes, even feuds. The older folks are still marked by the hardships of the past. I suppose you could call 'em old-fashioned, but don't count my generation out. We're makin' our mark, too. We can respect the past, but you know, we gotta make our own way in this old town.

Well, enough with the history lesson. I don't want to bore you and I can see you're anxious to get on with your visit. You've picked a fine time to visit our town. Christmastime . . . I just love it. We dress everything up with real greenery here. No shiny tinsel-shaped bells or flashing snowflakes hanging from our lampposts. Our gasburning street lamps decorated with red velvet bows from the town florist do just fine.

If you want to see displays of the electric variety, several of the old Victorians up on Ridge Road really do it up right. Particularly my brother's, Blake Ferguson's place. Not that I'm prejudiced or anything.

Ah, yes. This is what you could call an enchanted time in Angel Ridge. A time of miracles. It's also when folks feel loss and loneliness more than any other time of the year.

I guess you could say this is a story about loneliness and figuring out where you belong. A heartwarming story about a hometown boy and a city girl. Yep, I've got a feelin' that this year a couple of lonely

11

hearts will find something they've been waitin' a long time for. Who knows? If they open themselves up to the magic of Christmas and our resident angels, their hearts might just find a home.

So have yourself a cup of cheer, sit back, and enjoy your time in Angel Ridge.

# CHAPTER 1

They say you can never go home.

Janice Thornton glided up to the curb in front of the old two-story Victorian and killed the engine. It looked much the same — gingerbread trim in the eaves, wide wraparound porch with wicker furniture. The house was huge, but in the short time she'd spent here as a child, it had felt cozy to her.

Sitting here looking at it through adult eyes, she realized the appeal had never been the house itself, but the home her grandparents had made in it. Their house had been her ideal of what a home should be. A home she'd longed for as a child. A home she'd never had with her own parents.

Janice slid her sunglasses off and laid them in the empty passenger seat next to her. She always got sentimental around the holidays. She didn't know why. Her formative years had been spent at exclusive boarding schools. Christmases always involved a trip, either with her parents, or more often, with school friends. Each year, her grandmother had invited her to spend Christmas break in Angel Ridge, but her mother wouldn't hear of such a thing. She'd always been embarrassed by her humble roots and didn't want her daughter revisiting them.

Janice hadn't been in Angel Ridge, Tennessee since she'd gone behind her parents' backs and borrowed a friend's car when she was sixteen to come during her spring break. It hadn't changed much. Tall, old houses lined one side of a street that ran high above the Tellassee River, with church steeples just visible a few blocks over. It was a sleepy little town that time seemed to have forgotten, but for some reason, it burned in Janice's memory like a warm, inviting fire on a cold winter morning.

A movement in her peripheral vision made her refocus on the old Victorian. She noticed that a man had appeared from behind the house carrying a ladder. The sun glinted off a pile of tangled Christmas lights, bunched near the steps of the porch, drawing her attention. Janice smiled. She was glad to see that this man, whoever he was, continued her grandfather's tradition of decking the house out in grand style for Christmas.

The man leaned the ladder against the house. As he turned toward the mound of lights, he noticed her and smiled. Her breath caught and hung inside her chest. It was an easy smile, full of good humor that enticed a person to come sit a spell on the porch and enjoy the unseasonably warm, late autumn sunshine.

Tall and lean with whipcord muscles, he wore faded and well-worn jeans with a T-shirt that looked like it had once been black, but now was more a soft charcoal dotted with paint stains. A tan leather tool belt slung low across his narrow hips. A lock of thick, dark hair fell across his tanned forehead as he bent to retrieve the lights.

Janice shifted and the leather seat creaked. A sheen of sweat misted her forehead, and she cracked the window.

What must the home's owner be thinking? But he acted as if seeing a strange woman in a new, silver BMW parked outside his house was an every Saturday morning occurrence. He turned, and without giving her a second glance, started up the ladder. Stopping about eight rungs up, he leaned to his right, toward one of the bay windows on the ground floor.

Shifting the lights to his other hand, he reached out to pull at something above the window. He teetered. One foot went up in the air as he tried to shift back to find his balance. But the ladder tipped sideways with the movement, and Janice watched in horrified disbelief as he began to fall.

Years of medical school, emergency room rotations, residency, and private practice had honed her instincts so that she didn't even give it a conscious thought. She was out of her car and at his side almost before he hit the boxwoods and rolled to the ground.

"Ah, jeez . . ." he groaned.

Janice had already clicked into professional mode. "Don't worry, I'm a doctor. Try not to move." She ran her hands down his arms, checking for broken bones. "Where does it hurt?"

The man chuckled. It was a low rumble that had a crazy effect on her. And that smile . . . it should be registered as a lethal weapon.

"If I said everywhere, would you keep doing that?"

Her hands froze on his hard, muscled thigh. *Get a grip,* she told herself. The man had fallen at least ten feet. He needed to be checked out. Thoroughly. She gave him what she hoped was a look that conveyed that this was a serious matter and continued down his leg. Firm muscles contracted and bunched beneath the soft, nearly threadbare denim.

Janice cleared her throat and tried to speak around the knot that had formed there. "That was quite a fall. Does anything feel broken? Strained? Any pain at all?"

The man tried to sit up, but she restrained him with a firm hand at his shoulder. "You really shouldn't move."

"Dr., *um* . . ."

"Thornton. Janice Thornton."

"Dr. Thornton, I'm fine. Really," he insisted, grabbing her hand as she began checking his other leg. "I'd have to fall further than that to hurt anything other than my pride."

Janice frowned. She was almost completely distracted by the crinkles at the corners of his eyes that said a smile came easy to him, but she knew that often one could have injuries that didn't present with pain after a fall like that. She turned her attention to his head. "You could have a concussion."

She sank her fingers into his thick, dark hair at the place where a nearly indiscernible sprinkling of gray fanned out from his temples. His scalp felt warm, and her fingers tingled as she checked for knots. She faltered when she looked into his eyes. Fringed

17

by incredibly long, inky eyelashes, they were a striking silvery blue that stood out against the framing of his dark hair and skin.

He propped himself up on one elbow so that his torso almost touched hers. When she felt his breath, warm and enticing against her cheek, she stopped breathing. He reached out to touch her face, but Janice sat back on her heels.

"There doesn't seem to be any knots. No bruising or contusions." She couldn't stop herself from removing a sprig of rich, green boxwood leaves from his hair. "*Um,* what about your neck? Does it hurt?"

Before he could answer, she slid her fingers around to the back of his neck and grasped his chin with her free hand. He had a strong jaw. She'd always been a sucker for guys with strong jaws. "Gently," she whispered, as she turned his head from one side to the other. "Any pain?"

She felt a sensual web forming around them, powerless to extricate herself from its seductive weave. Janice watched in fascination as the Adam's apple bobbed in the tanned column of his throat.

He wrapped a big, callused hand around her wrist and said, "I wish, because despite the fact that I know your interest here is purely professional, I'm enjoying having your hands on me . . . too much." He turned his head then, and with his fascinating mouth slightly opened, pressed a warm kiss against the pulse point at her wrist.

She stood and shoved both hands into her pockets.

He stood as well, immediately contrite. "I'm sorry. I — I don't know what got into me."

Ignoring that and the tingling spot on her wrist that his lips had just touched, she said, "You're lucky those boxwoods broke your fall. You could have been seriously injured."

A lopsided grin lent his chiseled features a boyish charm. "Happens all the time in my line of work."

"What would that be?" Janice found herself asking.

"I'm a carpenter, but I make a living as a contractor."

"I see."

He was the most physically appealing man she'd met in . . . Well, she'd never felt this sort of sudden, intense elemental attraction. He also had her feeling off-balance. She couldn't remember not being in control of a situation since she'd reached adulthood.

He nodded towards her car. "I thought when I saw you sitting over there that you must be an insurance salesman. They like to make their rounds on Saturday mornings when folks are usually home."

She felt herself blushing. She couldn't remember the last time she'd blushed either. "I hope you don't mind. I have an appointment in Angel Ridge later today. I came early because I wanted to see this house. My grandparents used to live here."

He rested his hands lightly on his hips. "No kidding? The Prescotts were your grandparents?"

"Yes."

"Really? Man," he said softly, "it's been a while since they passed on."

"Yes." She inclined her chin and sucked in a deep breath. The thought of never seeing them again still brought pain, even after all these years.

"Oh, I'm sorry." He reached out and gently squeezed her shoulder. "I could have handled that better. Guess the fall addled my good sense." He smiled.

She smiled, too, to put him at ease. "Did you know them?"

"No. We were just passing acquaintances. I grew up just outside of town, so I didn't know the folks up here too well."

She nodded her understanding. "Well, I don't want to keep you." She took a couple of steps back. "Be careful on that ladder," she called over her shoulder as she retraced her steps to her car.

"Wait. Why don't you stay awhile? I mean, you drove all this way."

Turning, she squinted into the bright morning sun to look at him.

"That is, I'm guessing you drove a long way."

"I drove in from Knoxville," she confirmed, "but I don't want to trouble you. I can see you're busy."

He took a step forward. "You live in a house there?"

Janice frowned. What did her living arrangements have to do with anything? "I live in a condominium," she heard herself saying.

"See there," he said. "You won't get a chance to hang lights at your place unless you do it from the inside. I bet it's in one of those big high rise complexes."

"Yes." Her smile widened.

He got a mock serious look on his face then. "Everyone should get a chance to help hang out Christmas lights, don't you think? It just isn't Christmas without 'em. And besides, I'd like to hear about your grandparents. Your memories of the place must be strong to bring you back here after all these years."

She looked up at the house, remembering. "Yes." As a little girl, Janice had desperately wanted to meet the grandparents who'd cared for her despite the fact they'd never met her.

"Good. So, you'll stay."

It wasn't a question. He gathered up a jumbled mass of lights and held them out to her. "Think you could straighten this out?"

Blake gave the woman standing on his front lawn a sideways glance as he busied himself righting the ladder. She was the most beautiful thing he'd ever seen. A cool, green-eyed blonde wearing expensive dark slacks, leather loafers, and some kind of a silky, loose white blouse that shimmered in the soft breeze and caught his imagination, starting all kinds of forbidden fantasies spinning around in his head.

She laughed. "Don't you think we should be properly introduced first?"

"Oh, sorry. Blake Ferguson."

He held out a hand, and she shifted the lights to her other arm so she could extend hers to him.

"Janice Thornton."

"It's a pleasure," he said, and meant it. It was pure pleasure standing there holding her soft hand in his. He wondered what her hair would look like hanging loose around her shoulders instead of pulled back in a long ponytail . . . She gave a gentle tug, and he reluctantly released her hand.

She looked at the tangled mess in her hands. "I don't know how to break this to you, but I'm not a surgeon."

Blake chuckled. "You'll manage. Feel free to go sit on the steps while you work at it. Would you like something to drink?"

"No, thank you. I'm fine."

Such a proper response. Unless he'd missed something, she hadn't been feeling so proper a few moments ago. The doctor had been good and rattled. He was still feeling a little rattled himself with her sitting at least twenty feet away.

"So, tell me," he began as he repositioned the ladder and started back up it, "has the place changed much over the years?"

"Not a lot. I remember there was always paint peeling somewhere on the house. My grandfather seemed to continually be scraping or painting a portion of the place. It was yellow then instead of white. The color of sunshine," she said softly as she looked up at it.

He'd go out tomorrow and buy yellow paint if it would make her happy. There was just something about her. She had a melancholy, faraway expression that made her seem so . . . sad. She must really miss her grandparents. Still, with them being gone so long, he wondered what had brought her back to their home after so many years.

"But the yard was always immaculate." She touched the boxwoods near where she sat with the tips of her fingers. "Grandmother loved planting flowers and trimming the bushes." She looked up, "And those trees, they seemed perfectly round. I think they must have had men come every spring to prune so they'd stay that way."

"Did you come here often?" He righted the hook he'd been trying to reach earlier.

"Not as often as I would have liked."

She had spoken so softy, he barely heard the words before she bent to the task before her.

"You know, I think they make plastic things to wrap lights around so that they don't get in this kind of mess."

"Yeah, but that sucks the fun right out of it, don't you think?"

She smiled up at him. "I don't know. I've never helped put up Christmas lights."

"Come on. You mean your folks didn't decorate for Christmas?"

She shook her head. "Not with outdoor lights. My mother thought it was tasteless."

"But you helped decorate the tree, right?"

She shook her head again. "Mother had a decorator do the tree. That is, when we spent Christmas at home. Otherwise, she wouldn't even bother with one."

"Where'd you grow up?" he asked, trying hard to keep disbelief from lacing his words.

"My parents had a home in Connecticut, but I didn't spend much time there."

Blake scratched his head, trying to follow. "Why not?"

"I lived at boarding schools."

Why would anyone want to send their child off to live in boarding schools? "But you came home for the holidays, right?"

"Sometimes."

"I see." A picture formed in his mind of her as a little girl. A princess locked away in an ivory tower who wasn't allowed to play or do any of the fun, traditional things that made holidays special.

"What about here? Didn't you ever come here for Christmas?"

"I did once. Mother had planned a trip to Switzerland, but I got sick and couldn't go. So, she sent me here to stay with Grandmother and Grandfather because I begged her to let me come. Since she couldn't find a nurse to take care of me on such short notice with it being the holidays, she agreed." She laughed. "Getting sick that year turned out to be one of the best things that ever happened to me."

"What was it like?"

Her face lit up, and he was glad to see that she had at least one happy Christmas stored in her memory. "There were lights everywhere. All around the house, in the bushes, along the walk. Inside," she pointed, "a Christmas tree stood in that bay window. Grandfather cut it himself and brought it in from the woods at the edge of town. The tall pines, I think he called it. Anyway, some of the branches had fallen off from where he'd dragged it through town and the shape wasn't perfect, not like the trees Mother had. But I thought it was beautiful.

"Grandmother made popcorn and taught me how to make a garland out of it. She let me help her bake shaped cookies and decorate them. And after I went to bed on Christmas Eve, she wrapped the presents herself and put them under the tree."

Sounded like typical things families did at Christmas. He got the feeling nothing about her upbringing had been typical.

Blake studied her more closely then. The wistful look on her face went straight to his heart, creating an irrational yearning to give her fifty or so Christmases like that one she'd had with her grandparents. The thought should have scared him senseless. After all, he knew nothing about her. But instead, for some reason, it just felt . . . right.

"She knitted me a green scarf. I thought it was the most wonderful gift I'd ever received."

The softness playing about her mouth vanished, replaced by an affected look of indifference. "Mother wouldn't allow me to wear it. She said it was the ugliest thing she'd ever seen. When we arrived back at home, she took it from me and threw it away."

"That's cruel!" The words were out before he could stop them.

A slight smile lifted the corner of her luscious mouth. "I sneaked out that night and rummaged through the garbage until I found it. I took it up to my bathroom, washed it out, and hid it in my closet to dry. I still have it."

"Good for you."

"Finished."

He hadn't noticed that while she spoke, she had arranged the lights she'd been untangling into a neat circle at her feet. "Well, there's plenty more where that came from." He tipped his head toward the pile in front of the bay window.

She stared at it a moment, considering.

"Or you could string those you just did around those bushes there in front of the porch."

"I don't know how," she admitted.

Finished with his task, he backed down the ladder and said, "I'll let you in on the secret of putting out Christmas lights if you promise you won't tell anyone."

She stood as he approached. "Cross my heart."

He looked over his shoulder as if making sure no one eavesdropped on the quiet, tree-lined street. "There's no real method to it. You just throw 'em on there, plug 'em in, then spread 'em out so the lights aren't too bunched up in any one spot."

She nodded, a mock-serious look etching her lovely features. "I had no idea."

He bent to pick up the lights at her feet then took her hand and led her to the box-woods. "Well, it's top secret. If you tell anyone, I'll have to shoot you."

Janice laughed and smiled up at him. He now knew how it felt to be pole-axed. Lord, she was stunning.

With fingers that felt like five thumbs, he grabbed the plug at the end of the lights and said, "We'll drop this here in back so it'll be easy to get to."

"Where's your family?" she asked as she, despite his instructions, methodically wrapped the lights around the first bush.

He frowned. "In their homes doing the kind of stuff families do on Saturdays, I guess."

"Oh." She seemed surprised. "You live here alone?"

"Yep. Just me and the mice." He smiled. "They're too smart for traps. I'm in desperate need of a cat."

"It's an awfully large place for just one person."

He leaned an arm against the porch railing as he watched her move to the next bush. "Well, I hope to fill it up with about half a dozen kids some day."

There was that surprised look again, except this one held an element of shock. "Do you have someone lined up to supply those for you? Or were you planning to adopt?"

"Well," he rubbed the stubble lining his chin wishing he'd shaved, "I'd like to fall head over heels in love first. Then get married. You know, manage it the old-fashioned way."

She didn't comment or look up at him, and he wondered . . . "How 'bout you? Do you have kids?"

29

"No."

He wanted to ask about a husband, but figured that would be too forward. She didn't wear a wedding band or engagement ring. That was encouraging, but she could be one of those modern types who didn't go for the sort of relationship where the woman wore her man's ring and took his name.

"I guess being a doctor keeps you pretty busy." Probably too busy for a relationship of any kind. He thought of Doc Prescott, the town's doctor. He'd never married. Doctors had a lot of demands on their time.

"Yes," she agreed, still working at the lights.

"What's your specialty?"

"I'm an internist. Finished."

He'd been watching her face again and not paying any attention to her task. "Great." He straightened away from the railing. "Let's plug 'em in."

Stepping up onto the porch, he retrieved a long, green extension cord, plugged it into a receptacle, and unwound it as he carried it down to the bushes. He found the end of the cord and plugged in the lights. The miniature, multicolored bulbs twinkled against the dark green bushes.

Janice's smile told him she was pleased

with her effort. "Perfect," Blake confirmed.

"Can I do those over there, too?" She pointed to the bushes across the sidewalk.

"Sure. Use the lights in that pile."

She retrieved the lights and primly sat on the steps untangling them as she had before. He shook his head. She'd probably never slumped a day in her life. He left her to it as he concentrated on getting the lights up on the house. Plain white lights in strings around the windows and icicle lights in the eaves. His progress was admittedly slowed by frequent glances in his guest's direction.

After they'd been working for some time, he noticed that Janice had allowed herself free rein in the placement of the lights. She'd finished the bushes and had started looping some of the strands with large multicolored bulbs around the porch railing. He didn't mind, but wondered if she was putting lights in places she remembered seeing them when she was a kid.

A car stopped in front the house, and he turned from watching Janice to see who it was. *Great.* Just what he needed. His brother, Cory. Did the guy have radar or what? He stepped out of his red Mercedes sports coupe, dripping designer clothes and pricey cologne.

"Hey, big brother. I see the annual day

after Thanksgiving hanging of the lights is under way. Who's your charming assistant?"

*Here we go,* Blake thought. He backed down the ladder and made the introductions when he reached the bottom. "This is Dr. Janice Thornton. Janice, this is my brother, Cory Ferguson."

Cory took Janice's hand and held it entirely too long. "A doctor. Well, now, they sure do make them younger and prettier these days, don't they?"

Blake watched fascinated as Janice pulled her hand away from Cory's and rubbed her palm down her thigh as if trying to remove the feel of him. Blake smiled. He couldn't remember ever meeting a woman who wasn't affected by his brother's good looks and charm.

"What are you doing in town, Cory? I thought you were skiing this weekend."

"Yes, well, that was the plan." He eyed Janice like a choice piece of meat at the butcher shop. "Bebe's a little green around the gills and running me ragged fetching things for her. I'm thinking about hiring a nurse."

Wife number four was pregnant with his brother's first child. A child was the greatest gift a woman could give a man, but to Cory, it was just an inconvenience.

32

"You stop by for a reason, Cory? Or is this just a social call?"

Janice eyed the two men with open curiosity.

"Mom and Dad asked me to come by today so we could discuss their Will." Cory turned to Janice.

Here it comes, Blake thought. *The pronouncement.*

"I'm an attorney."

Janice didn't look particularly impressed. Blake's smile widened.

"So, I was driving by and saw you out here. I just thought I'd stop and say hello."

Blake nodded. If Cory was fishing for an invitation to stay, he was doomed to disappointment.

They all stood looking at each other for an awkward moment.

"Well," Cory finally said, "guess I'll get on out to the farm."

"Give Mom my best. Remind her I'll be by in the morning to help her with her decorations."

"Sure. A pleasure to meet you, Dr. Thornton."

Janice nodded, but didn't offer him her hand. Instead she slipped it into her pocket.

"Later, Bro."

Cory slapped him on the shoulder and

then turned to stroll back to his car. Janice and Blake watched until he pulled away from the curb.

"How many siblings do you have?" Janice asked.

"Five. I'm number three. Cory is number four."

"He looks much older than you," Janice commented.

He stood a little straighter at hearing her compliment. "There's only thirteen months between us. Mom had us all right together, except for my baby sister. She was a late-life surprise after all us boys."

"Your mother must be an exceptional woman."

He smiled down into Janice's upturned face. "She's pretty amazing. How 'bout some lunch?"

Janice glanced at her watch. "Oh, I didn't realize how late it was getting. I'd better be going. I have that appointment to get to, then I should call the hospital. I may need to do rounds later."

"On a holiday weekend?"

"Someone has to do it, and since I don't have a family, I feel sort of obligated to let my partners spend time with theirs."

Confirmation. No husband. "That's mighty considerate of you."

She shrugged and just stood there, making no movement toward her car. Despite her words, she didn't seem in a hurry to leave.

"Maybe you could come back later. I'd hate for you to miss the lighting ceremony after all the hard work you've done. I'm going to be finished in record time, thanks to you."

She looked up at the house, shielding her eyes from the sun. She wanted to. He could see it in her eyes and in the way she nibbled on her full, lower lip.

"I could make dinner." Now where had that come from? He should just let her get in her car and drive away. He didn't know much about her, but if he would just think rationally, he'd realize he knew more than enough. She was a city girl. She lived a couple of hours away. She had a demanding, time-consuming job. All that added up to no time for a relationship, especially with someone who enjoyed the laid back, slower pace of a small town. He was at a point in his life when he didn't want or need to waste time on a dead-end relationship based solely on attraction.

But he could dream. He hoped she was tempted. If circumstances were different, he wouldn't mind having the chance to get to know her a little better. To explore the feelings she evoked in him.

"I'm on call. I shouldn't be so far from the hospital."

Yet she'd spent the entire morning with him, hanging lights. He wondered again what had brought her here. It must have been something pretty compelling to pull her away from work when she was on call. Who in Angel Ridge would be important enough for her to drive all this way?

"It was a pleasure meeting you."

She looked up at him then. Her slow smile fired his already overwrought senses.

"Likewise."

She turned to walk away, and he followed, appreciating the view. Her pants hugged her curves in all the right places. When they reached her car, he opened the door for her. She turned and, with her hand beside his on the top of the door, said,

"Thank you for letting me help with the lights. I really enjoyed being here again."

"Come back by any time." As the words left his mouth, he told himself that he'd made the offer strictly because of her family connection to the place.

"Thank you."

She got into the car and turned the key in the ignition. When the engine purred to life, he shut the door and watched her drive away, unsure if he'd ever see her again. He returned to the task of hanging the lights, but his joy in it had gone with his unexpected visitor.

has shut the door and wrapped her loose-ly, unsure if I'd ever see her again. He promised to do his best during that eight-

# CHAPTER 2

"Here you are. Come in, come in."

The elderly man who met Janice at the door of his home-office did not jog one memory in her, despite the fact that he was her great uncle.

She took his hand and kissed his cheek above a downy white beard. "Hello, Uncle Charles."

"My, you've grown into a beautiful woman, Janice. I must say, you look just like your mother."

Janice wrinkled her nose, hating the comparison, but she supposed it was inevitable. He, on the other hand, reminded her pleasantly of her grandfather. Just looking at him brought another rush of warm memories to the surface. Memories of just-baked cookies and milk and crawling up into his lap and being rocked to sleep. . . .

"Come and have a seat in the back parlor."

With the front of the old Victorian serving

as waiting room and patient examination rooms, Charles Prescott kept an office and comfortable sitting room in the back for his private use. Funny, she couldn't ever remember visiting Angel Ridge's only doctor for either professional or personal reasons. Surely she must have seen him the Christmas she'd been sick and had stayed with her grandparents.

"It's good of you to come out here on a holiday weekend." He indicated a pairing of wing chairs with a sweep of his hand, and they both sat.

"I must admit, I was intrigued by your call and a bit curious. May I be honest with you, Uncle Charles?"

"Please."

Best to begin diplomatically. "It's been years since I've visited Angel Ridge, and honestly, I don't remember ever meeting you." She didn't mention that her mother had never spoken of him.

"I'm not surprised. I saw you just once when you were a little thing, even though your grandfather was my brother. You had a high temperature and were sleeping fretfully when I came by. Your mother had left you with Bill and Edna while she went off to Europe or some such thing."

"That's my mother." She'd also been two

39

days late picking her up from school that year because of a shopping trip to New York.

"I left a prescription that seemed to help. We never did figure out the source of your infection, but you were better by Christmas. Probably the flu."

"Were you there? At Christmas, I mean?"

"Oh, sure. Don't you remember?" He chuckled merrily. "You thought I was Santa himself."

"That was you?"

The kind, older man nodded, still laughing.

"I thought you *were* Santa." Janice laughed as well.

"I'm sorry I wasn't able to spend more time with you that Christmas." He rubbed his beard. "A lot of folks were sick that season. The other couple of times you visited Bill and Edna, I think I only managed to have dinner with you once. The doctor's life. You understand."

"I do." Too well. She didn't remember that dinner either. "I'm sorry I never got to know you, Uncle Charles."

"Don't worry about that now, dear." He leaned over and patted her hand. "I'm aware that your mother had little use for her family after she moved away and married your father."

40

"I always wondered why she hated Angel Ridge so much. Do you know what happened? Did she have a falling out with Grandfather and Grandmother?"

He removed his round, wire-rimmed glasses and polished them with a crisp, white handkerchief. "Your mother, she was a beautiful girl. Folks around town gave her anything she wanted, and, well, she was more than a little spoiled by all the attention. She won every local beauty pageant there was: Homecoming Queen, Snow Ball Queen, County Fair Queen. When she told her parents she wanted to go to Knoxville on a school night to be in the Miss Knoxville pageant, they told her *no.*

"Well, Dotty wasn't accustomed to the negative response. So, she sneaked out her window and went on anyway. Won the thing, too.

"When they read about it in the paper, Bill and Edna had a fit and grounded her. Wouldn't let her go on to the state competition. That made an awful anger stew inside your mother. As soon as she turned eighteen, she took the first bus out of town and went to New York City."

"Why did she go there?"

"To become a model or an actress, I suppose. We didn't hear much from her after she left. Broke Bill and Edna's heart."

"That's where she met my father." And became the quintessential trophy wife; the proper hostess who kept his house in order and looked good on his arm. Beyond that, they hardly ever saw each other, which seemed to suit them both.

"I enjoyed the time I had with my grandparents here. I wish I could have come more often, but my mother wouldn't allow it."

He leaned toward her. "They loved having you. They knew you would have come more often if you could. Your letters meant a lot to them."

Janice stared at her hands. "They always wrote back." She had kept their letters all these years, storing them in plastic boxes.

He eased back in his leather wing chair and said, "I don't know who was more pleased when we learned that you wanted to become a doctor. Them or me."

Surprised, Janice said, "I wasn't aware that . . ."

"That I had kept tabs on what you've been doing?"

"Yes."

"I didn't have children of my own. Too busy taking care of other folks' kids, I suppose. Bill and Edna shared your letters with me. I hope you don't mind."

"No, of course not."

He nodded and smiled. "I can't tell you how happy I was when they told me my only living descendant had chosen the medical profession as a career."

"I'm not your *only* descendant. There's Mother."

"Yes, well, she'd never claim the relation. But you, now you're another story."

He tapped his fingers against the armrest of his wing chair, then stroked his beard. A mantel clock ticked loudly in the quiet room, but the silence wasn't at all unpleasant. Janice could tell he was drinking her in as much as she was him. He removed his glasses and leaned forward, propping his arms on his legs. "My colleagues up in Knoxville tell me you're a fine physician. I'm so proud of you, Janice."

"Thank you." His praise gave her a warm feeling. Her parents had never told her they were proud of her.

"I'll come right to the point. I'm not gettin' any younger. I want to turn my practice over to you."

Janice blinked and straightened in her chair. She couldn't have been more surprised by his pronouncement.

"I know this is kind of sudden, but I've given it a lot of thought. Folks around here don't cotton to outsiders, so it helps that you're a Prescott." He paused a moment to let that sink in. "I wouldn't just quit and throw you in cold. I'd work with you for as long as you want, or at least until everyone becomes acquainted with you. Then after that, I'd come in a couple of days a week. I'd say you'd be fine to go it alone in no time at all."

"But I'm a partner in a large medical group in Knoxville. I have a full case load."

He leaned forward and gave her an honest look that demanded an honest reply. "Yes, but tell me, dear. Are you happy there or is something missing?"

Janice looked away, unable to reply. There'd been something missing for as long as she could remember. It was part of the reason she was taking some time off at Christmas.

"You belong here, Janice."

She had never belonged anywhere, but she'd managed to carve out a life for herself despite the fact. It might not be perfect, but it was hers. She loved her work. People depended on her. Needed her.

"Now, I don't expect you to start next week. Take until Christmas to give it some thought, then if you see your way clear, you could begin at the first of the year."

The first of the year! There was no way she could leave a thriving medical practice in the middle of winter. She hated to disappoint the man, but she had to be honest with him. "Uncle Charles, I'm flattered by your offer, more so by the confidence you have in me, but I can't just pull up roots and start over now. Since Knoxville is nearly two hours away, commuting and maintaining both practices would be out of the question."

"Your roots are here, my dear. Unless I miss the mark, you're not at all like your mother. You'd fit right in. People here would welcome you. I'd welcome having you nearby, to finally have a chance to get to know my only niece.

"The house would be yours," he continued. "I was plannin' to leave it to you anyway. I'll be movin' into my cabin on the mountain beyond the lake. If you don't mind, though, I'd like to keep a room here until you're settled in the practice."

"I don't know. This is all so . . . so sudden. Practicing medicine in a small town would be unlike anything I've ever done. Angel Ridge is so far from hospitals."

"This is the only hospital most folks 'round here have ever known. And I do make house calls. Ever done one of those?"

"No." Janice couldn't imagine practicing medicine with such limited resources.

"You'd be surprised. I'm pretty well equipped," he said as if he had read her mind.

"But what if you have an emergency you can't handle?"

"I try to stabilize the patient and then transport them to Maryville or Knoxville."

"What if it's more urgent?"

"Then we have them airlifted to the University Medical Center."

"Are you on call all the time?"

"It isn't so bad. Things seem to ebb and flow here. You'll go through periods when there are several emergencies and a number of calls to make. At other times, they'll be nothing to do for days."

"I'm used to a fast pace."

"The breaks are welcome. Everyone needs time to enjoy life a little. Don't you want to settle down? Start a family?"

"You never did," Janice pointed out.

"I had my reasons," he said without offering further information.

The look on his face told her those reasons were private. "Now, I know I've sprung this on you. You need time to let it sink in."

That was an understatement. No. She couldn't think about coming here for anything more than a visit. She had a life that she had created. A good life. Why should she give that up to come here, to uncharted waters, and reinvent herself with the temptation of Blake Ferguson living in her grandparents' house just a couple of blocks down the road?

Her uncle stood and walked to his desk. When he turned back, he passed a white business card to her. "You can reach me at this number anytime. I have an answering service that can track me down if I'm not in."

Janice took the card and slid it into her purse. She should turn him down now. She'd just be giving him hope if she didn't, but when she stood and looked into his kind, brown eyes, she couldn't do it. Suddenly, she wanted to get to know this man who only knew her through some letters that weren't even addressed to him, yet still had enormous faith in her.

"What are your plans for Christmas?" he asked.

"I'm taking a few weeks off. I thought I'd take a trip."

"Won't you be seeing your parents?"

Janice laughed. "Mother is taking a European cruise. Father isn't sure if he'll be able to join her. He's been working in London

47

for the past month."

"Why don't you stay with me? I'd so welcome having family around to fuss over at the holidays."

He was making it impossible to say no.

"You could still take your trip afterward, but come here for Christmas. You don't want to be alone and far away at a time when families should be together."

Janice had spent practically all of her Christmases lonely and in strange places. Even when she'd accompanied her parents on trips, she'd been cared for by a nanny. The thought of sharing this holiday with her uncle in Angel Ridge. . . .

"I'm tempted," she admitted.

"Splendid. Then you'll come?"

She wanted to say *yes*, but she held back. "Let me think about it."

He had a clear look of disappointment on his face, but he said, "Of course."

They walked in silence back to the front of the house. She surveyed the old two-story home, gazing up the beautiful open staircase in the foyer with yards and yards of gleaming hardwoods.

This house could be hers. She could get up in the morning, dress, and come down to work without ever getting in her car. No traffic hassles. No rushing around. She had to admit it seemed idyllic. Too good to be true.

When they stepped out onto the wide, front porch, an attractive woman who looked to be in her early thirties called up a cheery greeting as she hurried down the sidewalk. "Afternoon, Doc."

"Good afternoon," Janice said in unison with her uncle. They looked at each other and laughed.

"Strange havin' two doctors around." He shoved his hands in his trousers and rocked back on his heels. "I could get used to it."

Turning his attention back to the woman who was nearly out of earshot, he called out, "You need to slow down, Dixie."

"Rollin' stones gather no moss. I got pies to bake. One's got your name on it, Doc," she replied as she disappeared around a corner.

"I look forward to it," her uncle called a little louder as he walked down the front steps. "That's Dixie Ferguson. She runs the diner in town. Best cook around."

"Ferguson?"

"Yep. She comes from a good family. Why, her brother bought your grandparents' place."

"I stopped by before I came over," Janice admitted when she had reached her car.

49

If he seemed surprised, he didn't show it.

"So, you met Blake? Guess he's gussying the place up for Christmas."

"Yes. Maybe you could look in on him later. He took about a ten-foot fall from a ladder."

He raised a snowy eyebrow. "Oh, my. Did you check him out?"

"I tried, but I think I made him feel uncomfortable."

"I see. Well, I'll go by in a bit. Blake's a good man. Fine carpenter, too. He'll bring that old house back to its glory."

"I'm glad," Janice said softly, and she was.

"So, you'll call and give me the details of when you'll be coming?"

He was persistent. "I'm looking forward to getting to know you," she countered without answering his question.

"There's nothing I'd enjoy more."

He leaned down and kissed Janice's cheek. The love filling his eyes had Janice wondering if this could be the beginning of a journey she'd been afraid to begin, or even long for, most of her life.

As she drove down the oak-lined avenue out of town, she wondered. Did she dare consider the possibility of calling Angel Ridge home?

# CHAPTER 3

Janice hung up the phone. The intercom immediately sounded. So much for working on patient charts instead of having lunch. Sighing, she picked up the receiver. "Yes?"

"Dr. Thornton, you have patients in exam rooms two and three, Dr. Holliday is on line two with questions about Eve Carlisle's medication, and there's a Blake Ferguson on line three."

"I'll be with the patients as soon as possible, I'll take Dr. Holliday's call, ask Mr. Ferguson to hold, order me a turkey sandwich from the deli, and hold any other calls unless it's an emergency."

"Yes, Doctor."

Janice spoke with her partner about her most critical patient's pain medication. Mrs. Carlisle . . . The poor dear was declining more quickly than she'd anticipated. Focusing on her patient shouldn't be difficult, but throughout the discussion, she kept staring

51

at the blinking light on line three.

Blake . . . This wasn't the first time thoughts of him had distracted her since meeting him last weekend. She didn't know why he'd entered her thoughts at all. Sure, he was a good-looking guy and pleasant to be around. But with the typical hectic pace of her office, she hadn't had a moment to analyze those wayward thoughts.

Her uncle's offer hung temptingly before her. Could it be possible to have a home and family and still be a doctor? The fantasy of it bloomed in her mind. Working from home, light patient loads, and the too appealing man restoring her grandparents' home . . .

She shook her head. There she went again.

She disconnected the call with Dr. Holliday, took a deep breath, and pressed the button on the phone that would connect her to Blake. "Hello, this is Dr. Thornton."

"Hi. This is Blake Ferguson."

His voice rumbled through the line in a sexy vibrato that charged all her senses. "Blake. Hello. What a surprise."

"A pleasant one, I hope."

A hint of vulnerability that she found endearing laced his words. Now why would a man like Blake feel vulnerable or insecure? "Any excuse to get my head out of patient charts for a few minutes is pleasant."

"Glad to be of service."

Blake's rich laughter further warmed Janice's blood. Good grief. Why was she reacting so strongly to this stranger? Had it been that long since she'd engaged in a little casual flirting? She didn't have to think long before realizing the answer to that particular question was, *yes*. Working the kind of hours she did left zero time for a social life.

She tucked her hair behind her ear. "How did you find me?"

"I was in luck. Only one Dr. Janice Thornton in Knoxville."

"Oh, right." She should have thought of that. If it only took his voice over a phone line to turn her brain to mush, what would happen if he were just around the corner, able to drop by anytime to see her?

"The house looks real nice," he said.

"I'm sure it does."

"The thought occurred to me that you might want to come back by. I mean, after all, you should see what you accomplished."

"I'd love to, but I'm really tied up with work at the moment." Maybe she could run by his house if she spent Christmas with her uncle.

"That's too bad. What's your schedule like this weekend?"

"This weekend?"

"Yeah."

Janice picked up her electronic organizer and opened her calendar. The rest of the week was crazy, but her weekend was free. She'd forgotten that she wasn't on call. "I'm off this weekend." She should sleep as much as possible. The back-to-back eighteen-hour days were getting to her.

"When you say you're off this weekend, do you mean you're off Friday night?"

Janice frowned. "Yes. I don't have to work and I'm not on-call again until Monday morning."

"Perfect. Why don't you come over Friday evening?"

Friday? Day after tomorrow?

"Janice?"

"Sorry. *Um* — Friday. What time?"

"How 'bout six?"

She hesitated for a moment. They typically didn't schedule patient appointments on Friday afternoons. Janice usually spent the time dealing with paperwork. If she took some things home on Thursday evening —

"It'll just be getting dark about then, and you could see the lights as you drive up."

He held the temptation of her grandparents' house out like the proverbial apple. In the end, she found she couldn't resist the temptation.

"Okay. I'll come."

"All right, then. Can I pick you up?" he offered.

Janice frowned. "Thank you, but that isn't necessary. It would be such a long drive for you." And she'd have no means of escape.

"I don't mind. I'm sure you'll be tired after a long week at work. We could have dinner. You could even spend the night, if you want, and then I'd drive you back into the city on Saturday."

Spend the night? Janice wondered if he was just being gentlemanly or if he had some sort of agenda. Still, she wondered . . . What would it be like to stay the night in her grandparents' house with the enticing Blake Ferguson?

She shook her head to clear the images running amuck in her mind.

"You could still spend the night. I don't want you to feel rushed because of the long drive back. It'd be pretty late by the time you made it home." He paused then added, "I just put the finishing touches on the guest room."

There he went. Tempting her again. She wondered what it looked like now. Oh, how she'd loved that room. The little girl she'd been then thought if she could hide away there, she could have a normal life. A life where she was loved and wanted and a part of a real family. Her mother had dragged her out of that room kicking and screaming while her grandmother cried.

"Yep. It's not really decorated yet. I was hoping you could tell me how it looked when your grandparents lived here. I'd like for it to be the way you remember it."

"You would?" she said around the lump in her throat.

"Oh, yeah. I want the renovations to be historically accurate."

"I only visited there a few times. Besides, I don't think my grandparents were the original owners. I'm sure they made changes over the years."

"Still, you know more than I do, and I'd like to hear what you remember about it."

"I don't know what to say." The thought of his returning the house to the way she remembered it did funny things to her heart. God, she hated feeling this vulnerable.

"No need to say anything, except what time I should pick you up."

She closed her eyes. Twenty-four hours in Angel Ridge sounded like heaven compared to the week she'd had. She cleared her throat. "I'll drive myself. I insist," she said firmly. And if she spent the night, she'd stay with her uncle.

He hesitated, but at last said, "All right. I'll see you Friday about six, then?"

"Yes. Should I dress casually for dinner?"

"Of course. We do everything casual 'round here."

Janice smiled. The word "casual" implied a relaxed atmosphere. She couldn't imagine being anything but tied in knots around the very attractive, sexy man asking her to dinner.

"Casual it is. Why don't you give me your number, Blake?"

"Not planning to cancel on me are you?"

"I never know when there might be an emergency."

He gave her the number, then said, "I'll just hold a good thought that all your patients stay healthy until you arrive here safe and sound."

The way he said it made her feel like she was going home after a long day at work. The hole in her heart that had always wanted a real home and family to call her own gaped open. An intense longing rocked her to the core. She shouldn't go. She should run from anything or anyone that could so easily dredge up these old feelings. Including her uncle's tempting offer to

57

settle in Angel Ridge permanently.

It was so much easier to see things as they were while she was safe in her world, but one step inside the city limits of Angel Ridge and her safe world had tilted crazily. At the moment, her desire to see her grandparents' house was stronger than her desire for self-preservation . . . this time.

"I'll see you Friday," she said, then hung up.

"Well, all I have to say is she must be special for you to go to all this trouble."

"That'd be a switch if that was *all* you had to say." Blake glanced over his shoulder at his baby sister while he swished tomatoes in a colander under the tap. "What color is your hair this week? What's left of it, that is."

"It's Spiced Tea. And the shorter length makes it sassy. Thanks for noticing," Dixie said. "So, come on. Out with it. There's a price for my homemade pasta."

"What's that?"

She leaned back against the counter near the sink and crossed her arms. "Information. Who is she?"

He shrugged. "Just someone I met."

"Not someone from around here. It would have been all over town by now if you'd invited someone from Angel Ridge over to your house for a romantic dinner."

"Who said anything about romantic? It's no big deal. She's just comin' to see the house, and I figured she might be hungry."

Dixie slapped him on the arm.

*"Ow,"* Blake complained as he transferred the tomatoes to towels on the island.

"Do I look like I just rode into town? Look at this place. It is spot — less," she emphasized the last syllable in a typically Texan way. Their formative years spent in Austin still showed in her accent despite the fact that she'd lived in Tennessee for nearly twenty years. "That's saying a lot since you've been bustin' out plaster since you moved in. Add to that candles, flowers, *you're* cooking. Need I say more?"

"All right." Blake surrendered. He knew she'd just wear him down anyway. "I met her last weekend. Her grandparents used to live here."

"The Prescotts, right?"

"Yeah," he said as he began crushing tomatoes for the sauce in a big stainless steel bowl.

She brushed him out of the way and took over with the tomatoes. "I saw a nice lookin' blonde down at Doc Prescott's last Saturday. Is she a doctor?"

59

He wiped his hands on a towel. "Do you have ESP?"

"Nope. Just observant. When I said, *Afternoon, Doc,* they both answered."

"It amazes me that you observe anything as fast as you move. You never slow down."

"I slow down for the important stuff."

Blake's sister was known for bringing the party with her, but she had suddenly become quite somber. He knew why. "How's Susan?"

"Not good."

The words were flat. Spoken with little emotion. Dixie's best friend had found out several months back she had stage-four breast cancer. They'd gone to school together. Susan'd been around the house so much when they were growing up, Blake had always seen her as a second sister. "Are the treatments helping?"

His sister worked the tomatoes more vigorously as she spoke. "Doc Prescott said they wouldn't cure her, but might give her a few more months. So, she refused them. Said she didn't want to spend what time she had left sick as a dog from chemo. She'd rather have quality time with her children."

"I didn't know. The Mayor must be takin' it hard."

"Oh, you know him. Stiff upper lip and

all." She transferred the tomatoes to a large pot and began adding spices. "It's the kids I'm worried about. Sammy's so young, and Abby's just in denial."

"Patrick will see them through," Blake said. He wanted to pull his headstrong baby sister into his arms and comfort her, but he knew she wouldn't welcome it. Talk about stiff upper lip.

Dixie wiped her hands on a towel then swiped the container of pasta from the counter and placed it in the refrigerator, slamming the door shut. "That man doesn't know the first thing about parenting."

"He's their father. He has to have some paternal instincts."

"None that I've noticed. Susie handles the kids so he can tend to his job. It's like that's the most important thing in the world to him."

That statement gave him a moment's pause. Public officials pretty much lived their jobs, a lot like doctors. Their families were the ones that suffered.

He grasped Dixie's arm as she tried to blow by him and gently squeezed it. "They've got you."

"Got that right," she said, her back stiffening with resolve. "So, about this woman —"

Blake took a step back. "No more questions," he said firmly.

"All right." She held up her hands. "If you're gonna be that way, I'm not gonna tell you what I know."

Dixie picked up her purse and headed for the door at a pace that had Blake dodging around the island and running to catch up. He stopped her just as she reached for the Victorian doorknob. "What do you know?"

She crossed her arms and peered at him through squinted eyes. "Now why should I tell you anything?"

He gave her what he hoped was a winning smile. "Because I'm your favorite brother."

"I don't play favorites."

"Not even with your older brother?"

She propped a hand on her hip. "You're all older."

"Yeah, but you and me, we're connected at the mind." He tapped his temple. "We have a bond."

"Bond, schmond." She looked away. The look of disinterest on her face clearly there to make it seem like she'd lost interest in the conversation.

With a gentle finger at her chin, he brought her face around until she was looking at him again. "Come on, Sis," he cajoled.

"Oh, all right. You know I can't resist when you go all charming."

62

Blake smiled and crossed his arms, waiting. "Word is that she's Doc Prescott's long lost grandniece. Apparently, her mother grew up in Angel Ridge . . . a real beauty who had ambitions too big for this little backwoods town. So, she left and never looked back. Supposedly married some hotshot financial guru who was richer than Midas." She waved her hand in the air. "But I digress."

She hitched her purse up on her shoulder and finished with, "Word is that Doc's ready to retire, and he's wantin' your date, or whatever you're callin' her, to take over his practice."

That got his attention. "Really . . ." Janice in Angel Ridge permanently. That added a new dimension to things.

"Well, you know, it's diner gossip, but it's usually pretty reliable."

"Who'd you hear it from?"

"Miss Estelee."

Blake raised an eyebrow. "Doc Prescott tells her just about everything."

Dixie shrugged. "Well, it's been real, but I gotta run." She brushed Blake out of the way, opened the front door, and sprinted down the steps. "You'd better put that sauce on if you want it edible, and don't overcook my pasta."

She was already down the street and around the corner before Blake could form a reply. So, Janice might be moving to Angel Ridge. Did that really change anything? Sure, she'd be closer, but as the town's only doctor, how much time would she have for a relationship?

Then he remembered the way he'd felt when she'd touched him. He wasn't inexperienced by any means. Still, he'd never had such an intense reaction to a woman so quickly. And what a woman. He let his mind wander back as the shadows lengthened across his front lawn. . . .

Something like that was at least worth exploring, wasn't it?

He rubbed his chin, then turned and made his way back to the kitchen. He had a feeling things were about to get interesting.

# CHAPTER 4

When Janice parked in front of the house at 211 Ridge Road, she killed the engine and just sat there, staring. It looked like a Victorian Christmas card complete with smoke curling up from the chimney.

There were tiny white lights everywhere, hung in every eave, and looped around every window. The colorful ones she'd placed on the railing of the wrap-around porch and in the bushes added to the effect, and she was pleased that she'd had something to do with the spectacular display. The only thing missing was snow.

The front door opened. Blake stood there for a moment silhouetted by the light spilling from the interior. The thousands of exterior lights enabled her to see that he wore casual boots, crisply ironed, close fitting dark jeans and a heavy white cotton shirt with pearl buttons that twinkled when he moved down the steps to the sidewalk.

Janice eased out of the car. She wanted to believe the rush she felt was because of the house that held so many warm memories for her, but she knew the nostalgic feelings were intensified because of the man who met her at the end of the sidewalk.

"Hi."

A lazy smile that was pure sensuality lifted the corner of his mouth. Janice bit her lower lip. She desperately needed to pull on the reins of her control before her emotions ran away with her. "Hi."

He cupped her elbow in his hand and leaned down to kiss her cheek. "It's good to see you," he whispered near her ear.

She closed her eyes and inhaled deeply. His cologne conjured images of long, languid nights sitting in front of a fireplace wrapped in his arms . . . making love . . . She sighed. The man had entirely too much sex appeal. She blamed the rest on the town and the house.

When he had straightened, his gaze swept her body, missing nothing. She felt her skin flush with awareness as if he'd swept his hands down her body. "The house is beautiful," she managed, her voice hoarse with reaction to him.

Blake turned and took in his home with pride. "I'm sure your mother would declare it gaudy."

Janice smiled. He was right. "What does she know?"

He swung that sense-charging smile back to her. "That's what I like to hear."

They stood silently for a few more minutes, just gazing at the house. A navy sky dotted with countless stars provided the perfect backdrop for it.

"It's pretty chilly out here," Blake said. "Would you like to come in?"

Janice nodded. Blake took her hand and laced his fingers with hers. It seemed the most natural thing in the world, strolling with him up the sidewalk and into the house. As they passed through the oversized, open front door and into the foyer, Janice smelled something wonderful cooking.

"Are we having dinner here?" She hadn't prepared for that. Dinner with a man like Blake in a crowded restaurant was one thing, but a private dinner in his home — this home — would be another thing entirely.

Blake helped her out of her coat and draped it over a peg on the hall tree. "That's world famous Blake Ferguson spaghetti sauce you smell cooking. You'll find none finer in any restaurant," he boasted.

"Smells delicious," she admitted.

"You look beautiful."

"Thanks." The simple compliment, sincerely spoken, made her glad she'd taken extra time with her appearance. Janice smoothed her hands over black jeans. She'd picked a soft red sweater because it put her in the Christmas spirit. After the week she'd had, she needed all the help she could get.

She looked around the familiar home, remembering the love she'd felt here. A poignant sense of longing pierced her. Maybe this was a mistake. More than a week had passed. In that time, she hadn't been able to put Blake or her uncle's invitation out of her mind, despite her best effort to do so.

"We have time for a tour," Blake offered.

He seemed to know the right thing to say to draw her back in. "I'd like that," she admitted. In fact, she'd like nothing better than to become reacquainted with the place. She'd come this far; she wouldn't walk away now. Not yet, anyway.

They turned left out of the foyer and passed through a wide doorway into the parlor. A huge Christmas tree that nearly touched the high ceiling stood in the bay window, filling the room with its fresh pine scent. Covered in lights with homemade and antique ornaments, it reminded Janice of the tree her grandparents had placed there.

Blake leaned over her shoulder from behind and said, "I thought we could add a popcorn garland later."

Janice eased her hands into her back pockets, considering. Spending time with Blake here wouldn't be so difficult, as long as he kept things light and she didn't let her emotions get away from her. A voice inside her head mocked, *Right. You're way past that, sister.*

Ignoring it, she said, "Sounds good."

He showed her around the ground floor. Blake had made the identical room across from the parlor, which had originally been the music room, into a comfortable office and den. It had a large old desk and dark leather furniture arranged around the fireplace. Other rooms downstairs included a formal dining room, a washroom, and his bedroom. The room that her grandparents had shared took on a whole new dimension knowing that this was now Blake's room.

A king-size cherry sleigh bed dominated the latter, making it difficult to ignore. More antiques, a romantic fireplace, and an adjacent bathroom with a claw foot tub big enough for two made the room comfortable and inviting, but the images filling her head every time her eyes strayed to the bed marked it off limits.

They took the back stairs from the kitchen up to the room she remembered using when she'd stayed here. It contained only a white iron bed and a small white French provincial dresser. Blake remained in the doorway while she walked in and let her mind wander back in time. The memories were so bittersweet.

"Tell me what it was like," he said.

Janice ran her hand down a freshly painted strip of wood framing the old leaded glass panes of the window. "Billowing lace curtains that stirred in the breeze. There was a padded bench here, in front of the window, so you could sit, look outside, and daydream . . ." She walked over to the bed. "A white lacy bedspread with lots of colorful pillows. The walls had old floral wallpaper with a pale pink background. And there was a bookcase over there filled with all the books a child would love to curl up with. It was any young girl's dream of a room."

He walked over to where she stood. "I kept a swatch of the wallpaper before we tore the old plaster walls down and hung the sheetrock. I'm having it reproduced."

She glanced up at him. "Can you do that?"

"Sure."

She turned her focus back to the white walls. "I can't imagine what it would look like new."

"You'll just have to come back after I get it up and see for yourself."

She chewed on her lower lip. She should run in the opposite direction as fast as she could. But when she opened her mouth, the word "Okay," came out as if of its own accord.

"I would show you around the rest of the upstairs, but I've just started working on the walls in the other rooms, and it's a real mess." He swept another of those bone-melting looks down her body. "All that dust wouldn't be a good thing with those black jeans."

She gave into temptation and swept his body with a look of her own, pausing at his dark pants. "You have the same problem."

"So I do," he said in deep, hushed tones that sent liquid heat racing through her veins.

Janice turned back to the window and cleared her throat. "I'm glad that you're restoring the house. It makes me happy, knowing that someone who really loves the place is living here. Caring for it the way my grandparents did."

"I do love it. It's such a great house."

She trailed her fingertips down the window frame. There'd been a crack in it that Blake must have repaired. "You do excellent work."

"Thanks." He jerked a thumb toward the door. "You know, I'd better check on the pasta. My sister warned me about overcooking it."

As they retraced their steps down the back stairs, Janice said, "I think I sort of met your sister the other day. Dixie, right?"

"Yeah."

"She breezed by my uncle's as I was leaving last Friday."

"That's Dixie. Always in a hurry."

They entered the big airy kitchen at the back of the house. The scarred Formica countertops she remembered had been replaced with white and black granite. The faded linoleum with refinished hardwoods that must have been underneath, but everything else was still the same, right down to the big old stove her grandmother used to cook on. "Man, I can't imagine how old that thing is," Janice said aloud.

"Still works like a new one," Blake said. "And it fits. They don't make ranges this wide anymore." He pulled a stool from the island. "Make yourself comfortable." Taking her hand, he made sure she was settled comfortably before turning his attention to the pots on the stove.

"So, I heard Doc Prescott is your uncle." Steam rose in the air as he lifted the lid on the pot containing the pasta.

Word traveled fast. "Yes."

"I didn't know he had any family left. Guess I should have made the connection after I met you."

"I hate to admit it, but I didn't remember having an uncle."

Blake glanced over his shoulder and frowned. "*Hmm* . . . Dixie said . . ."

He turned a knob and picked up a wooden spoon. She propped her chin in her hand. "What did she say?"

"Oh, just that he had mentioned you over the years."

"I met him a couple of times when I visited my grandparents. Beyond that, I corresponded with my grandparents. They shared the letters with him."

As he stirred the sauce, she thought how strange he looked holding a wooden spoon, standing at a stove. He just didn't seem the domestic type. He had the rough, rugged look of the dark and dangerous bad boy. She couldn't tear her gaze away from him.

"That's odd. Looks like he would have written you himself."

73

She shrugged. "That's my family. Odd."

Blake chuckled and shook his head. "Dixie would say, *you can pick your friends, you can pick your nose, you can pick your friend's nose, but you can't pick your family.*"

She burst out laughing. "Your sister must be something."

"She is. We just haven't figured out what yet."

Blake set the long wooden spoon he'd been using aside and carried the pasta to the deep, white porcelain sink. Janice looked around the old, familiar kitchen again. When her gaze stopped at the back door, she asked, "Is there still a sun porch out there?"

"Yes, ma'am, complete with your grandmother's wicker porch swing."

She gasped. "Really?"

"Yeah. We can wrap up in a blanket and sit in it later, if you want."

Wrapped up in a blanket with Blake on a crisp winter night in a porch swing . . . if that wasn't a recipe for trouble, she didn't know what was.

He moved around the kitchen naturally, as if he spent a lot of time here. "Do you enjoy cooking?" she asked, ignoring his invitation to seduction on the sun porch.

"Yes, although my sister would argue my

74

skill. I'm not as good as her, but I do all right. I guess it's a good thing, too. I'd starve if I didn't. Don't know if you noticed on your way in, but the nearest fast food restaurant is about fifty miles down the road, and my sister usually closes her diner down after the dinner crowd clears out. That way she can do the next day's baking." He lifted a bottle and asked, "Wine?"

"Please."

"It's red. Hope that's okay."

"Perfect."

While he poured, she said, "That's one of the things I like about Angel Ridge. It seems to have missed development entirely."

Blake raised his glass. "Here's to keeping it that way."

He turned to pour the pasta into a colander. "How was your week?"

The scene was entirely too domestic for Janice's comfort. "Busy. Yours?"

"Actually, I took the week off and worked around here. So, I've enjoyed myself."

Janice couldn't remember the last time she'd taken a week off. What would she do for two weeks in Angel Ridge? And with whom would she do it? It was one of the things that bothered her about taking over her uncle's practice. The pace would be decidedly slower, leaving her more time for . . . what? Blake?

He turned and leaned against the island near where she sat, capturing her full attention. He had the most arresting blue eyes. That lock of dark hair fell across his forehead. Her fingers itched to brush it back into place.

"So, what'd you think of my brother?"

Janice frowned. Where had that come from? "Your brother?"

"Yeah. Remember? He came by last Saturday while you were here."

"He seemed nice, I guess." She supposed some women might consider him good looking, but he was nothing compared to Blake.

A huge, cheesy grin split Blake's face.

"What?"

"Oh, nothing. So, what are your plans for Christmas?" he asked.

Janice set her glass down in front of her and twirled the stem. This was certainly an odd conversation. "Well, my partners are insisting that I take a few weeks off. In fact, they suggested just today that I take off sometime next week and not come back until the New Year."

"Sounds great. Do you normally work at Christmas?"

"Yes."

"For the same reason you worked Thanks-giving?"

Janice shrugged. "I don't mind."

Blake just shook his head. "Will you be spending time with your folks?"

"Mother is taking a three week Mediterranean cruise. Of course, she invited me along, but being in a warm climate at Christmas doesn't appeal to me." And three weeks confined with her mother on a cruise ship didn't warrant consideration.

"So, what are you going to do?" he repeated.

"I've been thinking about going skiing, but I haven't made any definite plans." She didn't want to tell him she was giving serious consideration to spending her time off just a couple of blocks away. If she had any sense, she'd talk herself out of it. No need to mention it to Blake until she'd made a firm decision anyway.

He straightened away from the bar and went to stir the sauce. "You should come here," he said without looking back at her.

"Here?" she squeaked, then cleared her throat.

"To Angel Ridge. It's a great place to relax. Unwind. You could even spend Christmas Day with me. I usually rattle around here alone on Christmas. It'd be nice having someone else around who does the day solo like me."

"You?" Janice said incredulously. "Didn't you say you have brothers, a sister, and parents nearby?"

"They spend Christmas day at home with their spouses and kids. Well, except for Dixie. She's still single, too. But she hangs out with her friend, Susan, and her family."

"So, you don't see each other on Christmas?" Janice asked.

"We get together on Christmas Eve at my parents', go to midnight church service, then part ways."

A pregnant silence filled the kitchen. Janice knew he was waiting for a response to his invitation.

"Have you lived in Angel Ridge all your life?" She took a sip of her wine.

Blake gave her what could only be described as "a look." He walked to the refrigerator and removed a bowl of salad. "I'm noticing a pattern with you." He set the bowl on the island.

She was noticing some things as well, like how nicely he filled out those skin-tight jeans. But she lifted her eyebrows, questioning.

"You're good at changing the subject when you don't want to answer a question."

"Fair is fair. You've asked me all kinds of personal questions, but I haven't gotten to ask many of my own."

Blake set a plate in front of her and served salad. "Ask away, but the invitation stands."

He dished up salad. Janice ignored the invitation. Again. She decided to see if she could throw *him* off-balance. "Have you ever been married?"

"No."

"Really?" She had expected him to say he was divorced. He was an intelligent, charming, sinfully sexy man. She imagined he didn't lack in dating opportunities.

"Really."

He turned the burner under the sauce off and put the lid on the pot. When he joined her at the bar, he said, "No and nothing are the answers to your next two questions."

Janice stopped eating, her fork halfway to her mouth. "What questions would that be?"

"Are you gay? And what's wrong with you?"

Janice laughed into her napkin.

"Come on. I know you were thinking it. I've heard it often enough. A guy who's forty and never been married must either be gay or have something wrong with him." He leaned down and whispered in a con-

79

spiratorial manner. "I have a sister. She tells me these things."

"I see. Well, since you're not gay and there's nothing wrong with you, that leaves only one other explanation."

"I can't wait to hear this." He sat and poured a generous portion of creamy ranch dressing onto his salad. His thigh brushed hers and she nearly lost the thread of the conversation.

Ignoring the fat content he was about to ingest, she focused on her own salad before saying, "You must have impossible standards no woman can meet."

"What's wrong with having standards? Don't you have them?"

"I thought *I* was asking the questions."

"Right. Fire away."

While he chewed, she considered what she would say. "So, you admit that you have standards."

"Absolutely." He wiped his mouth. "I think that if more people had standards and waited until they found the person compatible with those standards, there would be fewer broken homes." He forked up more salad.

Skeptical, Janice crossed her arms on the island and said, "Tell me."

When he'd swallowed, he said, "First, she

has to be someone admirable. Someone people look up to."

"A spotless reputation," Janice supplied.

He shook his head. "No one is perfect."

"I'm glad you acknowledge that."

"Ready for the pasta?"

She looked at his clean plate and nodded, ignoring her own half eaten salad. "What else?"

Blake took their salad plates and busied himself filling two large bowls with pasta then smothered it with aromatic sauce. "Someone who appreciates quality rather than quantity."

"As it pertains to what?"

"Lots of things." He set her food in front of her and took his place on the stool beside hers. "Take this house, for instance. I could easily build a new home in one of the affluent subdivisions I've developed, use the best materials, fill it with top of the line everything, but the fact is, today's materials and building standards can't begin to replicate the work and craftsmanship put into building this place. The history and character of this house can't be reproduced. That comes with time, patience, and caring for something."

Janice twirled noodles around her fork, staring at him, but not eating. "So you're talking about material things. Quality as opposed to quantity."

"That principle applies to many things."

"What else?"

"Kissing."

Janice lost her grip on her fork. It clattered nosily against her dish. "Sorry," she mumbled, then picked up her napkin and pressed it against her mouth.

"Although quantity is somewhat important there," he continued, ignoring her unease, "taking the time to do it right, to let the act express what you feel inside for the person, is the most important thing. Wouldn't you agree?"

So much for throwing *him* off-balance. "Yes. Absolutely. This pasta is really good."

"You haven't eaten anything yet."

Add observant to his list of attributes.

"I'm not making you uncomfortable, am I?"

"No. I asked a question, you gave me an honest answer. I must admit I find this fascinating. So, are there any other standards?" Janice took a bite, hoping his next answer would not have anything to do with sex. She was having enough trouble trying not to focus on what it would be like to be kissed qualitatively by Blake Ferguson.

"We'd have to want each other beyond

reason . . . without reservation."

His voice had lowered, softened. Janice looked up, and when her eyes found his, she trembled at the intensity and depth of emotion she felt in the words. She wondered. . . .

"Have you ever wanted anyone that way?"

"Yes."

His answer had been immediate. His gaze on her did not waiver.

She leaned toward him, her body drawn to him as if of its own accord. "Did she feel the same way?"

"I'm not sure."

Janice couldn't imagine any woman who hadn't been waiting her entire life for a man like Blake to want her beyond reason.

"What happened?" She said quietly, her dinner forgotten. "Did she hurt you?"

"Yes."

Janice lowered her gaze. This was the worst-case scenario. The other reason a man like Blake would have never married. A broken heart. And now, no woman could ever replace the one he once loved.

She had to admit, if only to herself, that since meeting Blake, she'd held onto a fine, intangible thread — call it hope or curiosity — about something romantic developing between them. With that hope deflated,

Janice felt a disappointment so acute that it pressed heavily on her heart.

"I'm sorry," she said at last.

"Don't be. Christmas is a time of miracles. A time when hearts come home."

Janice frowned. The man was definitely giving mixed signals. Had she missed something here? Was he talking about lost loves or something else entirely? He was sitting there looking at her like he could devour her. Maybe she could force his hand. . . .

Janice pushed her plate back. "You're hoping she'll come here for Christmas?"

"I've asked her, but, for some reason, she won't give me an answer."

Janice let out her breath. He *was* referring to his earlier invitation. She looked away, still evading. "Maybe she's not interested."

Blake carefully placed his napkin next to his plate and stood. Janice looked up at him, surprised, when he took her hand and gently urged her off the stool.

"There's one way to find out," he murmured as he lowered his head to hers.

# CHAPTER 5

Janice reeled with the implication of his words and the shock of his warm lips on hers. He'd been talking about her all along.

Logical thought fled when Blake slid a hand down her spine and pressed her close as his lips slanted across hers. Janice sighed. He was so tall. At five foot nine, standing on her toes to wrap her arms around his neck made her feel almost petite. Blake deepened the kiss, swirling his tongue in and out of her mouth in a heady rhythm, inviting her to kiss him back. She surrendered completely, giving as well as taking, until she was beyond weak with wanting him.

When his lips left hers, she slid her hands across his wide shoulders, rested her forehead against his chest, and closed her eyes. A kiss had never made her feel so much. Want so much.

He enfolded her in his arms and held her,

his lips pressed to her hair. His heart beat fast and furious beneath her palm.

"I think she's interested," he whispered near her ear, "but get the feeling she's still going to hold back. I wish I knew why."

Janice traced a pearl button on his shirt with the tip of her finger. Without lifting her head from his chest, she surprised herself by saying, "Have you ever wanted anything so much that it frightened you?"

"Wanting someone beyond reason doesn't allow room for fear."

"There's always fear."

He placed a finger beneath her chin and tipped her face up until her gaze met his. "Not when the feelings are mutual . . . the desires the same."

Janice closed her eyes as he gently caressed her cheek. "We just met. We don't know each other."

"I know I haven't been able to get you off my mind since I found you parked outside my house last week."

She knew the feeling. Janice ran a hand down his muscular arm. It would be so simple to tilt her head and rest it against his impossibly wide shoulder, her face nestled against his warm neck. "But you don't know if I meet your standards."

He captured her hands and laced his

fingers with hers but maintained contact with their bodies pressed together from her shoulders down, his feet on either side of hers, thigh to thigh. "I know what we just shared was a quality kiss. I know you enjoyed it as much as I did."

"You can't know if I'm an admirable person. You don't know me well enough."

He pressed their entwined hands to the small of her back and intensified the contact of their bodies. She arched her back. "Saving lives on a daily basis makes that one pretty much automatic."

"It doesn't happen everyday. There are some I can't save."

"But you keep trying. And there's the fact that you work holidays so that your married partners can be with their families. That's admirable. Of course, that would change if you had a family of your own."

She started to point out that she'd still have to take her turn, but he short-circuited her thoughts by brushing his lips against hers in a slow, seductive slide that fired her already revved up pulse.

"Say you'll come for Christmas."

The tip of his tongue traced the seam of her mouth. She caught it between her teeth, then swirled her tongue around it. He moaned and buried a hand in her hair. She felt her barrette pop open, heard it bounce against the floor as her hair tumbled around her shoulders. She angled her fingers into the thick hair at his temples and he deepened the kiss, but the sound of Janice's beeper startled them apart.

"I'm sorry." She stepped out of the circle of his arms, shaken and more than a little weak. Pushing her hair back, she picked her purse up off the floor and retrieved her pager, then checked the number on the display. "May I use your phone?"

He ran a thumb along his tempting lower lip. "It's by the refrigerator."

As Janice walked away from him, she tried to ignore the feeling of loss produced by just a few empty feet between them. What would walking away from him forever feel like? She shook the thought away, then punched in the familiar number to the doctor's lounge at the hospital and waited.

"Holliday."

"Hi, Mark," Janice said. "What's up?"

"Sorry to bother you, Janice. I know you're off this weekend."

"That's all right. What do you need?"

"It's Eve Carlisle. She's taken a downward turn. I don't think she'll make it through the night. Thought you'd want to know."

"I'm nearly two hours away. Can I make it?"

"It's hard to say. She's been asking for you. I think if I tell her you're coming, she might hang on."

"Thanks for calling, Mark. I'll be there as soon as possible."

"Drive carefully."

Janice hung the phone up and turned to Blake.

"Emergency?"

"In a way." She didn't miss the look of annoyance that passed across his face. She was used to that. She'd dated several men, one in particular, who'd expected her to put him first. When they saw that wouldn't be possible, they dropped her. Another reason to take a step back. She had to admit, if only to herself, she was kind of glad to have an out. Things were getting entirely too intense, too quickly, between her and Blake.

"I have a patient who's been ill for some time. My colleague doesn't think she'll make it through the night. She's elderly and doesn't have anyone. I've treated her for so long, she sort of sees me as part of her family. I should be there. I'm sorry to cut our evening short," she said, and in a way, she was.

He shoved his hands in his pockets and

pinned her with a steady look she couldn't read. "Don't worry about it. Can I drive you?"

"Oh, there's no need. I have my car. Besides, I could be at the hospital all night."

He frowned. "Call me old-fashioned, but I don't like the idea of you driving alone all the way back to the city this late."

His tone was a bit too stern, and it rankled her. "I'll be fine," she insisted.

He shrugged. "Can I give you some food to take with you? You didn't finish your pasta."

"I should just go ahead and leave."

He nodded. "I'll walk you to the door."

They slowly made their way down the long central hallway to the front of the house. She couldn't help dwelling on how the mood had shifted since she'd gotten that page. She also couldn't resist stopping at the doorway to the parlor for one last look at the tree. "We didn't get to make the popcorn garland."

"Duty calls."

He helped her into her coat. When she turned to say goodbye, the intensity she saw burning in his eyes was unnerving. She thought he might kiss her, but instead, he opened the door.

"I hope your patient . . . I hope everything

goes okay. At the hospital," he added.

"Right. Thanks."

She walked out to her car, but stole one more look at the house before she got in. Despite her head's best remonstrations and the conflicting emotions swirling inside, seeing it and Blake silhouetted on the other side of the door filled her heart with a sweet, tender longing. A longing for home. A longing for Blake.

Blake closed the door behind Janice and slammed his fist into the wall. The new sheetrock gave, leaving a large hole. He looked at his hand then and noticed it was bleeding. He flexed his fingers. He hadn't even felt pain.

He pressed his injured hand against the palm of his opposite hand. Pacing the hallway, he used the self-talk and breathing techniques he'd learned years ago. Breathe in. Breathe out. She was a doctor. She had a patient dying. Sure, her partner could handle it, but the patient was special and had asked for her specifically. Of course she would want to be there for the woman.

He was just being selfish. He raked a hand through his hair and continued to pace. Breathe in. Breathe out. She was an independent woman. She'd be fine driving alone at night all the way back to Knoxville.

He had no reason to be upset. He hardly knew her. They'd seen each other twice now. Shared a mind-boggling attraction, but that was all it was. Clearly they were wrong for each other. They wanted different things. No harm. No foul. They should both just get on with their lives and forget they ever met.

And that got him to the source of his irrational anger. He didn't want to forget Janice. He put his back to the wall and slid to the floor. Sinking his head in his hands, he wondered how he'd gotten in so deep.

Better yet, what was he going to do about it?

When Janice arrived at the hospital, she went directly to the nurse's station. No one was behind the desk, so she found Eve Carlisle's chart and reviewed it. Her partner had ordered only pain medication to keep her comfortable.

Janice walked the short distance to Mrs. Carlisle's room. No family waited sadly outside in the hallway or crowded inside around the bed to say their final goodbyes. No minister stood by the bedside to comfort or pray. All machines and IV's had been removed. The frail old lady seemed dwarfed by the bed. Her snowy white hair blended with the pillowcase.

She checked the pulse at her patient's wrist. Thready and irregular. Respirations, infrequent and labored. Eve's eyes fluttered open and a smile played at her bluing lips.

"Dr. Thornton. Is that you?" Her voice came out in a raspy whisper.

"I'm here, Mrs. Carlisle. How are you doing? Are you in any pain?"

"No. No."

"Can I get you anything?"

"Please sit." She patted the bed. "Stay with me."

Janice sat on the side of the bed. How she hated this aspect of her job. The dying woman lifted her hand, and Janice took it. The bones stood out prominently, the skin stretched paper-thin.

"It won't be long now."

"No," Janice confirmed. "Is there anyone I can call, Mrs. Carlisle?"

"No. No one. I gave the nice nurse the name of a funeral home. They know what to do. The nursing home can do what they wish with the few things I left behind."

Janice nodded. Tears stung her eyes. No one should have to die this way. Completely alone with only her doctor to comfort her.

Eve patted her hand. "Now don't be sad.

I'm an old lady. It's my time. I'm ready to go."

Janice swallowed hard and tried to smile.

"I have something for you." Eve pointed toward the nightstand.

A large wooden box sat next to it. Janice pulled the old trunk over to the bed. Eve gazed at it lovingly.

"My father made it for me. It's a hope chest."

"It's lovely."

"Open." She drew in a labored breath. "Look."

A musty smell filled the room as she lifted the lid. The hinges creaked from lack of use. The inside was lined in faded blue velvet. An old quilt lay neatly folded in the bottom. A white Bible, yellowed with age, sat on top. A posy of dried flowers tied with a lace ribbon and several other mementos were also inside. Janice tilted the box so Eve could see the contents.

"My grandmother made that quilt. The church I grew up in gave me the Bible. All the brides were given one."

Janice picked it up and opened it to front page. *Presented to Eve Fields Carlisle by the Women's Auxiliary of the First Presbyterian Church of Eden's Crossing. April 3, 1940.*

Janice recognized the name of the town. It

was about an hour east of Knoxville, but she'd never been there. "You were married?"

Eve nodded. "But he never came back from the war." She took a labored breath. The gurgling sound indicated fluid filling her lungs. "He was unforgettable. His life so short . . . mine too long."

Janice replaced the Bible and closed the lid. "What would you like me to do with your hope chest, Mrs. Carlisle?"

"I want you to have it."

"Oh, I couldn't. Surely there's someone —"

Eve held up her hand. "You. There's still time for you. Don't waste it. Don't wait for tomorrow. You never know what it will hold. Promise."

Janice wasn't sure what the dear lady was asking of her, but she said, "I promise."

Eve smiled and looked up. A look of sheer peace transformed her face. "So beautiful . . . so . . ." She took a long, deep, unencumbered breath, and then took no more. Janice closed Eve's eyes and laid the hand she held atop the other at her waist.

After a moment, she walked out to the nurse's station. "Sharon, Mrs. Carlisle —" Her voice broke. What was wrong with her? She was a doctor. Dealing with death, part of the job.

"I'll take care of it, Doctor."

"Thank you. There's an old chest in there. Please have an orderly bring it down to my office."

"Yes, Doctor."

The nurse lifted the receiver on the phone to make the necessary calls. Janice took the elevator down to her office on the third floor. She went straight in without turning on any lights, shut her door, curled up in the corner of her couch, and cried. All of the loss and loneliness crashed in on her at once.

Like Eve, she was alone.

Dear God, she didn't want to end her life that way. No family to care. No children to be proud of. No husband to have loved.

She didn't know how long she sat there in the dark. Someone knocked on the door of the outer office, dragging her from her misery.

"Who is it?" she said sharply.

"Orderly. I have a delivery."

Janice hurried to the door in the front office and let the man in. Back in her office, she indicated where she wanted him to place the old box. She sank back into the corner of the couch, staring at the chest that had meant so much to Mrs. Carlisle. It rocked her back to a time when she'd had hopes for a future and a family of her own.

She'd met Joel while doing her residency. He'd been in law school at the University of Tennessee, just across the river from the Medical Center. Having grown up on a farm in a small town north of Knoxville, she'd been charmed by his large family. Loved the community he grew up in, because it reminded her of Angel Ridge. His family's farmhouse, loud with children and full of love, reminiscent of the warmth and caring she'd experienced in her grandparents' home.

She'd accepted his proposal without hesitation. When he'd suggested she abandon her medical studies and focus on staying home to start a family after their marriage, she hadn't taken him seriously. He knew how much she wanted to become a doctor. As time passed, the suggestion became a demand. Her flat refusal had caused him to call off the engagement.

The break-up had been devastating, but drove home the realization she'd never have the things she'd dreamed of as a little girl. She'd never have a home and a family. Would never be loved and accepted for who she was. Sitting up a little straighter, she rationalized. She had her practice. Colleagues who respected her. Patients that needed her. That was enough. Wasn't it?

Inexplicably, the tears came again. What was wrong with her? She grabbed a handful of tissues and buried her face in them.

The persistent pealing of her pager pulled Janice from her grief. She snatched the offensive device from the purse she'd dropped at her feet and punched a button that ended the nauseating beeps. The number on the digital display showed her answering service was trying to contact her.

She walked to her desk and dialed her service. Pulling several more tissues from the box on her desk, she wiped her nose while she waited for someone to pick up.

"Doctor's office."

"Yes, this is Dr. Thornton. You paged me."

"Yes, Dr. Thornton. A Blake Ferguson called. He asked us to tell you that he's in the lobby of the hospital. You can reach him at . . ."

Janice jotted the number down and disconnected the call. Why in the world would Blake be here at the hospital? Her uncle. Oh, God. . . .

She dialed the number and waited.

"Hello?"

"Blake?"

"Hi."

Janice wiped her nose again as fresh tears threatened. "My service said you were here at the hospital. Is something wrong? Uncle Charles?"

"No. Nothing's wrong."

"Then why are you here?" There was a long pause. "Blake?"

"I thought you might not want to be alone. I don't know. I guess it was crazy."

Blake was here. He'd seemed so detached when she left him. She couldn't believe he'd come all this way. For her.

"Where are you?" he asked.

"In my office."

Another pause.

"Maybe I shouldn't have come. I was just, I don't know, uncomfortable with how we left things. And I guess I was a little worried about you."

"I'm glad you're here," she admitted. "You're right. I don't want to be alone. Come up to the third floor, and I'll meet you at the elevator."

"I'm on my way."

Janice grabbed her keys and walked out to the elevators. A tone signaled its arrival, and then he was there.

He stepped into the hallway, hands in his pockets, to stand in front of her, a shy, uncertain look on his face. He wore a black

99

leather jacket that made him look entirely too rugged. Too sexy. She wanted like crazy to walk into his arms and stay there all night, but folded her arms against her midsection instead. "I can't believe you're here."

He raked a hand through his hair. "Neither can I."

Strain made the crinkles at the corners of his eyes more pronounced. Janice had to look away from the intensity of his clear, blue gaze. "My office is just down the hall."

She led the way. Blake followed. Unlocking the suite door, they walked back to her office. With a flip of a switch, she turned on a lamp in the corner of the room.

"Were you sitting here in the dark?"

Janice nodded and sat on the couch. She kicked off her clogs and tucked her feet beneath her. Blake sat next to her. He leaned forward, his hands folded loosely between his knees. There was that look again. The one that took in entirely too much detail.

"You've been crying. Is it your patient?"

Janice had to turn away again. "Yes. No." She shrugged, unsure of her own feelings, and propped her chin in her hand.

He took her other hand in both his, then dipped his head to meet her gaze. "I'm sorry."

The softness in his voice did her in. Janice turned away from him, pressing her fist to her mouth as the tears came again.

He squeezed her hand. "It's okay."

She brushed the tears away. "I don't know what's wrong with me. I've lost patients before."

"But something made this one different?"

She swallowed hard, struggled for control. "I suppose."

"It's okay if you don't want to talk about it, but I'm willing to listen if you do. It's sometimes easier to unload your troubles on someone you don't know very well."

"I never have. I'm not sure I know how." Sure, there were parallels between hers and Eve's lives, but there was more. "I guess she reminded me of my grandmother. Thinking of her brings back memories . . . regrets."

"Why regrets?"

Janice hesitated. She'd never told anyone what had happened. She'd been so angry and hurt all these years, and Eve's death just brought it all to the surface. Blake squeezed her hand, silently encouraging her to continue.

Janice took a deep breath and began. "I was finishing up medical school in Boston. I'd been offered residencies at Johns Hopkins and The University of Tennessee Medi-

101

cal Center at Knoxville. Much to my mother's dismay, I accepted the latter."

"What about your father? What did he think?"

"He didn't get involved. He never got involved."

"Johns Hopkins is pretty prestigious."

"I didn't care about that. I wanted to be close to my grandmother. Grandfather had died the year before. He had Alzheimer's."

"I'm sorry."

The warmth of his hands enfolding hers helped her go on. "His illness had been hard on Grandmother. I kept in close touch with her after he died. When I got the UT residency, we agreed that I would relocate to Angel Ridge and move in with her. She was quite elderly and needed help with the place. I didn't want her to be alone.

"I loved that house. Looked forward to living there and having someone to care for. Someone to . . ." She let the words trail into silence.

"Someone to what?"

"To care for me," she said quietly.

"But you never moved there," he supplied.

"No. She died before I finished school."

Blake squeezed her hands.

"She died alone, just like my patient tonight. Someone went to check on her

102

when she didn't show up for her Wednesday morning quilting circle at church. That's when they found her.

"The worst thing is that I didn't get to say goodbye." Janice laughed. It was an empty sound that held no humor. "My mother was out of the country at the time. Some weeks later, she broke the news to me in a postcard from Nice. The house and its contents had already been sold at auction."

"I remember that. Thought it was unusual."

"I guess that's when you bought the house."

"No. I only bought it a year or so ago. It stood empty until then."

So, no one had lived there since her grandparents until Blake moved in. It went uncared for all those years. Janice sniffed and wiped her nose. "My mother's a heartless, cold woman."

He handed her a tissue. "Mrs. Prescott had a nice funeral. The whole town turned out."

"I'm so glad," she whispered.

He tugged at her hands until she moved over next to him. He put an arm around her shoulders. "Like I told you, I didn't know her, but I knew of her. Everyone thought highly of your grandparents. They were good people. Active in church. The kind of folks that would give you their last dime if they thought you needed it."

"You know more about them than I did."

He squeezed her arm. The look in his eyes made her limbs go liquid.

"It's not your fault."

This situation was becoming entirely too intimate, and she wasn't so far gone that she didn't recognize her own vulnerability. Janice found her legs, stood and moved behind her desk. She shuffled a few files into a neat stack, thinking she should update these charts she hadn't gotten to before she left the office this afternoon, but first. . . .

"Blake, it was really nice of you to come all this way." She tucked her hair behind her ears. Doing that reminded her of the kiss they'd shared and how she'd lost her barrette. What now? She couldn't invite him back to her condo. Could she?

He rose and slowly approached her desk, hands in the pockets of his jacket again. He was entirely too appealing for her peace of mind. With her emotions so raw, it was a frightening combination.

"Let me take you to get something to eat."

"Oh, thank you, but it's late, and I don't think I could eat anyway."

He smiled an easy smile that did wild

things to her pulse and nodded. "I guess I'll be going, then." He turned and looked at the door, then back at her. "Can I at least walk you to your car?"

She doubted she'd get much sleep tonight. No need to go home and rattle around her empty condo. "I think I'll work on these charts before I go home." She stacked the files in the center of her desk and sat. Blake just stood there. Looking at her. He was clearly concerned about her.

"Thank you for coming. For listening." She gave him a weak smile.

"Sure." He picked up a crystal paperweight and turned it over in his hand. "What are you going to do?"

Janice frowned. She'd just told him she was going to stay and work. "These charts—"

"I'm not talking about work."

Her uncle's invitation to come to Angel Ridge. Blake's invitation to spend Christmas day with him. The promise she'd made to Eve she hadn't yet had a chance to analyze. "I need time to think, Blake. To process everything. I can't make a decision like that now."

He moved around the desk. Janice spun in her chair to face him. She had a strong urge to retreat to the other side. She felt much safer with the barrier between them, without him standing so close she could feel his heat. For one crazy moment, she imagined him pulling her up against his chest and kissing her the way he had at his house. Only this time, it wouldn't end at his door. It would propel them to her sofa and into something neither of them was ready for.

Blake leaned back against the desk, his knee touching hers. "Come to Angel Ridge. Take the time to get to know the town and its people. Your uncle. Me. See how it feels. No pressure."

"No pressure." Janice laughed and rested an arm on the desk. "You have no idea."

"Tell me."

She looked up into his amazing blue eyes and all she wanted to do was run into the safety of his arms. She couldn't go there. Allowing herself to depend on anyone always spelled disappointment. Her parents had certainly never been there for her. Even her grandparents had left her just when she finally had the opportunity to form a real relationship with them.

Blake trailed his fingertips lightly across the top of her hand. "Tell me," he repeated.

What the hell. "My uncle wants me to move to Angel Ridge permanently. He's ready to retire and thinks I'm the right person to take over his practice."

"I know."

"You — you know? How?"

"Dixie. There aren't many secrets in a small town."

Janice nodded. She should have realized that. She might have if she hadn't been so distracted by this attraction between her and Blake.

"So what's holding you back?"

"My life is here." She stood and walked over to the window and away from Blake. City lights winked at her instead of stars.

He followed. "You sure about that?"

She wasn't sure of anything. She felt like her life had been shaken up and poured out in a hopeless jumble on the floor.

"Like I said, I need time to think."

"Okay. Fair enough."

She could see him reflected in the window. He took two steps back, and headed for the door, but stopped before reaching it. Janice pivoted and watched him. He put his hands on his hips, his head dipped, and then he was facing her.

"At the risk of coming off like a complete idiot, I think there's something special between us. Call it attraction, a connection, I don't know. But I want to . . ."

He approached her in slow measured

steps. "I want to know everything about it. About you, about us together, about where this might take us."

He grasped her arms, then slid his hands from her shoulders to her wrists and back again. Janice grabbed the front of his jacket with both hands and willed her knees to keep her upright.

"I've never felt anything like what I feel when you're near me," he continued, his voice soft and low.

"I know," she breathed. Janice closed her eyes and leaned into him.

He smelled like leather, warm spice, and one hundred percent male. He was the culmination of every fantasy she'd ever had.

"The kisses we shared earlier . . ." He squeezed her shoulders and rested his forehead against hers. "I can't get it out of my mind."

She closed her eyes. All other kisses for the rest of her life would be measured against Blake's. The way he made her feel frankly scared her senseless. She couldn't let herself feel that way for anyone.

She released his jacket and balled her fists, then forced herself to move away from his touch. "I'm not free, Blake."

Blake raked a hand through his hair. "There's someone else?"

"No."

"Then what is it?"

She crossed her arms. "I thought you said something about no pressure."

He held up his hands. "Sorry." He backed away. "It's your decision to make. I won't pressure you, but . . . I'll be hoping."

The door closed softly behind him, and Janice was left in a state with which she was intimately familiar. Alone.

*You. There's still time for you. Don't waste it. Don't wait for tomorrow. You never know what it will hold. Promise.*

Eve Carlisle's words hung in the room like she'd just spoken them.

Time. Don't waste the time she had. Still time for her. . . .

Janice chewed on her thumbnail. Time for what? She had a life. A safe life. For as long as she could remember, she'd envisioned Angel Ridge as an ideal that couldn't possibly be real. She'd have to be insane to give up everything she'd worked so hard to achieve and move to a place that didn't exist.

*What if it does?* the voice whispered. *It's your time . . . if you let tomorrow come.*

# Chapter 6

Insane. She was completely insane. Hearing voices. Telling her partners she would take the rest of the month off as they'd suggested. Packing her bags. Sitting in front of her uncle's house, prepared to spend the holidays in Angel Ridge.

Janice eased her sunglasses off. She couldn't fault the weather. It was a beautiful day with nothing overhead but a wide expanse of cloudless blue sky. She opened the door and grabbed her coat from the passenger seat. After shrugging into it, she walked up to the front door.

Since it was a doctor's office, she tried the doorknob, but found it locked. She looked for a lit doorbell button, but only found a raised knob with something like a key protruding from it. Janice turned the key. The contraption made a loud whirring sound that resembled the sound of a bell. Very clever.

Janice stood back and waited. No one came.

"Check the note in the window. Doc's probably gone fishin' like he usually does on Saturday," someone said from the sidewalk below.

Janice turned. A little red-haired boy looked up at her from his bicycle. "Thank you," she said.

"You new 'round here?"

She walked down the steps before she answered. "I'm Janice Thornton. Doctor Prescott is my uncle."

"Ya don't say. Well, I'm Sam Houston. My daddy's the mayor."

"I'm pleased to meet you, Sam Houston." The adorable boy's smile revealed he was missing his front teeth. "I could show you to the fishin' hole, if'n you's a mind to go."

"That's very kind of you, but I think I'll wait around town until my uncle comes back."

"Suit yerself. See ya."

"Bye." Janice watched as the boy continued on his way down the sidewalk.

She walked back up the steps to the porch. As Sam Houston had said, there was a note on the window by the front door, and it read, *Gone fishing. Call Mable if you have an emergency. Doc Prescott.*

Janice turned and squinted against the bright noonday sunshine. The light reflecting off the lake was nothing short of brilliant. Might as well have a look around town while she waited.

She went to the car and retrieved her sunglasses, then strolled down the drive to the sidewalk that ran parallel to the street. Two steeples were visible a few blocks down to the right. To the left, nothing but a long row of houses with a spectacular river view below. She headed toward the steeples.

After covering only a block, she turned to find a very elderly lady approaching her from a walkway in front of what must be her house: an unusual, two-story white frame with two jutting wings that extended on either side of a trapezoid-shaped front porch. Janice squinted to make out a design in the gingerbread trim. Angel wings?

"Howdy-do there."

The woman, who reminded her a little of Eve Carlisle, was bundled into a royal blue wool coat with a fur-trimmed collar and matching fur cap. Snowy white hair with a bluish tint peeked out from beneath the hat and a wide, curious blue-eyed gaze peered back at her. At five foot nine, Janice dwarfed the diminutive lady.

"Hello," Janice said.

The older woman opened the gate and joined her on the sidewalk. "Well, it's a happy day to see you standin' here in front of my house, young lady."

Janice frowned. She didn't quite know how to respond, but she said, "Thank you."

The woman tugged at her black wool gloves. "We expected you sooner, but I suppose it's no matter. You're here now. *Mmm-hmm*."

How could this stranger know she was coming when she hadn't even known herself until this morning? "I'm sorry, ma'am. Do I know you?"

"I reckon not, but I know you. You're Dotty Prescott's girl. Got to be. You're the spittin' image of her."

"Yes, ma'am. I'm Janice Thornton. Dot—Dorothy Prescott Thornton is my mother."

"Well, I knew that. I might be old, but I ain't senile." She pointed toward town. "Let's get movin' before we freeze to the sidewalk."

"Of course." Janice couldn't hold back a smile. The woman certainly knew how to take charge of a situation. They moved out at a brisk pace. "I'm sorry, but you have me at a disadvantage. I'm afraid I don't know your name."

"Well, I'm Miss Estelee," she said it as if

everyone knew her name.

"I'm pleased to meet you, ma'am."

"No need to call me 'ma'am.' *Miss Estelee* will do just fine."

Janice shortened her strides to match Miss Estelee's. She seemed in good shape for a woman of her age.

"Doc told me you'd been in town."

"Yes, ma— *um* — yes, I came to see my uncle last week."

"*Mmm-hmm.* He didn't say you was a comin' back. In fact, he weren't sure a t'all that you would."

She also knew how to get right to the heart of the matter. Janice was at a loss again. "I'll be staying through the holidays."

"You'll be stayin' longer than that, but you'll see the light soon enough."

Janice bristled. She'd only be staying for the holidays, but saw no reason to dispute the point with this stranger. She wondered if everyone in this small town would feel the need to offer unsolicited advice.

After two more blocks, the road they were walking on ended at Main Street. Janice stopped and stared. "Oh, my . . ."

"Beautiful, ain't it?"

It certainly was. It looked like a Currier & Ives Christmas print. Evergreen garland and wreaths decorated the old Victorian storefronts and buildings and . . . real gas-burning street lamps? In the center of an honest to goodness Town Square stood a bronze sculpture of an angel with a huge Christmas tree rising behind it.

"Take it all in, honey. This is your home."

Janice blinked out of her reverie at the woman's words. Enough was enough. "Miss Estelee, this —"

"Come on, I'll show you around. Help you get acquainted."

Miss Estelee took off down the street, while Janice just stared after her. Apparently her straight, honey-colored cane was for ornamental purposes only.

She turned and pinned Janice with an astute gaze. "Don't make an old lady wait. It ain't polite."

Janice got her feet moving and caught up with the woman as she was saying, "This here's the grocery. Just let Jessie know what you need and she'll have that nice Houston boy bring it out to you."

Janice just nodded and let the lady talk. There was hardly anyone around. With it being such a chilly day, everyone must be indoors.

She pointed. "DeFoe's Hardware is just there. There's a nice young man — Cole Craig — who does all the handy work in town. He's put in an office over by the Hardware because he's an architect now, or some such. But if you've got anything that need's fixin', he'd be the one to call."

Janice found it odd that an architect would do odd jobs about town, but kept silent on the matter.

"Over there's the bank. The McKays run it. They're richer than the Rockefellers and snooty as the Vanderbilts. They own the library down there, too. That nice Cole Craig I just mentioned is marryin' our librarian, Josie Allen, in a couple of weeks."

"What a beautiful building." The red brick structure resembled a medieval castle. Not at all what she'd expect in a small town library.

"It's one of our oldest buildings. Served as Red Cross Headquarters during the Second Great War. Sherman's Headquarters in the recent unpleasantness with the North."

Janice frowned. "Sherman?"

"Oh, yes. He marched right through the middle of town on his way to Georgia and commandeered it. Stayed pert near three weeks. Some welcomed him. Most didn't."

"Didn't Tennessee fight with the south in the Civil War?"

"Some did. Some didn't. Most folks were

simple farmers, but around here, they was a lot of folk whose way of life was threatened by the Northern aggression. That's enough talk of discord and strife. This here's a happy day what with it bein' your homecomin' and all. No need for none of that."

The woman's references to Janice coming home were making her very uncomfortable. "Miss Estelee, I don't want you to get the wrong impression. I'm only here for a visit."

They stopped for a moment before circling around and proceeding down to the other side of the street. She tapped her cane. "*Mmm — hmm.* I hear you met our Blake Ferguson."

Janice puzzled at that statement. The woman certainly was forward. "Yes."

Miss Estelee stood still, resting both hands on the silver handle of her cane. "He's settled into your grandparents' house real nice. Like he belongs there."

She was about to agree when Miss Estelee continued. "You belong there with him."

The statement took her by surprise. The older woman took advantage of her speechless state.

"Your mama never belonged here. A fish out of water. But now you, you was meant to be a part of this town. And Blake Ferguson buyin' that house was no accident. No

117

siree, them angels was at work in that."

Janice found her voice then. "Angels?"

"Why sure. There's been angels a livin' up on this ridge for ages. They kinda watch over things, if you will, since we ain't too good at it ourselves."

Janice wondered if the poor dear suffered from dementia. That would explain a lot. She'd have to discuss it with her uncle later.

Miss Estelee continued down the sidewalk and Janice followed.

"That's the First Baptist Church up there. First Presbyterian's just there, at the other end of the curve. Don't know how they're gonna fair when they get to heaven. I reckon one'll set up at one end of the streets of gold. One on the other." Miss Estelee shook her head.

Might as well humor the old dear. "They're both beautiful churches. Which one do you attend, Miss Estelee?"

"Oh, I used to attend both. But now, most times, I just go up to the tall pines. If ya ask me, it's the closest a body can get to Heaven 'round here.

"Over here, right across from the bank, is where one of our newest businesses has opened. Girl who runs it is named Candi Heart."

Miss Estelee had to stop. She began to

118

cackle and tap her cane. Janice couldn't help it. She laughed along with her.

"O — Oh. She's a breath o' fresh air, I tell you." She elbowed Janice. "Givin' old lady McKay a time, too. Well, just look at that sign. Why it's enough to give Harriet McKay an episode every time she walks out the front door of her bank right across the street." Miss Estelee tapped her cane again, and laughed louder.

A big, heart-shaped, red sign above the door of the white wooden storefront read *Heart's Desire.* In the store window, one mannequin was dressed in a risqué red teddy with white fur trim and a Santa hat while another wore a more sedate, full-length red satin peignoir set. Cling stickers on the window read, *Naughty or Nice.* A platter of chocolates and an arrangement of flowers sat between the two displays.

"Interesting."

"It sure is. We ain't never had nobody like Candi here in town. She's a breath of fresh air if you ask me. If you ask Mrs. McKay across the way there at the bank, she'd just as soon run Candi out of town on a rail. I say, to each her own. There's room enough for everybody in Angel Ridge. If you live long enough you learn it's the differences in folks that make life interestin'." She laughed

119

and tapped her cane, "Some make it more interestin' than others!"

Without warning, Miss Estelee veered off the sidewalk toward the Town Square. She walked right up to the angel monument and stared up at it with a slight smile on her face. The exquisite sculpture stood on a brick pedestal and extended at least eight feet toward the blue sky. The warrior angel immortalized in bronze stood passive, his sword hilt held in both hands, its tip down. He had the most strikingly beautiful face. The most peaceful countenance.

"Somethin', ain't he?" her companion breathed.

Still looking up, Janice agreed. "He certainly is."

"He just sorta says it all, don't he?"

Janice puzzled. "About what?"

"The town."

Janice looked back up at the angel, giving the statement some thought. He did. Peaceful. Dignified. Surviving the test of time.

"Yes," Janice agreed. "I see what you mean."

"Good. I'll be on my way now." Miss Estelee moved away at a brisk clip. "Drop by on Monday to check my blood pressure with the doc." Her voice trailed off as the distance between them grew.

"Nice to meet you," Janice called after her. The old lady waved as she strode back toward her house. Janice moved around the monument and turned her attention to the impressive blue spruce taking up much of the square. Glass balls of varying sizes added color, but its most impressive decoration was the large angel sitting at its apex. She was a beautiful blonde in a flowing gold gown.

"Stunning, isn't she?"

Janice turned, startled by the sound of Blake's voice. He leaned against the angel monument, his arms crossed, looking sexier than any man had a right to in that black leather jacket, form-fitting, faded jeans, and an off-white ribbed sweater. That lock of raven hair fell across his forehead begging to be brushed back into place.

"Fancy meetin' you here," he said in a low, deep southern drawl that pushed her the rest of the way over the edge.

"Hi."

"I wasn't sure after last night if —"

"I wasn't sure either."

"But here you are."

"Yes."

He paused, staring at her with that intense gaze that seemed to miss nothing. "What does this mean?"

Janice shrugged. "It means I'm here . . . for now."

Blake looked away, then back again. "Was that Miss Estelee givin' you the grand tour?"

"Yes. An interesting lady."

Blake chuckled. "No doubt about that." He shoved his hands in his pockets and said, "I was just headed over to Ferguson's for lunch. Would you like to join me?"

"It was next on my list of places to see."

He pushed away from the monument and offered her his arm. Janice took it and walked with him to the diner.

"Been by to see your uncle yet?"

"Yes. He wasn't in."

"Ah, yeah. He's got a nice little cabin up on the mountain on the other side of the lake. It's got a creek where he can be found trout fishin' most Saturdays. Any season. Any type of weather."

"I call that dedication."

Blake laughed and held the door to the diner open so she could precede him. This must be where the entire population of Angel Ridge was keeping warm. The place was buzzing with conversation, until Blake followed her inside and stood next to her. A hush fell over the place, and Janice suddenly knew what it felt like to be on display as all eyes trained on her. The attractive young woman with the spiked red hair Janice remembered from last week emerged from behind the counter and elbowed her way toward them.

"Well, what's the matter with you people? Haven't you ever seen a person walk through a door before?"

Most returned to their conversations, but kept stealing glances in their direction.

"I was wonderin' if you'd make it in today, Blake." She said the words to Blake, but gave Janice an assessing glance. She extended her hand. "I'm Dixie Ferguson. Blake's much better looking sister."

"Janice Thornton." She put her hand in Dixie's for a firm shake. Height must run in the family. She was an inch or two taller than Janice.

"A pleasure. Was that you I saw last week at Doc Prescott's?"

Janice caught the look that passed between Blake and his sister and wondered what that was about. "Yes. Doctor Prescott is my great-uncle."

"Well, that means you're homefolk. Welcome to Angel Ridge. Let me get you a table."

There wasn't an empty seat in the place, but they followed Dixie to a corner booth where two older gentlemen were engaged in an intense discussion over cups of strong looking coffee.

"All right, fellas. Take it outside. You've beat that dead horse too long and have drunk enough coffee to float it, to boot." Dixie jabbed a thumb toward the entrance.

"But —"

"No *buts,* now. You've been takin' up this booth since breakfast. Why, I oughta start chargin' you rent." She shooed them out of the booth. "Go home to your wives before they forget what you look like."

"Oh, all right, Dix," one man said.

"See ya on Monday." The other rose with his friend.

"Blake. Ma'am." They tipped their caps to her.

Janice smiled. She removed her coat with Blake's help, then sat as Dixie cleared the cups away and swiped the crumbs off the table with a towel. "The special today is beef stew with corn muffins. If that doesn't appeal, there are menus on the table. Can I get you anything to drink?"

"Hot tea," Janice said.

"Coffee for me, Dix."

"Comin' right up."

When they were alone, Janice joked to cover her nervousness, "Nothing like making an entrance." She tucked her hair behind her ears and focused on the green Formica tabletop. A small potted poinsettia sat near the artificially frosted window.

"It's a small town. Newcomers draw attention."

"Guess I'll have to get used to that."

Blake winked at her. "If you stick around long enough, they won't give you a second look."

There it was. An unspoken question as to whether she was here for good or just for a visit. Might as well clear that up now. "I'm here through the holidays. Beyond that —"

Blake held up his hands. "Hey, you don't owe me any explanations. But I am happy to see you. I won't lie about that."

If she were the type to confess all, she'd have to admit she was happy to see him too. Good thing she wasn't that type, because she wasn't ready to have that conversation. In fact, she was unsure coming here had been a wise decision.

Dixie returned with their drinks. Janice thanked her.

"What'll you have?" She pulled a pencil from behind her ear and an order pad from the Christmas tree that made a pocket on her holiday apron.

"The special sounds good to me," Janice said.

"Can't go wrong with Dixie's stew," Blake said.

Dixie propped a hand on her hip and glared at her brother. "Can't go wrong with anything I cook."

"Of course that goes without saying," Blake agreed. "I'll have the same."

"Comin' right up. Two specials at table four," she called out as she threaded her way through the crowded diner back to the counter.

Janice smiled. "I like your sister."

"That's good, 'cause she owns the only eating establishment in town. You don't want to be on her bad side, if you know what I mean."

"No danger in that happening. I like a woman who can keep her brother in line."

Blake's smile was warm and easy. The effect was devastating to her senses. "All right, now. Don't go gangin' up on me."

"There's power in numbers," Janice teased, falling in with the easy banter.

Blake shook his head, a resigned look on his face. "I'm in big trouble."

She looked out the window as a horse drawn carriage rolled by. "Tourists," Blake explained. "We get tours from Knoxville midday on Saturdays. The Historical Society thought it would help raise money for their preservation projects."

"How nice." It made the town more picture-perfect in her eyes. A bad thing for a woman in her state of mind; one who was quickly falling under the influence of a Pierce Brosnan look-alike with a southern drawl.

"We'll have to finish your tour later."

She stirred a packet of sugar into her tea. "I don't know. Miss Estelee was pretty thorough."

He set his cup down. "You know, she's the town's oldest resident."

She sipped her tea. Perfect. "I'm not surprised."

"Where'd you two meet up?"

"I ran into her on my way into town, and she insisted that we walk together."

He propped his arms on the table and leaned forward. "Did she tell you about the angels?"

"You mean the monument?"

"No. I mean *the* angels." He raised his eyebrows to emphasize the word.

"She said something about angels living here, but I didn't think much of it. People her age sometimes go on with nonsensical things."

That earned another raised eyebrow. "I'd be surprised if that was all she said."

"She also said they sort of guided matters around her." She wasn't about to mention that these "angels" had also paired the two of them up.

Blake leaned back.

"Okay, I'll bite," she said. "What else should Miss Estelee have told me about the angels?"

"Well see, there's a legend —"

A young waitress set their food in front of them. "Thank you," they both said.

"Can I get you anything else?"

"No thanks, Abby," Blake said.

When they were alone again, Janice prompted, "You were saying?"

He crumbled his corn muffin in his stew and mixed it up. "There's a legend." He took a bite and chewed.

She sighed. "Yes, I got that."

"Sorry, I'm starvin'." He took another bite, chewed, swallowed, then continued. "The old-timers here say that angels appeared to the first settlers and told them to name the town Angel Ridge. Some believe the angels stuck around. That they watch over the town and its residents. Miss Estelee has been known to tell anyone who will listen that they guide the course of things 'round here."

Janice swallowed her first mouthful of the

delicious stew and almost moaned out loud. It was wonderful. The best she'd ever tasted. It was almost good enough to distract her from their conversation. She wasn't about to tell Blake Miss Estelee had told her as much. She wanted to hear his take on these supposed angels. "What kinds of things?"

Blake shrugged. "According to Miss Estelee, they have a particular interest in folks' love lives."

Janice nearly choked on her muffin.

"She'd probably also say they brought you back here after all these years. Nothing happens by chance in her book. *It's them angels a workin' their magic.*"

That was pretty much exactly what Miss Estelee had said. She took another sip of her tea. "What do you think?"

"I think it's an interesting notion. What do you think?"

"I've never been particularly religious."

"Yeah, well, that's the curious thing. Neither is Miss Estelee. She used to attend church real regular, but any more, about the only time you ever see her in church is for Christmas Eve services."

"She mentioned that she doesn't usually attend. She said something about feeling closest to God in the tall pines."

Blake laughed. "Well, now, I've heard tell

of people gettin', *um, close* up in the tall pines, but I doubt they were thinkin' about God while they were doin' it."

He winked at her, and Janice felt heat creep up her neck. She tried to cover the juvenile feeling by wiping her mouth, then sipping her tea. Blake wasn't fooled.

He touched her hand. "I'm sorry. I didn't mean to embarrass you."

"Oh, you didn't," she lied.

He was gentleman enough to let it pass and to change the subject. "How's the stew?"

"Excellent."

They continued to eat until Blake said, "You plannin' to join your uncle for Sunday services tomorrow? They turn lightin' the advent candles into a real spectacle."

Janice couldn't remember the last time she'd gone to church. "I'll probably just take some time to settle in."

That rakish grin that did wild things to her pulse pulled at the corner of his mouth. "If you'd rather, I could take you up to the tall pines . . ."

The look in Blake's eyes defined smoky.

"Young man, I am certain you did not just embarrass yourself *and* my grandniece by making untoward advances on such short acquaintance."

"Doc Prescott!"

Blake stood and banged his knee on the table in the process. He tried to straighten to his full, impressive height, but the effect was ruined because he felt compelled to rub the ache out of his injury. Twin flags of red colored his cheeks.

"Janice, I'm so sorry." Her uncle took her hands and kissed her cheek. "I would have thought you safe from this type of ungentleman-like behavior in our town." He swung his accusatory gaze back to her lunch companion. "You should be ashamed of yourself, Blake Ferguson."

"It's all right, Uncle. We were just talking about church."

"Indeed?" He continued to glare at Blake who looked like he wanted to sink into the black and white checkerboard linoleum tile.

"Yes. We were talking about church. Miss Estelee told me earlier that she feels closest to heaven in the tall pines. Blake was just offering to show me where it is in case I'd rather go there instead of church tomorrow." She regretted the words as soon as they left her mouth.

*"Harrumph!"*

"That didn't come out at all like I meant it to."

He continued to pin Blake to the spot with

his glare.

"Won't you join us?" Janice invited. "The stew is wonderful."

"Well," he transferred his gaze to Janice, "I was coming over for a bite when I ran into Estelee. She told me she left you in town."

"I'll get you an order of stew, sir," Blake offered and disappeared.

Janice tugged at her uncle's hand. "Please sit. I'm getting a crick in my neck looking up at you." She slid over to make room.

He shrugged out of a heavy canvas jacket with wide pockets. He must have come straight from his cabin.

"You can tell me, now, Janice. Was that young man bothering you?"

"No."

"He seemed overly familiar to be a passing acquaintance."

"Well, we had dinner last night."

"You were here in town? Tell me you didn't drive back to Knoxville alone when you could have stayed with me."

"I had an emergency at the hospital."

Her uncle clicked his tongue against the roof of his mouth. "Ferguson should have driven you. Ill-mannered chit. I could have driven you, for that matter."

"Blake offered, but I insisted on going

alone. It never occurred to me to bother you with such a thing. I'm not helpless, you know. I've done quite nicely on my own for some time."

"Yes, well, there's no need for that now." He patted her hand. "You have family to take care of you."

The soft look of love in her uncle's rich brown eyes melted her heart. Janice squeezed his hand. "That's very sweet, but I don't need taking care of."

"That's not what Estelee said."

"Miss Estelee?" What could the woman know about her? They'd only met a few minutes ago.

"She knows these things."

Not her uncle, too. Janice opened her mouth to speak, but no words came.

"Here's your stew, sir. I apologize for my earlier behavior."

"Think nothing of it, son. Janice explained. Sit. Sit."

"I really should be going. Janice?"

She looked up into his amazing eyes and tried to keep from turning into a puddle. "Yes?"

Her uncle looked from her to Blake and back again.

"That wallpaper I told you about came in today. I'd like to show it to you. Maybe tomorrow?" A hopeful expression settled over his handsome face.

"Yes. I'd like that very much."

"Good. I'll call you, then. Nice to see you, sir. Janice."

She watched Blake walk away. He had a great walk. Confident, easy, sexy. . . .

"*Harrumph.* Look at wallpaper. Well, that's got to be about the oldest line in the book."

"He's just interested in my knowledge of the house, Uncle. He wants it to look the way it did when my grandparents owned it. He even had some of the old wallpaper reproduced."

"Really? He never asked me anything about the house, and I'd know better than most. Why, he bought the place from me!"

Janice frowned. "You bought it?"

"Well course I did. I couldn't let some stranger come in and do who knows what to it. I grew up in that house."

Her eyes widened. "You did?"

"Sure. Your great-grandparents — my parents — built it."

"But you sold it to Blake."

"That boy's a first-rate carpenter. I knew he'd take good care of it. Besides, it had stood empty long enough. But you're gettin' me off the subject. We were talkin' about Blake Ferguson and his ploys to get you over to his house. The point I was tryin' to make was if you think his interest in you is purely for your knowledge of the house, your powers of observation are singularly lacking. That's a poor quality in a doctor, young lady." He shook his head, clearly disappointed.

She bit her lip against the smile that threatened to form. Blake was interested in her, and someone else had noticed. For some reason, that pleased her immensely.

After leaving the diner, Blake went straight to the hardware store and made arrangements to have his wallpaper delivered that afternoon. If he worked on it tonight, he could probably get most of the room papered by tomorrow. He also picked up some putty to repair the hole in the wall near the door. He didn't want to have to explain that. To anyone. He hadn't lost control like that in years.

He still couldn't believe she was here. After laying it all on the line last night, he figured she'd run in the opposite direction, but she was here.

"Hey, big brother. What's put that smile on your face?"

Blake closed his eyes and sighed. Leave it to Cory to ruin an otherwise perfect day

135

with his presence. He turned and faced him. "Been grocery shopping?"

"Yeah. Bebe ran out of crackers and ginger ale, and the delivery boy had already left on his last rounds."

Terrible he should have to come down to town and associate with the little people.

"You didn't answer my question. What are you so happy about?"

Janice and her uncle chose that moment to exit the diner. She saw him and gave a wave. Both he and Cory smiled and waved back.

"So, the good doctor is back in town. No wonder you're smiling."

He gave her a look that made Blake's blood pressure climb. He shoved his brother's shoulder. "Get your eyes back in your head."

"What? Just enjoyin' the view." Cory turned his attention back to Janice. "*Mmm, mmm, mmm* . . . That's about the hottest thing we've ever seen in this sleepy little town. Yeah, kinda makes you wanna come down with something just so she'll have to give you a thorough examination. Stripping down in front of her would be no hardship at all."

Rage roiled up inside Blake. He crushed Cory's designer jacket in his fist and shoved him up against the brick wall behind him. He'd like the satisfaction of smashing his fist into his perfect nose.

Self-talk. Breathe.

Not working.

"You make me sick. You've got a pregnant wife at home and you're standing here on the street ogling women."

Cory pushed against Blake's chest, and he released him. "I'm married, not dead. And I don't know if you've noticed or not, but that's not just any woman. I'd wager I wasn't the only man in town today thinking the same thing. Young, old, married, single. When a woman like that walks by, men notice."

Blake shot a hand through his hair.

"Oh, give it up, Blake. You could never be with a woman like that. You're not man enough. She'd never be satisfied with someone like you." He snorted. "You were more of a man before you let Mom and Dad send you away. Now, you're just a pathetic pansy."

Self-talk. Breathe. Walk away.

"That's it. Scurry off to that big empty house of yours and lock yourself in it. Wouldn't want that nasty temper to get the better of you."

Blake turned and took two steps back

137

toward his brother, but stopped. "You should be glad that I learned some restraint, Cory, or you'd be needing more than the services *this* town's doctor could offer."

"Oh," he held out a steady hand, "I'm so scared."

"What's goin' on out here, boys?" Dixie stepped between them, giving both an even look.

Cory did what he always did. Turned on the charm. He put an arm around Dixie and kissed her cheek. "Nothing, Sis. Man, you get prettier by the minute. I can't understand why some good lookin' guy hasn't snapped you up."

Dixie actually blushed and swatted at his chest. "You're a silver-tongued devil, Cory Ferguson."

Cory looked over at Blake and winked. Blake clinched his fist and took a step forward.

Dixie stopped him with a hand at as chest and a frown. "What's got your dander up, Blake?"

"Yeah, Blake," Cory chimed in. "What's up?"

He pointed a finger at him and leaned across his sister. "If you don't get out of here right now, I swear I'm going to plaster you to that brick wall."

"Blake!" Dixie protested.

"It's all good, Sis. You know it's just empty threats. He doesn't have it in him any more."

Blake took another step forward and Dixie put her back into his chest. "Maybe you better get on home, Cory. I don't think he's jokin'."

"Yeah. Gotta get back to the puking wife. Joy." He moved to step around them, but turned back and said, "Hey, maybe that new lady doctor could give her something for it. Women know about these things." He waggled his eyebrows. "Maybe I'll ask her over."

Blake nearly mowed his sister down, then. He had to give her credit. She blocked him like a pro linebacker.

"Cory Ferguson. You get yourself home right now," she snapped.

Cory just laughed and strolled down the sidewalk toward home while Dixie did her best to keep Blake from following. When Cory had turned the corner and was out of sight, Blake slumped against the wall.

"You wanna tell me what that was about?"

He pulled in several long, deep breaths, desperately trying to regain control. When he was able, he said, "That slime bag was drooling —"

"Watch it, now. That is our brother you're

referring to."

"I can't help that."

"Help what?"

"That he's my brother."

"Blake Ferguson —"

He held up a hand. "Don't start in on me, Dix. I'm in no mood."

"I can see that. What's got you so riled?"

"Nothin'," he lied. "I gotta get goin'." He turned and started toward home.

"Okay. I'll stop by later and check on you."

He gave a wave, but didn't look back. Why had he allowed himself to lose control like that? His brother had just been goading him, and he'd let him. He hadn't lost control like this in years. Now it had happened twice in two days. What the hell was the matter with him? He knew he couldn't give into anger that way. Not with a temper like his. He wouldn't allow his worthless brother to erase what he'd worked years to achieve, not now. He had wallpaper to hang. And a possible relationship to consider.

But first, maybe he'd make a detour to his workshop. Yeah. Hammering out his frustrations on that china cabinet Pastor Strong had ordered for his wife's Christmas present was just what he needed.

# CHAPTER 7

Janice woke early. After years of getting up in the pre-dawn hours to complete rounds before going into the office, sleeping-in apparently would take some time. Earlier, she'd heard her uncle moving about. He must have decided to let her rest, because she also heard a door open and close downstairs, then a car started and moved away from the house.

Janice gave up and headed for the shower. Downstairs in the kitchen, she smiled when she saw that her uncle had left the coffeepot on with a plate of muffins beside it. A note read, *Back about one. Make yourself at home.*

Enticed by the sun, she stepped out onto the sun porch. Windows all the way around let in the warmth while keeping out the cold. Still, she wrapped up in a blanket she found on the back of a chair and sank into a wicker chaise lounge filled with soft, over-stuffed cushions.

Sipping her coffee, she enjoyed the view of a frost-covered lawn until some sound at the door interrupted the peacefulness of the moment.

She frowned. There it was again. Faint, but definitely a distressed sound. She hurried to the door. The blast of cold took her breath, then frosted it as she blew it out. She looked down along the side of the house. Nothing. Then she heard it again, this time clearer. A pitiful meow. She looked down into the upturned face of the tiniest kitten she'd ever seen. Huge blue eyes dominated the tiny face. It looked like a little ball of soft, gray fuzz.

"Well, hello." She bent and held out her hand to let the kitten get her scent. The cat didn't move. It shook as if it were freezing. It didn't protest when she scooped it into her hand. "Come inside where it's warm, little one."

She stroked its tiny back. The kitty meowed its pleasure. Janice closed the door and walked into the warmth of the kitchen. "Are you hungry? *Hmm?* I bet you are. Where's your mommy?"

The little kitten just stared up at her with huge ice blue eyes. Janice had never had a kitten, or a pet of any kind for that matter. For one thing, she'd never been home. For another thing, her mother would never have allowed a pet in her pristine house. She couldn't even stand to have Janice around.

Setting the kitten on the counter, she searched the cabinets, moving several cans around until she found what she was looking for. "Here we go. Tuna. Yum." She popped the can open and set it in front of the kitten. It sniffed the fish, then looked up at Janice as if to say, *What am I supposed to do with this?*

Janice frowned. Maybe she was too young to eat solid food. "Would you like a little milk, instead?" She pulled a glass bottle from the refrigerator and poured a bit into a saucer. Fifteen seconds in the microwave warmed it to tepid. Janice tested it and licked her finger. Perfect.

"Here you go. Eat up."

The cat tasted the milk experimentally with the tip of its pink tongue. Satisfied, it went after the treat with gusto. Janice laughed as it buried its face in the saucer. Even put its front paws in it. When the kitten had had its fill, it looked up at Janice and meowed its thanks. Milk dripped from its whiskers and chin. Janice picked up the kitten and dried it off with a kitchen towel. "There now. That's better." After a quick check, she found it was a female.

The two sat at the kitchen table. While Janice stroked her fur, the kitty curled up in the crook of her arm and fell asleep. "Where did you come from?" She wondered if her mother were nearby? If she'd just wandered off and couldn't find her way back? And what if she didn't have a home? What if she was a stray?

What would her uncle think? She couldn't saddle him with a kitten after she went back to the city. Taking it with her wasn't an option. Her condo association didn't allow pets.

Her thoughts wandered to Blake. He'd said he was in desperate need of a cat. It was the perfect solution. Maybe he could look after her until they found her home. If she didn't have one, maybe he could keep her.

That was it. She'd take the cat to Blake and get her settled in before she got attached to Janice.

No time like the present. Janice bundled into her hat and coat, settled the kitten in her pocket, then wrapped a scarf around her neck and pulled on gloves. Outside, she headed down the walk, and turned onto the brick sidewalk toward Blake's house.

"What did I do to rate this?"

Blake greeted his sister at the back door just as he was zipping his jeans and slipping his arms into a plaid shirt. Seeing who it was, he didn't bother buttoning it.

"I come bearing hot muffins. You'd better have coffee."

"You're in luck. It just finished brewing."

Dixie came inside and unbuttoned her coat. Blake helped her out of it and draped it over a kitchen chair.

"I'm surprised you're here," she said. "I saw your car in the drive as I passed by on my way to Susan's. I promised to sit with her while the rest of the family goes to church, so I can't stay long."

"I overslept."

"You?" She opened the bag and the aroma of blueberries filled the room. "I wasn't aware you knew how."

He pushed his wet hair off his forehead. "Guess there's a first time for everything."

"Don't suppose it'd have anything to do with a certain blonde sleeping a block away warm and snug in her uncle's house?"

He gave Dixie what he hoped was a look that clearly stated he didn't want to discuss Janice Thornton. Fact was, he'd been up most of the night hanging wallpaper and trying to decide what his next move with her would be. If there would be one.

"I just got a passing glance at her last week, but seein' her standin' there with you in the diner yesterday, I gotta tell you, I think she's the most beautiful woman I've ever seen."

The statement reminded him of the exchange with Cory yesterday. The anger that had been simmering since then threatened to rise to the surface.

"Of course, it shouldn't surprise me. I heard her mother was a real looker, too."

Blake gave her a look again when he set a plate in front of her.

Dixie held up her hand. "Just coffee for me. I gotta get movin'. Can't keep the mayor waitin'. You know how he can be. But I got a piece of advice for you before I go." She pinched a bite out of his muffin and popped it into her mouth.

"What if I said I don't need any advice?"

"You're gettin' it anyway. If you're really interested in this woman, don't beat around the bush about it. Go after her. Women like that don't stay on the shelf long." Dixie brushed the crumbs off her hands and stood. "Now don't give me that look. I know you. You were probably up half the night plannin' your next move, and that's why you look like six miles of bad road."

He saluted her with his cup. "Thanks,

Sis." He took a long draw of the strong liquid and closed his eyes while the caffeine worked its magic.

She shrugged into her coat. "Word is she's only going to be here until Christmas, then she's jettin' back to the city. You got no time to waste, and you sure don't want to let someone else around here get the jump on you."

"Dixie . . ." He couldn't think of anything worse than having his baby sister telling him what he needed to do to snag a woman. He definitely didn't want to hear that he might have competition.

"Okay, okay. I'm outta here. Think about what I said."

Her voice trailed off as she hurried down the hallway to the front of the house. "Well, good mornin', Doc. I was just on my way out. Come on in. Blake's back in the kitchen."

Blake stood and made it to the doorway of the kitchen in time to see Dixie leave and Janice come in.

"Bye," Janice said to a banging door.

Blake leaned against the doorframe and looked his fill. She was all bundled up in an off-white coat, her cheeks pink from the cold. Dear Lord, one look at her and every doubt or reservation he had fled.

Janice pulled her hat off. "Hi." She looked back over her shoulder at the door. "Was that a whirlwind or your sister that just blew through here?"

"That's Dixie. She's hard to pin down for more than five minutes."

Janice removed her gloves and swiveled back to face him. "I hope you don't mind me dropping by un— *um* — unannounced . . ." Her words trailed into nothing.

"Of course not."

She took a breath and looked away, biting her upper lip. "I'm sorry. You must have just been getting dressed."

He glanced down at his shirt hanging open. "Oh, sorry." He secured the two middle buttons and buttoned his jeans. "I'd just gotten out of the shower when Dixie showed up." She still stood near the door, looking unsure of what to do or where to look.

"Join me for a cup of coffee?"

Watching her walk toward him was pure pleasure. Even bundled up so that only her face showed, she was stunning. When she stood before him, he couldn't help himself, he reached out to unwrap her long green scarf. "Are you in there?"

She smiled up at him then and it seemed

the most natural thing in the world to lean down and kiss her cheek. "Man. You're like a human ice cube." He rubbed her arms. "Come in the kitchen and let me get you a cup of coffee."

"Thanks."

She preceded him into the kitchen and went directly to the coffeemaker. "It must be ten degrees out there."

Blake peered at the thermometer outside his kitchen window. "Fifteen."

Her laugh seemed a little nervous. "Is there really a difference between fifteen and ten? If you ask me, anything under twenty is just cold. Really cold."

Blake poured a large mug of coffee. "Spoken like a true southern girl."

"Considering the fact that I grew up in the Northeast, I have pretty thin skin. I admit it."

"You take it straight?"

"Absolutely."

He handed her the steaming mug and she held it with both hands, sipping the hot liquid. "Thank you."

He frowned. She still wasn't looking at him.

"So, what brings you my way?"

Her gaze made it as high as his chest before she set the mug on the island and

149

said, "I have something for you."

She reached in her pocket and scooped out a handful of gray fur. A wiggling handful of gray fur that said, *Meow,* and looked up at him with huge, curious blue eyes.

"I found her at my uncle's this morning. I wasn't sure what I should do with her. With it being so early, I couldn't go knock on doors to see if she belongs to someone. Then I remembered that you said you were in desperate need of a cat, and I thought you wouldn't mind taking her in for now."

He rubbed the soft fur under the kitten's chin. She closed her eyes and extended her neck to give him better access. "She hardly looks old enough to be away from her mama."

"I know. Do you think she'll be all right?"

The concern lacing Janice's words made him want to ease her mind. She brought out every protective instinct he had and then some. "Well, if we can't figure out who she belongs to, we could take her in to the vet in Maryville. Have her checked out."

"Tomorrow?"

"Sure." He had a full day, what with things wrapping up at the library and another crew starting two houses in a new subdivision in Lenoir City, but he'd make time. Somehow.

She moistened her lips with the tip of her tongue. "If she doesn't already have a home, will you keep her?"

If she kept looking at him like that, he would promise her anything.

"Are you sure you wouldn't rather have her? I think she's bonded with you."

She stroked the kitten in a rhythmic motion. "Oh, no. I couldn't."

"Why not?"

"I'm not sure how my uncle feels about cats, and the complex I live in doesn't allow pets."

"That won't matter if you move into your uncle's place permanently. I'm sure he wouldn't mind you having a pet until then."

"I can't make the commitment right now. There's a lot to consider. You know that."

"Tell you what. I'll keep her under one condition."

She chewed her full lower lip and her gaze dipped to his chest again.

"What's that?"

"That you exercise liberal visitation."

"Deal. I'll even pay the vet bill."

"Can't beat that."

He bent his knees and caught her gaze. Her cheeks immediately flamed. He took the cat from her and set it on the floor. It rubbed against his ankle. "You okay?"

"*Um*, sure. Now that I know you'll keep her, I'm, *um*, fine. Fine."

That incredible emerald gaze dipped. Again. And she licked her lips. Again. Desire, hot and fast, washed over him and he couldn't resist teasing her. "See anything you like?"

She gasped and would have turned away, but he caught her wrist, halting her retreat. Pulling her forward, he pressed her palm flat against his chest.

"Oh . . ."

Her breath came out in a little puff that teased his neck. Her cold hand felt like a branding iron on his overheated skin, then it shifted inside his shirt, out and down over his flat, taut nipple. She scraped his ribs with her fingernails.

He unbuttoned her coat and eased his hands inside. She wore a heavy pink cotton sweater that almost reached the waistband of a pair of black, hip hugging knit pants that fit her real nice. In that moment, he thought every morning should start this way. With Janice standing in his kitchen inviting him to seduce her back into his bed with only a touch. A heated glance.

He pulled her forward with a hand at either side of her hips while she worked the buttons on his shirt. When she had it open, she smoothed her hands across his chest. Sliding his hands to the backs of her thighs, he pulled her up tight against him and did what he'd wanted to do since she walked into his kitchen . . . he kissed her. He didn't wait for a warm-up kiss, just slanted his mouth on hers, open, hot and hungry. Judging from the way she responded, she'd been more than ready.

He plunged his tongue into her mouth. She dropped her hands letting her coat fall to the floor, then stood on her toes to wrap her arms around his neck. God, she fit so perfectly against him, they felt like two parts of a whole finally coming together.

While their tongues did a wild dance, he slid his hands up over her bottom until he found that enticing gap of warm, smooth skin between her stretch pants and her sweater. He swept his hand up under it and found she hadn't bothered to put on a bra. He groaned deep in his throat, but before he could regain a shred of control, she started an exploration of her own. She trailed hot hands down his chest, his sides, then swept them around to his back and lower. . . .

"Doc Prescott!"

Both Blake and Janice jumped apart at the sound of Dixie's voice.

Blake groaned again as his sister burst into the house and rushed into the kitchen. The cat skidded across the hardwoods and hid under the kitchen table.

"Doc Prescott, I need you. It's Susie."

It took Blake a second to figure out his sister was speaking to Janice, who didn't waste time correcting her.

"Slow down," Janice spoke in a calm, re-assuring voice to his sister. "Tell me what's wrong."

Lord, he wondered how she could regain control so quickly? She trailed a shaky hand down her thigh, and he smiled. She was feeling it, too.

"It's my friend, Susie. I was walking her to the bathroom and she passed out on me. You have to help her."

Janice picked up her coat and moved toward the front door with Dixie. Blake stepped into some shoes, grabbed his car keys and coat.

"I don't have my medical bag."

"We'll swing by and pick it up," Blake said.

"I'll meet y'all there." Dixie had run out the door, down the sidewalk, and around the block before Blake had Janice in the front seat of his truck. Blake fired the ignition and put the truck in gear.

"Has your sister's friend been ill?" Janice asked.

"She has cancer. It's pretty advanced."

They made it to Doc Prescott's in record time. Janice jumped down from the truck and ran to her car. She was back in a moment with her bag. Blake grasped her hand and helped her up. As soon as she was in, he continued down the road to the mayor's house.

When they arrived, Janice didn't wait for Blake to help her out of the truck. She hopped out of the cab before he'd brought it to a complete stop and sprinted up the sidewalk, into the house.

"Dixie?"

"Up here."

Janice took the steps two at a time. He wasn't far behind. They found Susan, wrapped in a blanket, lying on the bedroom floor near the bathroom. Dixie was at her side, cradling Susan's head in her lap.

"How long has she been out?" Janice asked as she checked the prone woman's pulse.

"She passed out right before I came for you. Is she —"

"Her pulse is weak and thready, breathing shallow." Janice dug in her bag for some-

155

thing. "How did she seem when you got here?"

Blake squatted with the women and squeezed his sister's shoulder while Janice worked.

"Weak. Like always."

"Tell me what you know about her condition."

Janice lifted her eyelids and shined a light in Susan's eyes.

"She has advanced breast cancer. She's known for a few months. Refused treatment because the doctors said it wouldn't cure her."

"Has my uncle been treating her?"

"He's been trying to keep her comfortable. She's really gotten worse in the past couple of weeks."

"Is she eating? Able to take fluids?"

"Not much."

"We need to get her to a hospital. Blake, call an ambulance."

"No!" Dixie grabbed Blake's arm so he couldn't move away. "No hospitals. She can go to Doc's clinic, but not the hospital. She'd never forgive me if — if I let her die in a hospital."

"She's severely dehydrated. She needs an *IV*. If we don't get her the treatment she needs immediately, her condition will worsen. I'm not familiar with my uncle's clinic —"

"I'll get him from church," Dixie said.

"I can't take her in my truck."

"Take my car. I'll take your truck."

Blake exchanged keys with Dixie, then lifted Susan into his arms. She weighed no more than a child. She felt so fragile. This happy, carefree woman who'd been like a sister to him shouldn't be fighting for her life. She was too damn young. The same age as Dixie.

Emotion clogged his throat as he carried her downstairs. Dixie and Janice followed. He settled her in the back seat of Dixie's Explorer with Janice, then got behind the wheel and drove the short distance to Doc Prescott's.

Blake gathered Susan in his arms and followed Janice into the clinic. He passed her and carried the unconscious woman into the large examination room. It was where Doc Prescott did the more complicated procedures. Janice was digging through drawers when Doc Prescott and his nurse, Mable, came in with Dixie and the mayor close behind.

Doc Prescott spoke to Janice as he rolled up his sleeves. "What do we have, Doctor?"

"Severe dehydration. She needs an *IV*. I

can't find —"

"Mable, let's start a line."

The large woman who'd been Doc Prescott's nurse for as long as Blake could remember moved Janice out of the way.

"Janice, this is my nurse, Mable Calloway. Mable, this is my niece, Dr. Janice Thornton."

"Doctor," the efficient nurse acknowledged Janice as she gathered the supplies she needed while Doc Prescott washed up at the sink. Janice moved to Susan's side, her hand on her wrist.

Patrick Houston had had about all he could take. He and Dixie crowded around Susan. "Doc, tell me what's going on."

"Patrick, you and Dixie can either wait in the reception area or stand back and let us work. There'll be time for discussion later."

Blake grabbled his sister's elbow and with a firm hand at Patrick's shoulder, urged them both back out of the way. "Do as he says."

"Pulse fifty-four, respirations ten and shallow," Janice said.

Blake put his arm around his sister. The fact that she leaned into him and rested her head on his shoulder was telling. His unflappable, strong, independent sister was shaken to the core.

"Let's get her some oxygen, too."

"Yes, doctor."

Janice took the needle and alcohol swabs from the nurse. "If you'll hand me some gloves, I'll do this while you get the oxygen," she said to the nurse.

Mable hesitated. She looked up at Doc Prescott. When he nodded, she handed Janice a pair of latex gloves then left the room. Janice expertly inserted the needle in Susan's arm, then connected it to the *IV*.

She punched several buttons on a keypad the thing was connected to and fluid began dripping through the tube.

Mable re-entered the room as Doc Prescott was taking a blood sample. She rolled in an oxygen tank. In a matter of seconds, she had Susan hooked up to it with clear tubing tucked behind her ears. The life-giving air flowed out the tubing into her nose. Doc Prescott handed the vile of blood he'd just taken to Mable. She left the room with it.

"What do you think?" Doc Prescott asked Janice.

"I think she should be in a hospital."

The older man nodded his agreement and rubbed his beard. "You're probably right, but we promised her when her time came, we wouldn't."

159

"Oh God . . ." Dixie murmured and pressed her face into Blake's chest. He held her tight against him, his throat constricted. He wanted to tell her it would be all right, but they both knew it would just be a lie.

Despite the doc's warning, Patrick moved to his wife's side. He took her hand in his. "You hang in there, sweetheart. It's too soon. You hear me? Too soon."

Janice and her uncle exchanged a look, but gave the grieving man no encouraging words. No reassurances.

"Patrick . . ."

They all looked at the woman lying on the table. She'd opened her eyes, and they were trained on her husband.

Dixie sniffed. "Well, ain't that just like Susie," she whispered. "He says *jump* and she says *how high.*"

Blake smiled.

"You gave us a right good scare there, Susan," Doc Prescott said.

"Sorry."

He patted her shoulder. "Rest. Let's get you perked up with these tubes."

"I want to go home."

Her voice was hoarse and weak, but the words were clear.

"Now, Susan, I know how you feel about doctors' offices and hospitals, but you're gonna have to stay here. At least for several hours, until we can get you some fluids. I'll have Mable get the guestroom ready, and we'll move you in there. How's that sound?"

A wispy smile played at Susan's lips, and she nodded her agreement. "Thanks, Doc."

He squeezed her hand and led Janice from the room. Blake and Dixie followed, leaving Patrick a moment alone with his wife.

"What do you think, Doc?" Dixie asked.

He removed his glasses and slid them into his shirt pocket. "I think we got lucky. That's one tough customer in there, but there's only so much a body can take. How long has it been since she stopped eating and taking fluids?"

"I see that she at least drinks something when I'm there, but I haven't been able to get her to eat for a couple of days."

"Why didn't you and Patrick tell me?"

"She didn't want us to."

"Well, I'll have a word with her about that when she's a bit stronger. But you, young lady," he pointed a finger at her, "you should know better."

Dixie raked a hand through her short hair. "I know, Doc. It's a fine line, tryin' to honor her wishes and doin' what's practical."

"We agreed, all of us, to do what we could to keep her comfortable. That means if she can't take fluids or food, we'll give them to her in a way she can accept."

"I know, but she hates tubes and needles," Dixie said.

"Better than the alternative," Doc Prescott said succinctly.

"She needs a scan," Janice said. "In order to treat her, we need to know the extent to which the cancer has spread."

"Yes, that would be useful, but she won't go near a hospital. She won't even discuss it," he said.

"Why did she refuse treatment?"

"When we found the tumors in her breasts, the cancer had already metastasized to her brain and spine. The head of oncology at the University Medical Center saw her. The type of cancer she has is aggressive. They told her surgery followed by chemotherapy and radiation would prolong her life by a few months, but it wouldn't cure her."

"She wanted to spend the time she has left enjoying her family, not puking from the treatments with her hair falling out," Dixie added.

"But there are excellent drug treatments that alleviate the side effects of the chemo," Janice pointed out.

"She was advised. She declined," Doc

Prescott said.

"How old is she?"

"Thirty-two. I'm going to see how Mable is coming with that blood work."

"I'll check on the patient," Janice offered.

Blake turned to his sister. "You okay?"

"Course I am." She moved away from him as if she'd never allowed herself a moment's weakness. "I should head back to Susan's. The kids will be home from church soon and starving."

"Want me to drive you?"

She shook her head. "No, I'll take my car. Are the keys in it?"

"Yeah."

"Thanks for your help."

He ran his hands up and down her arms. "No problem. Anything else I can do?"

"I'll let you know."

Blake nodded and walked his sister outside. He stood on the front porch as he watched her drive away. The church bells from the Baptist and Presbyterian churches in town rang in tandem indicating Sunday School was over and church services would soon begin. A typical Sunday.

He looked up at the sky and wondered, not for the first time, why a woman like Susan should have to deal something like this. A young woman with two children and her whole life ahead of her shouldn't be facing the fact that she didn't have much longer to live.

He slammed a fist into his palm as impotent rage boiled up inside him. Susan was one of the most giving, caring people he'd ever known. She was always the first to welcome newcomers to town with a warm smile and a home baked treat. Usually a cake. She put in more volunteer hours in the community than anyone he could think of. Why her? Why now?

He felt a light touch on his arm.

"Are you okay?"

He turned, surprised to see Janice standing next to him. "I didn't hear you come up."

"You were pretty deep in thought."

"How's Susan?"

"Improving. We got to her just in time. Another half hour, and I don't know."

He unclenched his fist and took her hand. "You were great in there."

"I was useless. I couldn't find anything."

"Don't be so hard on yourself. You just got into town. Your uncle hasn't even had a chance to show you the clinic yet."

She pulled her hand back and rubbed her arms. "I should have made time to at least have a look around."

"You knew what she needed so that Doc and Mable could go to work when they got here."

Janice didn't respond.

"How long will you keep her?" he asked.

"She should stay overnight. She needs tests. Tests we can't perform here."

"Doc Prescott usually makes do."

"So I'm told."

"Mable?"

Janice nodded. "She wasn't happy about my rummaging through her drawers. Said it would take her the rest of the day to get everything back in order."

Blake laughed. "That's Mable."

Janice didn't seem amused.

He scrubbed a hand down his face. "I guess I should go. Can I get y'all anything?"

"I think we're okay for now." She grabbed his hand, frowning. "What happened?" She brushed her thumb across the fresh scabs.

"*Aw,* it's nothing. I'll check back with you later, then." He squeezed her arm, and then started down the steps.

"Blake?"

He turned on the bottom step and glanced back up at her.

"Thanks for your help. I don't know what we would have done without you." She shaded her eyes against the sun, shielding her expression from him. He nodded and shoved his hands in his pockets as he strolled to his truck.

He sat behind the wheel and watched Janice walk back into the house, wondering how he would feel if she walked out of his life forever in a couple of weeks? He needed more time with her to see if there was anything beyond the attraction. In any case, Dixie was right. He shouldn't waste time. Susan was proof that time was not a limitless commodity.

Yes. He'd check on the doctors later. If Susan was okay, maybe he'd just whisk Dr. Thornton away. Lay his cards on the table and see where the chips fell.

# CHAPTER 8

"Hello?"

Janice heard the voice just as she put the coffee on to perk. She stepped out into the hallway in time to see Miss Estelee heading for the kitchen with a large basket, as if she knew the layout of the house.

"Miss Estelee?"

"Oh, hi-dee, Doc. I brung you lunch."

"Here, let me help you with that." Janice took the heavy basket of food from Miss Estelee. "This is very nice of you."

"Estelee?" Janice's uncle joined them in the hallway. "Estelee," he said warmly and kissed the woman on the cheek.

She swatted at his arm. "Here now, there's no need for all that."

Her uncle just smiled. "You brought lunch."

Was Miss Estelee blushing?

"Well, course I did. It'd be a shame to have all that food go to waste."

Janice turned and walked back into the kitchen. Her uncle and Miss Estelee? She seemed a little old for him, but then, she really had no idea how old her uncle was. Miss Estelee either for that matter.

The two followed her into the kitchen. She opened the basket and an enticing aroma filled the room. "This smells wonderful," Janice said.

Miss Estelee shooed her away. She pulled out bowls and plates covered in plastic wrap and set them on the counter. "You got any plates around here?"

"Of course. Janice, get us some silverware from that drawer right there. What's in the thermos?" he asked as he took plates down from the cabinet.

"Tea. You know I can't abide yours."

"You mean mine doesn't stand alone like yours."

"Well, you don't have to drink it, Charles Prescott."

Her uncle chuckled. Miss Estelee uncovered containers of beef roast, potatoes, carrots and rolls. She put an apple pie in the oven and turned it on to warm.

"There's enough here to feed an army," Janice commented. Her mouth watered and her stomach growled.

"Better too much than not enough. I

figured the Houston boy would be needin' to eat, too." She started dishing food onto plates. "His wife's holdin' her own."

It was a statement, not a question.

"She's a strong woman," her uncle said.

"It ain't her time. You needn't worry," Miss Estelee said.

Her uncle nodded, not bothering to correct her, even though Susan was in very bad condition. Miss Estelee set one plate aside and began filling another. There was something about this woman. Something perplexing. Janice felt she should tell her where things stood with Susan, but in her gut, she knew Susan would pull through, too. This time.

Janice picked up the plate she'd set aside and said, "I'll take this in to Mr. Houston."

Patrick refused the food as he continued to watch his wife sleep. Janice left it just in case, along with a glass of iced tea. Miss Estelee and her uncle retired to the back parlor after eating. Janice cleaned up the dishes then checked on Susan. Still sleeping. No change.

Miss Estelee left sometime later. Janice was curled up on a couch in the reception area with a blanket and an outdated magazine when her uncle came in.

"I looked in on Susan. She's resting

169

comfortably, but I told Patrick we needed to keep her overnight."

She smiled up at her uncle. "I concur, Doctor. How advanced is her cancer?"

He sat next to her on the couch. "She was diagnosed around seven months ago. Since she refused treatment, I've only done what I can with my limited resources to monitor her condition. Keep her comfortable."

She restated her earlier opinion. "She should have a scan to see how far the cancer has progressed and what organs are affected."

"I agree, but getting her to do it," he shook his head and removed his glasses, "that's another matter entirely. I'm sorry, my dear. This was not the first day I had envisioned for you."

"No need to apologize. I'm accustomed to the patient emergencies."

"Why don't you go up to your room and rest for a bit?"

"I'm fine."

"Maybe you'd like to take a walk, then. Stretch your legs?"

Janice laughed. "Are you trying to get rid of me?"

"No, no. It's just, you've been out here all day. I thought you could use a break."

Janice grasped her uncle's hand. "You'll

have to be patient with me. I'm not used to having someone worry about me."

He raised her hand to his lips and kissed it. "Well, get used to it, young lady, because I intend to see that you are completely spoiled."

Janice couldn't hold back her smile. Just being around him made her happy. "I think I will go upstairs, if you're sure you don't mind. I never got a chance to unpack this morning."

"Of course, of course. Do you have everything you need? If not, just call down to the grocer and they'll bring over whatever is lacking. I'm not used to having a woman about. I'm sure there are some creature comforts I've overlooked."

"Thank you for taking me in on such short notice."

"Oh, sweetie. You've no idea how happy having you here makes me."

She slid off the couch and walked to the doorway that led to the stairs. Before leaving the room, she turned back and admitted, "It makes me happy, too." She didn't understand how someone could love her simply because she was family. But she wanted to understand, because in her experience, being a part of a family meant never being worthy of love. Looking into

171

her uncle's eyes, she saw only acceptance.

She could get used to that.

Janice woke disoriented. Dark shadows filled the strange room, and she wasn't sure where she was or what had woken her.

"Janice?"

The familiar voice was followed by a knocking at the door. Then she remembered. She'd come to her uncle's. They had a critical patient.

Susan.

Janice pushed her hair back out of her face and stood. She heard a meow as she padded over to the door. Did her uncle have a cat? She hit the light switch before she opened the door. She squinted against the light. "Uncle Charles? Is everything all right? Susan —"

"Oh, everything's fine, dear." He patted her shoulder. "Just fine. She's doing much better."

"I must have fallen asleep. I didn't mean to."

"It's not a crime to have a Sunday nap." He chuckled. "In fact, it's darn near a town ordinance." He bent and looked down. "What do we have here?"

Janice looked down, too. The kitten she'd taken to Blake's earlier looked up at them with big eyes. *Meow.*

Janice scooped the kitten up into her hand. "How did you get back in here?"

"Well, now. She's a beaut! Where'd you find her?"

"Outside the sun room this morning. You wouldn't know who she belongs to would you? Have any of your neighbors' cats recently had kittens?"

He stroked his beard, considering. "None that I'm aware of."

"I took her to Blake Ferguson's this morning. He said he'd look after her for now." Her uncle sneezed. "God bless you."

"Thank you. I'm a bit allergic. Nothing an antihistamine won't cure. *Uh,*" he jabbed a thumb toward the stairs, "speaking of the Ferguson boy, he's downstairs dishin' up supper. I told him you were restin'. He looked so disappointed, I figured I'd do him a favor and come up here to get you."

"Oh. Just let me splash some water on my face, and I'll be right down."

"Sorry I woke you."

"No, I'm glad you did."

"There's some back stairs that lead to the kitchen at the end of the hallway. You can take those when you're ready to come down."

Janice hurried into her adjoining bathroom

and set the kitten on the counter while she washed her face and pulled a brush through her hair. She picked the kitten up and found her way downstairs using the narrow back stairway, stopping just inside the kitchen.

Blake sat at the kitchen table with her uncle while the older man ate, but stood when he saw her. She drank in the sight of him. He wore those faded blue jeans that fit him like they had been molded to his thighs and . . .

"Hi."

"Hi." She shoved her free hand into her back pocket and approached the kitchen table. Why did this man have the ability to make her as nervous as a schoolgirl out on her first date?

"I was wondering where she got to." Blake stroked the fur under the kitten's chin.

Janice shifted her focus to the cat. "I was reading in my room and fell asleep. When I woke up, she was there."

*"Ah — choo."*

"God bless you," Janice and Blake said in unison.

"I'd better get that antihistamine. Thank you again for the dinner, Blake. My compliments to your sister."

"You're welcome, sir."

He sneezed again as he walked down the

174

hall. "He's allergic to her," Janice said. "I don't know how she found her way back, or how she got inside."

"Maybe we should name her Houdini. Here," he took the cat and said, "have something to eat while it's hot."

Janice rubbed her stomach. "I'm still stuffed from lunch."

Blake put a plate of chicken and dumplings in front of her anyway. He held out a chair and she sat. "What'd you have?"

"Miss Estelee brought beef roast, roasted vegetables, and apple pie."

"Sorry I missed it." Blake sat back in the seat he'd recently vacated. The kitten curled up in his lap and went to sleep. "I hear Miss Estelee's a good cook, but the only person she ever cooks for is your uncle."

"Really. I wondered . . ." The food smelled and looked wonderful. She would be as big as a house if she kept eating like this. She forked up a bite and nearly moaned. The dumpling melted in her mouth.

"Wondered what?"

*"Umm."* She swallowed. "Oh, I don't know. I just got a vibe about them. It's probably just my imagination."

"I doubt that. They're close, I can tell you that much. Good?"

Janice rolled her eyes and chewed. "Fabulous. Did you make this?"

He absently stroked the kitten's fur. "No, Dixie did. She didn't want y'all to go hungry over here."

"Not much danger in that happening. I'll have to make sure I get in a couple of extra workouts this week or none of my clothes are going to fit."

Blake wiggled his eyebrows. "Now there's an image. You in tight-fitting clothes."

Janice tried not to blush. "Blake Ferguson, are you flirting with me?"

"Absolutely." His smile was wide and unrepentant.

Janice didn't know how to respond to that. Most of the men she associated with were either patients or colleagues. Flirting would be inappropriate. She couldn't remember ever really flirting with a man. At least not a man like Blake. One teasing look from those intensely blue eyes and she was toast.

"I guess speechless is good," he chuckled. "What are you doing tonight?"

"I'm going to sit with Susan so my uncle can get some rest."

There was that look of annoyance again. To his credit, it passed over his features so fast, she almost missed it. "You're keeping her overnight?"

Janice nodded and took a sip of her tea.

"She needs the *IV* fluids."

A cloud shadowed his eyes. "I guess she was in pretty bad shape when we got her here."

"Yes."

"Does it mean that she — that she'll —"

"It's hard to say. She needs tests. Tests we can't perform here."

"Talk to Patrick. He's the only one she'll listen to."

Janice moved food around in her dish. "How many children do they have?"

"Two. A boy and a girl."

"I think I met their son. Cute little red-haired boy?"

"That's Sam. The daughter works part-time for Dixie over at the diner. She was our waitress yesterday."

Janice nodded. "I remember her. Abby, wasn't it?"

"Yeah. She's only fourteen and not really old enough to work, but Dixie figures running plates from the kitchen to tables will keep her busy. Maybe help keep her mind off her mom's illness."

"Gorgeous children."

Blake dipped his head until he could look in her eyes. "What's that look about, beautiful?"

Trying to ignore the compliment that

177

made her go warm all over, she said, "I just keep thinking that surely something can be done for her. She's so young."

"All the doctors have said there's nothing."

Janice chewed on her thumbnail.

"What are you thinking?"

"I have a colleague I'd like her to see."

"Like I said, she doesn't want to be poked and probed if nothing can be done. Can't say as I blame her."

Still, she'd talk to Patrick about it. If Jeremy declared Susan's case hopeless, then, and only then, would Janice let it go.

"You're not going to drop it, are you?"

It should concern her that he could read her so easily. "Not just yet."

Blake shook his head. "Well, since I can't convince you to come out with me, mind if I stay and keep you company for a bit?"

"I'd like that," she admitted. With only one patient and no charts to work on, having someone to talk to would help fill the time. It was a practical thing to do. Nothing more.

But when she looked at him and felt her heart rev into overtime at just being near him, she knew it was a lie. She had a little over two weeks. She wouldn't worry about what happened beyond that. She'd just live in the moment and enjoy the time with her uncle in this town. Getting to know Blake, spending time with him at her grandparents' house, that could be a special bonus.

They tidied the dishes and retired to the parlor. Janice curled into the corner of a small couch. Blake joined her. The kitten snuggled on a plush pillow between them. Spoil sport. Well, maybe it wasn't such a bad thing having the cat there. It would remind him to keep his distance so he and Janice could talk.

Neither of them spoke right away. They just stared at the lights on the tree that sat near the fireplace.

"Nice tree," Blake said at last. "Did you help decorate it?"

"No. It was already here."

"Seems like you've just been missing out."

She just shrugged and sipped her coffee. Blake watched her. He'd wanted to take her for a ride to show her the outskirts of town, the farm country, where he had grown up and his parents still lived. But, again, her job came first. He didn't really understand why she couldn't come out with him. Doc Prescott was here.

"You sure you don't want to go for a drive or something? You've been cooped up in here most of the day."

"I'm afraid I slept most of the afternoon. I should stay and give my uncle a break."

"I'm sure he wouldn't mind. He's used to going it alone here."

"But I want to help. He's getting older. The long nights have to be getting harder for him."

Couldn't argue that point. He settled back into his corner of the couch. It would appear she wasn't in a talkative mood. How could he get her tongue moving? He closed his eyes and grinned. Bad analogy. That had him thinking about kissing her. Again.

The other night, she'd complained about him asking her a lot of questions, but not giving her the same opportunity. Maybe if he took that angle. "When we were having dinner at my house, you said something about me asking all kinds of personal questions and not giving you the opportunity to ask any of your own. So here's you chance. Ask me anything you want." That earned him a slight smile. He'd take it.

"Anything?"

"Anything."

She paused, considering. "Have you lived in Angel Ridge all your life?"

"No. I was born in Austin, Texas. We moved here when I was a teenager. That's when Dad opened the diner."

"Did you have family in town?"

"No. Dad had an old army buddy who used to live here. He and mom visited him once and fell in love with the town."

"So, you just picked up and moved?"

He nodded. "Pretty much."

She sipped her coffee. "Must have been hard, leaving all your friends behind and moving to a strange place."

She had no idea. Oh, well. He'd opened this can of worms. Might as well expect them to squirm all over the floor. "I guess you could say I had a little trouble adjusting."

"Sounds like there's a story behind that."

He rubbed his jaw, wondering how he should put this. "I was angry about the move, angry that no one seemed to care that I was angry, and by the time it was over, I was just angry."

She laughed. "You? I can't imagine it. You're about the most laid back person I've ever known."

"No. It's true. My brothers and my sister loved it here. They fit in. Had friends. Especially my brother, Cory. He was the most popular guy in school."

"I got the feeling there was some bad blood between you two."

Blake set his mouth in a hard line. "He

181

made it his mission to antagonize me back then. Not much has changed."

"Why would he do that?"

He cocked an eyebrow. "It's what makes him a good lawyer. He sniffs out his opponent's weakness and goes for the kill."

"What was your weakness?"

He shrugged. "I guess I wanted to fit in."

"Did you try? To fit in?"

"Naw. I sat around, sulked . . . and got into trouble." Shaking his head, he gave a wry laugh. "I sure had everyone's attention then. Mom and Dad were constantly on my back. They tried to put me in counseling. Nothing helped."

"Apparently something did. You're not that way now."

He smiled. "I have good days and bad days."

Her eyes widened.

"Now I've shocked you. Don't worry. Nowadays I take my frustrations out on nails and wood. Back then, I got in a lot of fights."

She glanced down at his injured knuckles.

He flexed his hand. "Let's just say I wound up on the wrong end of a disagreement with some sheetrock."

She raised an arched brow, but didn't probe further. Instead, she leaned forward and squeezed his hand. "It's admirable that you were able to turn your life around. What made you want to change?"

He turned his hand over and laced his fingers with hers. "When I was sixteen, my parents sent me away to Louisiana to work with a preacher who dealt with kids. I helped him build and repair homes for single moms and the elderly when he wasn't counseling me. What really made me want to get control of the anger was the day I left. When it was time to go to the airport, I found out my brother was driving me instead of my parents." He looked away from her then. This particular memory was still hard for him.

She just waited, and after a moment had passed, he continued. "I thought they didn't care about me. That they just wanted to be rid of me. As we were driving away, I saw my mom and dad outside in the garden. They were crying in each other's arms."

He stood and walked over to the fireplace. Leaning a forearm against the mantle, he added, "Mom wrote me everyday. I must've come home with a hundred letters." He turned back and faced her then.

"Your family loves you." She lowered her eyes before adding, "That's a wonderful gift."

"One I had forgotten I had. It made me want to control the rage. I didn't want to hurt them anymore."

She shook her head. "I just can't imagine you as the kind of person who loses control."

She should have seen him yesterday in town, or the other night when he slammed his fist into the wall. "I have my moments."

He rejoined her on the couch. Now was as good a time as any to probe. Weighing his words carefully, he stretched his arm out along the back of the loveseat. Cupping the back of her head in his palm and pulling her forward for a kiss would be so easy. . . .

He shook his head. Talk. They needed to talk. There was no question about the attraction between them. He needed to know if he should pursue anything beyond that with her. He clenched his fist to keep from touching her.

"So, why'd you decide to become a doctor?"

That brought a hint of a smile. "There were a lot of reasons, but at base, I guess I was being rebellious."

She had his attention. "You mind explaining that?"

"My mother is an extremely domineering woman. Her plan for my life was pretty straightforward. I should be educated in the finest schools, then marry someone fabulously wealthy and high-profile."

"Like mother like daughter?"

"So you've heard."

"Bits and pieces."

She set her coffee cup on the table in front of them. "I was determined to be nothing like my mother. I didn't want to be the kind of woman whose sole purpose in life was looking beautiful on her husband's arm, while spending the rest of her time seeing that the home is lavishly decorated, traveling, and shopping."

"And that the child is safely away in school."

"And out of the way," she finished flatly.

He took her hand in his then. He couldn't help it. She quickly pulled away.

"Don't feel sorry for me, Blake."

He held up a hand and gave her space. She crossed her arms and glared at him. He'd clearly touched a nerve.

"So, you chose to be a doctor because . . ."

"I wanted to make a difference. Do something worthwhile with my life."

"And now that you've attained that goal?"

"I keep accomplishing that goal, every day, by doing what I do."

"It must be hard. Never having time for

yourself."

"It's part of the job. You know it going in."

"Doesn't make it any easier."

Janice frowned. "Doesn't make what any easier?"

"Giving up your personal life."

"When the work is important and fulfilling, you don't mind."

She had such an earnest expression on her face, he knew she believed in what she did. He rubbed a finger along his chin. "Is that all you want out of life, Janice?" he asked quietly.

Her laugh sounded harsh. "Don't tell me you're one of those men who believes a woman can't possibly be fulfilled unless she has a home and children."

"Seems like having only a career could get pretty lonely."

"Maybe that's all I need."

"Everyone needs to be loved."

She stood and moved toward the fireplace, her hands in her back pockets. "Most men can't deal with the kind of work I do. They expect me to do things like drop everything, and say, oh I don't know, go for a drive with them?" She leveled him a pointed look. "Having relationships is a little difficult when most men just don't get it."

He moved to the edge of his seat, resting his arms on his thighs. He needed to weigh his words carefully. "Relationships involve give and take."

"Right. And the woman does all the giving."

"Is that how it's been for you? Dating guys who expect you to put them first?"

She turned, leaned back against the mantle, and crossed her arms. "Is this where you tell me you're not that kind of guy? If it is, don't bother. You've already tipped your hand. Several times."

He stood then and approached her. "What do you mean?"

"Friday night when I had to go to the hospital, you were less than thrilled. And tonight, you weren't happy that I wouldn't leave with you."

"I wouldn't be upset if it were an emergency. But in both cases, you didn't have to be there. The other night, you weren't on call, and tonight, you're making excuses to stay. Maybe you're avoiding getting too close to me because you're afraid of getting hurt."

"That's ridiculous."

"Is it?"

"I think you should go."

She took a step toward the door, but Blake

reached out and snagged her arm, stalling her retreat.

She stared at his hand on her arm. "Let go of me."

He dropped his hand immediately. He'd pushed hard, but he'd needed to know what she wanted out of a relationship or if she even wanted one. Her answer had been pretty emphatic.

She surprised him by taking a step toward him. "I'll tell you what you want to know, Blake. My job is my life. Anyone I become involved with will have to understand that my work always comes first. It has to, because I deal in life and death situations."

He took a chance and reached out to her then. He caressed her face with a thumb at her cheek, his fingers threaded in her silky hair. "Your patients are fortunate. They benefit from your dedication and caring nature." He placed his other hand so he could frame her face. "But what about you? You deserve to be cared for, too."

She squeezed his forearm and closed her eyes against the emotions filling them. "When I find the man who gets it, I'll have it all. Until then, I have my work."

She opened her eyes and stepped back, away from his touch. "Goodnight, Blake."

She left the room, the kitten trailing after

her. There it was. She expected any man she became involved with to be on the sidelines, waiting for her to find time for him. For a man who felt he'd been on the sidelines most of his life, he was selfish enough to want to be the focus of someone's life. Seems like he'd always been in somebody's shadow. His brother's. Hell, even his baby sister's life was more high profile than his.

The only things he could call his own were his business and his home. The business, well, it pretty well ran itself. He'd hired great people who saw to that. And his home stood empty at the corner of Ridge and Angel Avenue. Even the kitten wouldn't stay there with him.

He moved toward the door, grabbing his coat off the rack and shrugged into it before stepping out into the cold, dark winter night. He turned up the collar as he walked down the steps to the sidewalk.

Maybe Janice was right. Maybe he did have impossible standards no woman could meet. Maybe he was doomed to be alone forever.

Monday afternoon, Janice was about to climb the walls. Her uncle had taken Susan to Knoxville for tests. Susan had agreed after Patrick convinced her she should explore these new treatment options Janice had told him about. Susan hadn't been able to say no when he'd pleaded with her, saying if there was any way to keep her with him and the kids a bit longer, they deserved all the time they could get.

So, Janice had arranged for her to see Jeremy Mears, her colleague and the finest oncologist in the area. Uncle Charles had instructed Janice to "hold down the fort" with an assurance that Nurse Mable would show her the ropes. The rope showing had taken all of ten minutes. Instructions not to mess up her neat, orderly storage system took somewhat longer.

So far, the highlight of the day had been when Mable had left for lunch at eleven thirty and returned promptly an hour later. Her sleepless night wasn't helping matters. She'd like to blame it on the nap she'd taken, but her mind racing from the exchange she'd had with Blake was the more likely culprit. At one, Janice had had enough.

"Mable?"

"Yes, Doctor?"

"I think I'll walk into town."

"Yes, Doctor."

Janice jotted her cell phone number down

on a sticky note and handed it to the older lady. "You can reach me at this number if you need me."

"Yes, Doctor."

Nothing like stimulating conversation to warm you on a cold winter's day.

The sun played hide and seek with white fluffy clouds. Janice tucked her hands in her pockets and tried to enjoy being outdoors. A typical Monday for her involved early rounds at the hospital, seeing patients at the office, updating charts, then back to the hospital for more rounds before getting home late and falling into bed. She felt so useless here. Like she was wasting time when she should be busy caring for people who needed her. She hated feeling useless.

She stopped at the sidewalk and looked both ways. Not a soul in sight. Shrugging, she turned toward town feeling unsettled and out of sorts.

She didn't pass anyone along the way. When she got to town, she knew why. Main Street was buzzing with activity. People milling around, moving from shop to shop. Some window shopping, others hurrying inside to take care of their Christmas lists.

Christmas. She should think about doing her shopping. That would be using her time wisely. Even though she didn't spend the holidays with her mother and father, they went through the motions of shipping presents to each other. A formality to make their bizarre relationship seem familial. And since she'd be spending the holiday with Uncle Charles, she should get him something. She chewed on her lower lip. She'd enjoy watching him open a gift from her.

"Afternoon, miss."

A man in a police officer's uniform tipped his hat.

"Good afternoon," she checked his nametag, "Officer Harris."

"It's Constable. Constable Henry Harris. Don't believe I've seen you 'round here before."

"I'm Dr. Janice Thornton. Dr. Prescott's niece."

"You don't say? Well, I'll be. A lady doc. Pretty as a picture too. Welcome to Angel Ridge. If you need anything at all, you just let me know. I'm here in town most everyday."

She couldn't imagine what she'd need him for, but said, "Thank you," anyway.

"Nice meetin' you, miss — *um,* Doctor." He tipped his hat again.

"Nice to meet you."

The cordial man moved away from her, and Janice continued down the sidewalk.

She surveyed Town Square, noting the nearby hardware store. Surely they'd have something there her uncle would like for Christmas. Maybe some fishing supplies.

She moved in that direction, but the display in Heart's Desire caught her attention. She could get her mother something there. The thought lightened Janice's mood and she laughed. She'd likely be appalled since she wore nothing that wasn't designer. Maybe they'd have some cheap perfume.

"Pardon me miss, but I heard you laughing. You mind sharin' what's got you so tickled?"

Janice turned to find another man in uniform standing before her. This one was tall, young, and very handsome. He had a wide, easy smile that formed crinkles at the corners of his hazel eyes, suggesting one came easily to him. Reddish-brown hair curled over the collar of his tan uniform. No necktie for this officer.

"I don't mean to intrude, but I could use a good laugh. It's been a slow day."

"I can relate to that."

"I'm bein' rude." He removed his hat and held out a hand to her. "Sheriff Grady Wallace."

She put her hand in his. "Janice Thornton." She decided to get into the casual atmosphere of the town and leave the "Dr." off.

"Well, it's a real pleasure. What brings you to Angel Ridge?"

"I'm visiting my uncle, Dr. Prescott."

"Of course." He rocked back on his heels, hands on his hips. "He's told me plenty about you over the years. You're a doctor, too."

"Yes." For some reason the fact that her uncle had told this stranger about her made her uncomfortable. She wasn't used to this kind of attention. She lived her life quietly and on her own terms.

He nodded. "Your uncle and me, we share a fishin' bank from time to time. Well, I'll be. It sure is nice to meet you. What's Doc up to today?"

"He took a patient into town to see a specialist."

His pleasant expression turned serious. "Not Susan Houston, was it? I heard she collapsed yesterday. It's real sad about her. Real sad."

"I can't really say." In fact, she'd probably said too much. She'd have to remember this was a small town and that everyone knew everything about everybody. But she definitely agreed with the sheriff. She hoped her colleague could recommend a course of treatment that would help Susan.

"I understand. Patient confidentiality and all." He looped his thumbs in his belt loops and assumed a relaxed stance. "So, did you come into town for lunch? Dixie's got fried chicken on for the special down at Ferguson's."

"Actually, I thought I'd do a little Christmas shopping."

A voice laced with static interrupted. "Grady, you copy?"

"Excuse me." The sheriff spoke into a walkie-talkie he removed from a leather pouch on his belt. "Yeah, Clara. What do you have?"

"Your mama stopped by and said something about a problem out at her place. I had a hard time getting the right of it. She wanted to talk to you, and when I told her you were out, she started talkin' in circles. You know how she can be."

"Yeah, Clara. I'll run by there."

"Ten-four."

The sheriff returned the walkie-talkie to its leather holster. A wry smile pulled the corner of his mouth up. "Duty calls." He held out his hand. "Pleasure meetin' you, Janice. If you need anything at all, give a holler. Just dial the Sheriff's Department and Clara will find me."

There it was again. Was there something about her that screamed she'd need help? And from police officers, no less. Janice shook the man's proffered hand. "Thank you."

He replaced his black, western style hat and walked down the sidewalk away from her. She checked her watch. Maybe she should get back to the office. What if there was an emergency? Would Mable call her?

*Sheez.* She hated being indecisive. It was so unlike her. Janice turned back to the shops in front of her. Curiosity got the better of her. She'd just run in Heart's Desire and then head back.

A jingling bell announced her arrival. Someone called from the back, "Be with you in a sec."

Janice looked around. The shop was large and consisted of several rooms. The front contained the window display, a glass case filled with mouth-watering chocolates and another larger cooler held floral arrangements.

The strong aroma of perm solution wrinkled her nose. A door to the right had a sign over it that read *Naughty.* The doorway across from it, *Nice.*

A petite woman in four-inch heels hurried toward her, drying her hands on a white towel. She had olive coloring and straight, waist-length, jet-black hair and the most amazing eyes. Violet.

"Hi. I'm Candi. Candi Heart."

Her accent was decidedly slow and southern. Janice shook the woman's hand. "Candi Heart?"

"What can I say? My mother had a sense of humor."

"Janice Thornton."

"Welcome to Heart's Desire."

The woman's outfit was as unusual as her name. She wore a one-piece, red mini-dress with white fur at the neckline and wrists. On closer observation, Janice noticed that the tall heels were actually black ankle boots. Dark hose and a wide black belt completed the look. The only thing missing was a Santa hat.

"So, what can I do for you?"

"I'm looking for a Christmas gift for my mother."

"What'd you have in mind?"

"I'm not sure. Maybe perfume."

"Okay, since it's for your mother, you should definitely see what I have in the Nice Boutique." Janice followed Candi down the hall. She tipped her head toward the Naughty Boutique. "Everything in there's designed to drive a man wild. Not an image most folks want when shopping for their parents."

Janice laughed. "My parents are rarely in the same room."

"Not even for Christmas?"

"No."

"Divorced?"

"No, just not your typical family."

"That's too bad." She moved behind a display case that had several perfume selections sitting on top. "So, tell me about your mom."

"Mother is very sophisticated. A snob, if you will. She drips designer everything."

The lovely woman nodded. "How about this?"

Janice smelled the perfume Candi handed her. Soft, clean, subtle, floral. Very classy. "*Mmm.* What is that? Rose?"

"It's rose with a hint of lavender."

"It's lovely. The bottle is exquisite." The container was an intricately cut, blue crystal atomizer.

"I make all of the scents myself. The bottles are antique."

"I'll take it. Thank you. It's perfect." Her mother might actually like it. She enjoyed the unusual.

"Wonderful. Now what can we do for you?"

"Me? Oh, I'm not shopping for myself."

"All the more reason to indulge." Candi set the perfume in a velvet-lined silver foil box, then pulled out a festive gift bag filled with tissue. "Do you have a dress for the dance?"

Janice frowned. "Dance?"

"Of course. The Snow Ball is this Saturday. Why, everyone will be there."

"I'm new in town. I hadn't heard."

"It's the social event of the holiday season. They hold it down at First Presbyterian's fellowship hall since the Baptists won't allow dancin' in theirs." She took Janice's hand and led her out of the Nice Boutique. "You're in luck. I have just the dress for you."

They would have continued into the "Naughty Boutique," but Janice put on the brakes. "Oh, no. I mean, I appreciate your assistance, but I'm sure I won't be attending."

"You're Doc Prescott's niece, right?"

"Yes. How did you know?"

"Dixie Ferguson was in this morning. She tells me you've been seein' her brother, Blake."

Janice was shocked. She was not at all accustomed to everyone knowing her business. "Well, I wouldn't say that."

199

"If he hasn't gotten around to asking you, I'm sure he will. And even if he doesn't, your uncle will expect you to go with him and Miss Estelee."

"I don't know."

"Just have a look. No harm in that."

Janice passed through the purple beads separating them from the Naughty Boutique. Inside, there was everything imaginable. Perfumes. Lingerie. All types of seductive clothing. A display of massage oils and, Janice frowned just before her eyes widened, edible underwear. Candi just smiled.

"A little something for everyone. Here it is."

She pulled a dress from the rack that was, in a word, incredible. The softest cinnamon-colored sweater material fell in folds to the floor. It was a wrap-style dress, but all around the hem and up the front and neck, the material gathered to form a gentle, feminine ruffle. But why was it in the Naughty Boutique? It didn't look at all naughty.

Janice held the long sleeve up to her cheek and sighed. "Is this cashmere?"

"The finest."

"It's beautiful."

"Try it on."

"Oh, I couldn't."

200

"It won't hurt anything to try it on, now. Oh —" Something at her belt began beeping. "That's my perm. I need to rinse her. Be right back." She handed Janice the dress. "Try it on, honey. There's matchin' shoes on top of that rack."

Janice bit her lip. She held the dress up to herself and looked in the full-length mirror. The material was so soft. She couldn't help wonder what it would feel like next to her skin. Oh, why not. She had nothing else to do. Like Candi said, no harm in trying it on. She stepped into the dressing room and pulled the curtain.

Wearing nothing but her bra and panties, Janice eased her arms into the dress. The material flowed over her like a second skin, hugging her figure, molding to every dip and curve. She wrapped the belt and secured it at her waist. The neckline plunged below her bra, leaving it visible. She tried to adjust it, but the dress had a mind of its own. She chewed on her lower lip then thought, what the heck. She wriggled out of the bra.

She stepped out of the dressing room to stand in front of a full-length, triple mirror. Janice was stunned. Definitely naughty.

She hardly recognized the siren staring back at her in the mirror. The dress and even the slip on shoes with four-inch skinny heels were a perfect fit. She'd never owned anything so decadent in her life. On giving her reflection a closer look, she noticed that her black panties showed through the material. She turned and walked over to the display of underwear on the other side of the room to see if there was something the color of the dress.

The jingling bell at the front of the shop signaled the arrival of another customer.

"Come on in," Candi called from the back. "I'm neutralizing a perm. Be with you in a minute."

"No problem, Candi. I know how to find what I . . . want."

Before Janice could react to the sound of his voice, she was standing face to face with Blake.

# CHAPTER 9

"Janice."

"Blake," they said in unison.

"Wow. You look . . . amazing."

She dropped the panties she'd been holding and pulled the neckline of the dress together. "Oh, I was just, *um*, you know . . . Candi insisted I try this on. I'll just," she sidestepped her way to the dressing room, "just change."

"No. Wait."

Blake blocked her path.

"No, really. I should be getting back to the office." Any excuse to get out of such an embarrassing situation. To be found trying on provocative dresses in Candi's Naughty Boutique in the middle of a workday. What must he think when she wasn't sure what she thought? But when he touched her face with the back of his hand, all thoughts of embarrassment short-circuited.

Last night, she'd walked out on him. Their

conversation had taken a turn she hadn't expected. Had become too deep. Too personal. It had also brought to light differences she couldn't overlook. But now, in this moment, the attraction between them sizzled. With him standing a breath away devouring her with his eyes, Janice was rocked with desire for him despite her misgivings. She leaned into his touch and braced her hands against his chest.

Blake plunged his hand into her hair and circled her waist with his arm, and then his lips were hot and hungry on hers, leaving her weak and wanting more. Much more. He broke the kiss suddenly, skidding his lips across her cheek to her ear.

"Janice. I'm sorry." He grasped her arms and pulled away a little.

She blinked. "Sorry?" The starched cotton material of his Oxford-style shirt felt rough against her palms.

"Yes." He looked over his shoulder. "We're not exactly in a private place here. It's just, I wanted to kiss you so badly. Seeing you here, looking so beautiful and sexy, I couldn't help myself. Can you forgive me?"

Janice leaned into him again. Blake groaned. "Only if you stop apologizing," she said. "After last night, after the way we left things . . ."

He smoothed a hand down her hair and pressed his forehead to hers. "I know."

She focused on the buttons of his shirt. "I wasn't sure you'd want to see me again. Not everyone is willing to deal with the demands on a doctor's time. When I make plans, I never know —"

"Now, stop right there. What you do is important. Any man that can't see that is just plain stupid."

"But you won't get to pick and choose what's important. Can you handle that? Giving someone else that much control?"

"Would you give me that chance?"

Janice had to look away from the intensity and passion filling his eyes. There it was again. Hope. It flooded her heart like a long overdue soaking rain on dry, parched land.

"There's more." Blake tipped her face up with a finger beneath her chin. "Don't pull away. Don't. Tell me what you want."

Janice shook her head and took a step back, out of his arms. "I can't."

"Can't or won't?"

"Does it matter?"

"Hell, yes it matters!"

For every step of retreat she took, he advanced. "I can't give you what you want, Blake."

He propped his hands on his hips in a

defensive stance. "What is it you think I want?"

"A wife. Children to fill your big, old house."

"Okay, yes. I admit it. I want those things, but not now. Not right this second. I mean, I think I should have a girlfriend and then a fiancée."

Janice tugged at the dress's plunging neckline, her arms wrapped around her midsection. "I can never be those things for you, Blake. I can never give you what you need. I can't be there for you the way you need me to. My job must come first. So, why bother with any of this? It'll just lead to one or both of us getting hurt."

"Listen to yourself. You're making excuses to keep me at a distance. Again."

Janice took another step back. "You don't know anything about me."

"I think I do. You're from this dysfunctional family that's taught you love equals disappointment and hurt." He took another step toward her, and another, until her back met the wall. "Well, I'm not afraid. It might not be easy, but I'm not afraid to take a chance at proving you wrong. Proving that some people come into your life and stay. I'm won't bug out when you need me most. I'll be right here."

"That's impossible, Blake. We live in different worlds."

"We don't have to."

Janice stepped around him. "Coming to Angel Ridge was a mistake. I should have stuck to my plans and gone skiing."

"That's your parents talking."

Janice spun to face him. "What?"

"Isn't that what they would do? Leave you alone? Take a trip? Run away from you when you need them the most?"

It was her turn to advance on him. "Don't do that. Don't presume to analyze my family and me, because you can't begin to understand. You had it all. A traditional upbringing in a huge, loving family, with all of them still close by."

He surprised her by framing her face with his hands. "You're right. I can't understand how someone could know you and not want to love and cherish you."

"Hey, how are you doing in he— Blake Ferguson! You know men aren't allowed in here unchaperoned. I'm so sorry, Doc."

One second he was holding her, and the next he was holding air as Janice disappeared into the dressing room. Blake turned to Candi and said, "Anybody ever tell you that you have rotten timing?"

"What are you doing in here, Blake?"

"I came in to get some perfume." He raked a hand through his hair, shaken by what was happening between him and Janice. At some point, she'd not only gotten under his skin, but into his heart.

"Well, what do ya know? I'm havin' a run on the stuff today. You'd think I was having a sale."

Blake barely noticed that she'd spoken as he walked out of Candi's Naughty Boutique and into the front room. How could this be happening? He knew where he stood with Janice. To have a relationship with her, he'd have to give up his dream of a traditional family. Maybe even move to the city. He couldn't be sure he was willing to do that, but he knew he cared about her. He propped both hands against the counter, hung his head, and pulled in a ragged breath while conflicting emotions ripped him apart.

He pulled out his wallet and threw several bills down on the counter. "I need some flowers delivered to Susan Houston." His cell phone rang, and he stepped out onto the sidewalk to take the call.

"What about the perfume?" Candi called after him.

"Not today. Yeah," he barked into the phone.

"Take my head off, why don't you?"

"What do you want, Dixie?"

"I need you to watch the diner for me."

"You know, I have other things to do besides jump when you say —"

"Look, Blake Ferguson. My best friend is dying, her husband is in the city with her finding out exactly how much longer she has, and her son is sick. That leaves me to get him to the doctor, so just get over yourself and haul your ass down here."

He held the phone away from his ear as Dixie slammed the receiver home. Blake holstered the cell and turned to go back into Heart's Desire. Janice was just coming out of the side room. They met at the counter.

Candi ignored Blake and spoke to Janice. "So, can I box up that dress and send it over to Doc Prescott's?"

"No. I'll just take the perfume."

"But —"

"I'm sorry, Candi, but I'm really in a hurry."

Seemed the plan was for her to ignore him, too. "Janice, I just spoke with Dixie. Little Sammy Houston is —"

"I know. I just got a call from Mable."

She handed Candi some cash, thanked her, and bypassed him on the way to the door. She left without looking back.

As he watched her walk away, something

snapped inside him. Determination straightened his back. He'd backed down too many times in his life. Some things were worth fighting for. He didn't know how it would turn out, but he knew in his gut, if he didn't give it shot, he'd live with the regret.

"Candi, I need another arrangement of flowers. And can you box up that dress Janice was trying on?"

"Now you're talking. What about the accessories?"

"Those too."

"What do you want the card to say?"

"No card. I'll deliver the message myself."

"How are you doing, Sammy?" Janice asked.

"Not so good."

The adorable little red-haired boy looked up at her with huge green eyes. She brushed her hand across his hot forehead.

"Where's the doc?" he asked.

"Sammy, Doc Prescott went into town with your Mommy, remember?" Dixie said. "This is his niece. She's a doctor, too. She's going to have a look at you instead."

He shifted his wide-eyed focus back to Janice. "A lady doc?"

Janice smiled. "Yes."

"Wow . . . I never seen a lady doc before. You sure are purdier than old Doc Prescott."

"Sammy," Dixie scolded.

"Well she is, and she smells nicer, too."

"Thank you, Sammy. Do you mind if I take your temperature?"

"Nope." He opened his mouth and stuck out his tongue.

"How about if I just stick this funny looking thing in your ear?"

"Will it hurt?"

"No, not at all."

"Okay."

Janice inserted the thermometer in boy's ear and took the reading. "All done." She made a notation in his file. Mable hovered nearby to make sure she did it correctly. Janice shook her head.

"How long have you been feeling bad, Sammy?"

The little boy shrugged.

"I let him stay out of school today. He was spendin' the day with my mother because he didn't feel well when he got up this morning. She keeps some of my nieces and nephews from time to time, so one more's usually no bother. Anyway," Dixie continued, "she called me at the diner. Said he'd been throwin' up all morning."

Janice made another note.

"Oh," Sammy groaned. Just the thought of the morning he'd had seemed to make

211

him go green.

Janice rubbed his stomach in what she hoped was a soothing motion. "Okay. Mable, could you get us —"

The nurse handed her a stainless steel, kidney-shaped pan. "Thank you. What did you eat this morning?"

"Pancakes."

"Anything else?"

"I had a big glass of milk. Oh . . ." he closed his eyes and moaned.

"I'm sorry, sweetie. We won't think about that. So, you go to school?"

The boy took a breath and said, "Yep. I go to Kindygotten. But I didn't go today. Dixie said I didn't have to 'cause I was feelin' poorly."

She smiled and smoothed his unruly curls. "That's a very good thing. Has anyone else at your school been sick?"

The little boy shrugged. "Tommy Thompson puked all over the bathroom last week. It was gross."

She nodded, then looked at Dixie. "It's probably just a virus or the stomach flu. There's not much you can do for it other than let it run its course. It'll probably last twenty-four to forty-eight hours. I can give him something for the vomiting. It will help him rest and keep some fluids down. It's very important that he not become dehydrated."

Dixie nodded.

To Sammy, Janice said, "I can give you something to make your stomach feel better. There's two ways to take it. The choice is yours."

Sammy nodded, a serious expression in those huge green eyes.

"I can give you a shot."

He screwed up his face to show his displeasure.

"Or I can give you something called a suppository." She explained how that worked.

That garnered a more serious look of displeasure. "Shot," he said.

She patted his hand. "You're a brave little boy."

The nurse prepared the syringe. Dixie held the little boy's hand.

"You get all the ice cream you want when this is over, sport."

Janice administered the injection, then handed the tray back to Mable.

"You did that real easy, Doc. I hardly even noticed."

"Thank you." She pulled a blanket up and tucked it under Sammy's chin. "Can you stay here and try to rest while I speak with Dixie?"

Sammy nodded.

She smoothed his curls off his forehead. "If you need anything, Miss Mable will be right here, okay?"

"Okay."

The nurse smiled and sat next to the bed where the little boy lay.

Janice and Dixie stepped out into the hallway and shut the door to the examination room. "The shot should make Sammy feel better right away. It will also make him very drowsy. I can give you some suppositories to use when it wears off if he starts feeling sick again. If he doesn't want to use them, just give me a call and I'll be happy to come out and give him another injection. There's no need to bring him back in."

Boy, was she really getting into this small town swing of things. Already volunteering to make house calls.

Dixie ran a hand through her short-spiked hair. "Thanks, Doc. I really appreciate it."

Janice laid a hand on her arm. "Dixie, these types of things are very contagious. You should make arrangements to have him stay somewhere other than with Susan. An illness of this nature would be very hard on her."

"Of course. She's gonna have a fit. She'll

want to take care of him herself, but I'll handle it. I may need restraints. Can you help me with that?"

Janice laughed. "We'll see what Mable can scare up." She noticed the dark smudges under Dixie's eyes. "How are you doing?"

"Me? I'm right as rain."

"How are you sleeping?"

"Oh, you know. Sleep's over-rated."

Janice crossed her arms and affected her best *don't mess with me* doctor's voice. "I know you're very involved with your friend's family. If you don't take care of yourself, you're going to be the one lying on that examination table."

"I'm fine."

"Is there anything I can do for you? There are medications that can help you rest. Help soothe your nerves."

Dixie cocked a hand on her hip. Janice didn't think she'd ever seen red pants with jingle bells trimming the pockets. "You treat upset with pills, and don't get me wrong, that's well and fine. But my recipe for just about anything is a nice chocolate cake."

Janice laughed.

Dixie squeezed her hand. "If there's ever a point when chocolate stops helping, then I'll come see you. Promise."

"Anytime."

"Now, about you and my brother —"

"I'll just have Mable get those meds together."

"Hang on, Doc. I got something to say and you're gonna hear it."

Janice took a deep breath. She'd heard about enough today from Blake about whatever this was between the two of them. As far as she could tell, they were at an impasse.

"He'd never admit it, but my brother's been pretty unlucky in love. Fact is, he's been burned so many times, I thought he'd given up. Then you came to town, and I'm noticin' that he has that look in his eyes again. I don't mind tellin' you that it's been a very long time since I've seen him act this way over a woman."

"Dixie —"

She held up a hand. "Now, let me finish. Please. I'm not one to meddle, but Blake's special to me. In my humble, biased opinion, you couldn't do any better than him. Still, I get this sense that you're in some weird place where you're not sure which direction your life is headed, and while that's your business, I just don't want to see my brother get hurt."

Janice crossed her arms. "For the record, I told your brother he didn't want to get involved with me. He doesn't seem inclined to take my advice."

Dixie nodded. She had a resigned look on her face. "So, I'm a day late and a dollar short."

"I don't know what you mean," Janice said.

Dixie began pacing. The bells jingled with the movement. "This is my fault. I told him to go for it. That he shouldn't waste any time if he wanted to pursue something with you. I just had no idea he'd fall this hard and this fast." She shook her head.

Janice didn't catch half of what she said. "Dixie, what are you talking about?"

"Okay. A different angle. I need to approach this from a different angle."

Now she was mumbling. "What?"

"Okay, I get that you're attracted to Blake."

That was to the point. "Excuse me?"

"Come on, Janice. Do we have to be so formal? I mean, this is my brother we're talking about. What I'm trying to get at is this. What would it take for you to give him a chance?"

"We really shouldn't be having this conversation."

"Well, I'm not givin' you a choice. As I said, I'm very protective of Blake. So, what would it take?"

"A change of address to start. I'm only here for a visit. I haven't agreed to move yet." Janice wished she could snatch the words out of the air, but it was too late.

Dixie pounced. "Yet. You haven't agreed to move yet. So you're saying you might. That's good enough."

"There's more, Dixie. Much more."

Dixie held up her hand. "Blake should be able to take it from here with a little coaching."

"Dixie —"

"I should take Sammy over to my place now, Doc. His sister's gonna be gettin' home from school anytime. Could you get me that medicine?"

Janice frowned. "Sure."

Why did she feel like she'd just propelled herself into something she'd didn't have a prayer of controlling?

"Delivery for Janice Thornton."

Janice and Dixie both turned as a teenage boy walked into the clinic carrying a huge bouquet of roses.

"I'm Janice Thornton."

"I'll take care of this," Dixie said.

Janice stepped into the exam room where Sammy was sleeping. She gave Mable some instructions about getting some nausea meds for Dixie to take with her, then walked back out into the hall in time to see Blake rushing into the office. He entered in such a hurry the door banged against the wall before he could grab it and swing it shut.

"Janice —"

"Blake —" Dixie intercepted him. "What are you doin' here? You're supposed to be watchin' the diner."

He grabbed Dixie's arms, his breathing labored like he'd run all the way from the diner. "I called Dad to come in. It's Bebe. She needs a doctor."

"What's the problem?" Janice interjected.

"She's pregnant. Says she's been bleedin' all morning."

"Did she say anything about cramps?"

"Yes."

"I'll get my bag."

"Blake, can you carry Sammy to the car for me?" Dixie asked.

"Sure. Is he okay?"

"Yeah. Just a stomach bug."

Janice said, "Mable, can you give those meds to Dixie and then get me some Demerol, Terbutaline, a couple of syringes, and a biohazard box?"

"Certainly, Doctor. Who is it?"

Janice looked at Blake.

"My sister-in-law, Bebe Ferguson."

"Do we have a fetal monitor?" Janice asked Mable.

"Yes. We also have a portable ultrasound."

"We do?" Janice said, surprised they would have such an expensive piece of equipment.

"Yes."

"Good. I'll need that, along with any file we may have on Mrs. Ferguson."

"Yes, Doctor."

Mable moved surprisingly fast for her size and girth. Janice walked back to her uncle's office, retrieved her bag, then found Mable.

"Here you are, Doctor."

Janice took the medicines and put them in her bag. The file, she tucked under her arm while she juggled everything else. "Thanks, Mable. Do you know if Mrs. Ferguson has been having difficulty with her pregnancy?"

"No, Doctor. She's been seeing a specialist in Maryville."

Janice nodded as she headed for the door. "I'll have my cell phone. Call if you need me."

"Yes, Doctor. If your uncle returns, I'll tell him where you are."

Out on the porch, Mable handed her a paper with two names and numbers on them. She performed an impressive balancing act to take it. "If you need to transport her by ambulance, call Carl. If she needs to be airlifted, call Willie."

"Thank you, Mable."

"Godspeed."

Blake held the door to his truck open for her. He took her bag and the ultrasound and put them away behind the seat, then he helped her up into the cab. When he was behind the wheel, Janice asked, "How far away are we?"

"It's not far. They just moved into one of the old Victorians."

"Good. Why did she wait so long to call?"

Blake's mouth was set in a hard line. "She's been trying to get my worthless brother on the phone all morning. When the cramping started and she still hadn't reached him, she called the diner." He paused and took a couple of deep breaths. "Is she losing the baby?"

"I don't know. I need to examine her."

"No offense, but can you handle this kind of thing?"

"If she's miscarrying, there's little anyone would be able to do."

She opened the woman's file and flipped through it. A positive pregnancy test. No previous pregnancies. Nothing to indicate if this was a high-risk pregnancy.

Blake slammed his palm against the steering wheel. "If I could get hold of my brother right now, I'd kill him with my bare hands."

"Let's focus our energy on your sister-in-law."

They came to a stop in front of a beautiful two-story home, but Janice hardly took time to give it a cursory glance. She rushed up the steps with Blake to the front door. "I hope it isn't locked."

"No one locks their doors in Angel Ridge." The door swung open to prove his point.

"My uncle locks his."

"Well, we wouldn't want teenagers walking off with drugs."

"Good point."

"Bebe? Where are you?" Blake called out.

"Upstairs," came a weak voice.

Janice ran up the stairs with Blake right behind her.

"In here," Blake said.

A small woman with an ashen face lay in the center of a large four-poster bed. Sweat beaded her forehead and she was obviously in pain.

"Thank God you're here," she said.

Blake went to her side and knelt by the bed. He took her hand and brushed sweaty bangs off her forehead.

"Where's Doc Prescott?"

"He's out of town. This is his niece, Janice

Thornton."

"*Dr.* Janice Thornton," Janice corrected.

"Right. Sorry. She'll take real good care of you."

Janice shrugged out of her coat. "Blake, if you could step out while I examine Mrs. Ferguson."

"Of course."

"Could you get me some cool water and a towel?"

"Sure. I'll wait outside the door. You can get it from me when you're ready."

"Thanks. Bebe, how far along are you?"

"Twelve weeks."

"Blake tells me you've had some bleeding."

"Yes. Am I going to lose my baby?"

"I'm going to do everything I can to see that you don't. Try to stay calm, okay? That's very important."

The woman nodded, her gray eyes huge and frightened. Janice squeezed her hand. While she checked her pulse and blood pressure, she asked several questions to determine how much bleeding there'd been, if she was having contractions, if she'd been as still as possible or moving around.

Not liking the answers she'd been given, Janice opened the case containing the ultrasound. She removed it and found an electrical outlet.

"Do you know what this is?"

Bebe shook her head.

"It's a small ultrasound. Have you had an ultrasound?"

"No. The doctor said there was no need unless there's a problem."

"I'm going use it now to see how the baby's doing." Janice raised the woman's gown and squirted the gel, then rolled the monitor over Bebe's flat stomach. She made some adjustments to get a good picture on the small screen. There it was. The fetus was normal size. Janice rolled the wand to get a profile, then moved to get a reading on the heartbeat. She made another adjustment, praying she'd find it. She moved the wand again . . . and again. Nothing.

"Can you see my baby? Is my baby all right?"

Janice turned the machine off.

"Doctor?"

Janice took Bebe's hand. This was one of the worst parts of being a doctor. Delivering bad news. "Mrs. Ferguson, I'm afraid you're having a miscarriage. I'm so sorry."

"Are you — sure?" her voice broke and tears fell from her eyes.

Janice pulled a couple of tissues from a box on the bedside table and handed them to her. "I'm sorry," she repeated. She wiped the gel from her stomach, lowered her gown, and pulled the covers back up to her waist. "I need to consult with your OB/GYN, but I would recommend that you go into the hospital for a D&C."

"Oh, God."

She began to sob. Janice squeezed her hand and shoulder. She wanted to hold her, but as her doctor, she had to remain detached and professional.

"What's wrong?" Blake came into the room. "I heard — Bebe?"

He rushed to the bed, knelt and put an arm around the distraught woman's shoulders. Bebe pressed her face into his shoulder. Blake looked at Janice, an unspoken question in his eyes. Janice shook her head. She stood and put the ultrasound back in its case.

After a moment, when the sobs had lessened, she said, "Mrs. Ferguson, if you could give me your doctor's name . . ."

Bebe sniffed and pulled away from Blake. "Kendell Griggs."

Janice opened the nightstand drawer and found a phone book. She dialed the number, and after a few moments, spoke with Bebe's doctor to make arrangements for Bebe to go to the hospital. She hung up and explained to Bebe and Blake. Janice opened her bag and took out a syringe and a vial of Demerol. "I'm going to give you an injection. This will ease the pain and will also help calm you."

Bebe just nodded. The tears continued to stream down her ashen face.

"Blake, can you call Carl?" Janice asked. "Tell him we need a transport?"

"Is that necessary?"

"She'd be more comfortable."

Janice administered the injection while Blake made the call.

"I got here as soon as I could. Oh, my dear girl."

A tall woman with gray hair and Blake's eyes came into the room. She went straight to the bed.

"Oh, Mom Ferguson. My baby's gone. It's gone." And the tears came again.

"Oh, my. Oh." She enfolded Bebe in a hug and looked at Blake. "Where's Doc Prescott?"

"He's in town with Susie. This is Dr. Thornton, his niece."

"I'm so sorry, Mrs. Ferguson. I'll just wait downstairs for the ambulance and leave you all alone."

Almost as soon as she stepped out into the hallway, her cell phone rang. "Hello?"

"Dr. Thornton, this is Mable."

"Yes, hello Mable."

"Doctor, I've just received a call from Hoyt Crawford. In fact, I have him on the other line. His wife, Sally, is in labor. It's her fourth child and she's had all her babies at home. She was planning to do the same with this one, but there seems to be a problem."

"Yes?"

"She's been in labor too long and the pain is real bad."

Janice frowned. "I don't understand, Mable. Labors are typically long and painful, especially without anesthesia or pain medications."

"She says this is different from the others."

"In what way?"

"She's been in labor too long and the pain is real bad."

Janice sighed. "Tell Mr. Crawford he should take his wife to the hospital."

"They live too far away. He says they need help now. They want you to come."

Her? Deliver a baby outside a hospital?

"Mable —"

"When should I tell them you'll be there?"

Janice set her bag by the front door and rubbed her stiffening neck. "Mable, if there

227

are complications with the delivery, there's very little I'll be able to do without the proper equipment."

"All the more reason for you to be there. I'll put him through so he can give you directions."

"No! Mable —"

"Hello? Doc? Is that you?"

Janice took a deep breath and let it out. "Mr. Crawford, this is Dr. Thornton. Mable tells me your wife is having a difficult delivery?"

"Yep. Real bad. You sure got a high-pitched voice for a doctor."

Janice looked up at the ceiling. "I'm settling a patient into an ambulance at present. As soon as she's transported to the hospital, I'll be happy to come to your home. Could you give me directions?"

"Right. Well, you head outta town towards the mountains."

"Okay. What road would I take?"

"The road out of town. You go a ways, and just before you come to the river bridge, you turn left."

Janice jotted the directions down. "Okay, does that road have a name?"

"The river road."

"Yes. Does it have a name?"

"The river road, I done said!"

"Sorry."

"Then you go down to the big cedar barn just past the post office and take the next road to the left and head up into the hills. At the first fork, bear to the right. At the next fork, bear to the left."

Janice swallowed. She was queasy just thinking about it. "Got it. Left then right."

"Here's where it gits tricky. Look for the driveway at the old oak tree with the split trunk, then take the second drive after that. I hope you got four-wheel drive, 'cause most of our gravel washed down to the road in the last rain."

Janice pushed her hair back from her face. "Do what you can to keep your wife comfortable. I'll be there as soon as I can."

Janice disconnected the call when she saw the ambulance parallel park in front of the house. Bebe's husband pulled in right behind it. She quickly made several notations on a blank sheet of paper in Bebe Ferguson's file, then opened the door for two men bringing in a gurney followed by the husband.

"What's going on here?" Cory asked.

She took Cory aside and quietly gave him the news. "I'm glad you're here. Your wife's been asking for you."

He dropped his briefcase and took the

steps two at a time. As she turned her attention to the other two men, she heard Blake say, "About time you hauled your sorry ass home."

"Blake!" a female voice remonstrated.

"I'm Dr. Janice Thornton." She shook hands with the men. "Mrs. Ferguson is upstairs, second door on the left. She needs to be transported to Blount Memorial Hospital." She pulled the paper out of the file. "I have instructions here for you to give to her doctor when you arrive."

"Carl Jamison. I'll get that from you after we've loaded her up. What's the problem?"

"She's having a miscarriage. I've administered fifty milligrams of Demerol."

"Did you start a line?"

"No. Her vitals are stable. I think it can wait until she gets to the ER."

The older man nodded and said, "Let's get her loaded up, Sonny."

Blake made it down the stairs just as the men started up. "Carl. Sonny."

"Blake. Sorry about your sister-in-law."

"Thanks, Carl."

Janice punched the number to the office into her cell phone, but before hitting *send*, she asked, "How is she?"

"Calmer. The shot helped."

"Good. Did I hear you chewing your

brother out?"

Blake's face flushed. She wasn't sure if it was the result of anger or embarrassment. "He should have been here."

"Well, he's here now. I shouldn't have to tell you that Bebe doesn't need to be upset further."

"Now you sound like my mother."

Ignoring that, she held up the phone. "I have to call Mable. As soon as we get Bebe in the ambulance, I have to go deliver a baby."

"Who is it?"

"Crawford . . . I can't remember the first name."

"Sally Crawford?"

"Yes, that sounds right. Can you take me by my uncle's to pick up supplies and to get my car?"

"Don't bother. You'd never make it to their place in that BMW."

"I have to."

"They live up in the hills outside of town. They've got a real steep driveway, and I'd bet it's washed out."

"Yes, Mr. Crawford mentioned that. I thought I'd walk up."

He propped his hands loosely on his hips, looked away, and then said, "It's too far and straight up the side of a mountain. With you not being familiar with the area, it'd be a miracle if you found it."

"I'll manage. If I get lost, I have my cell. I'll call them."

"You won't get a signal up there." He paused. "I'll take you."

"No. You should be with your family."

"Mom's keeping Bebe calm, and she's got Cory to go with her."

"And I'm guessing it wouldn't be a good idea for you to be in the same room with him right now."

"Yeah," he said harshly. "Look, I know I'm probably the last person you want to take you up there, but right now, I'm all you've got."

She checked her bag, as much in an effort to hide her emotions as to assess what she'd need to add if she had to deliver a baby. What if the woman needed a C-section? She pushed the hair back from her face. She hated to admit it, but she felt horribly out of her depth. How did her uncle manage?

She should take Mable with her, but with her uncle gone, the nurse would have to stay at the clinic in case someone came in needing medical attention. She looked up at Blake, "I don't suppose you've delivered a baby before?"

"No, ma'am. A couple of colts, but no

babies." He dipped his head and looked into her eyes, a sideways grin on his face. "I'm real good at boilin' water. Will that do?"

Janice smiled, too, her earlier testiness with him melting away. "I suppose it'll have to."

"You'll do fine."

Heaven help her, but standing here, seeing the confidence Blake had for her shining from his pale blue eyes, she felt like she could do anything with him by her side.

# CHAPTER 10

In just under an hour, Blake pulled up to the Crawford house. Well, house was perhaps overstating the matter. It was more like a trailer with a room added on to the front of it. Old, rusting cars were parked all around the property. A few old appliances added to the ambiance. On the front porch, there was an old couch, a refrigerator, and a sleeping hound who raised his head and yawned when Blake killed the engine. She'd heard about people living like this, but she wasn't sure she'd ever believed —

"We'd better get in there," Blake suggested.

Janice focused on the man beside her. She took a breath and willed her stomach to settle back into its normal spot. The drive had been a nightmare of hairpin curves, dips, and nearly vertical climbs. "Right. Let's go."

Blake got out and came around to help

her down from the truck. He retrieved her medical bag from behind the seat and handed it to her.

Carrying the ultrasound under his arm, he followed her up to the front door. When he knocked, a dog from inside began barking. The dog on the porch peered up at them, but didn't move.

"Git the door, Marissa," someone called out.

The door swung inward and an imp with a mass of strawberry blonde hair and huge blue eyes said, "Is you the doc?" She was looking up at Blake.

Janice bent and said, "Yes, I am. Can you show me where your Mommy is?"

The little girl looked at her warily. She grabbed Blake's hand and led him to a back room. He gave her an apologetic look over his shoulder, and Janice followed. A small dog danced around their feet, yapping loudly.

"Hush, Barney."

A younger girl feeding yet another little one called the dog down. The dog quieted immediately and backed off. For all the disarray outside, the inside was spotless. The furniture was old and worn, but clean.

In the back room, they found a young woman lying in the center of a bed. Her light brown hair lay limply against the pillowcase. Her pale cotton gown was damp and clinging to her skin. A large man with curly red hair sat next to her. He looked like he'd been to hell and back. When they entered the room, he stood.

"Blake." He held out his hand and the two men shook. "I didn't expect to see you here. Where's the doc?"

"She's right here. This is Dr. Janice Thornton. She's Doc Prescott's niece."

"You gotta be kiddin' me? Ferguson, my wife's in a bad way. She needs a real doctor, not some nurse or midwife."

"Hush, Hoyt," the woman in the bed said. She held her hand out to Janice. "I'm Sally Crawford."

Janice took her hand. "I'm pleased to meet you, Mrs. Crawford."

"Please, call me Sally."

"Thank you." She sat on the side of the bed. "How are you doing, Sally?"

"Not too good. Somethin's wrong. I can tell. I never had this much trouble havin' the girls. Why, with the baby, I barely had to grunt and she shot right out."

Janice removed a blood pressure cuff from her medical bag. "I'm just going to check your pressure."

The woman nodded.

"What kinda nonsense is that? How's that gonna help her have the baby?"

Janice looked up at Blake.

He tipped his head toward the door. "Hoyt, why don't you and me go see about boilin' some water?"

Blake clasped the man's shoulder and ushered him out of the room.

On their way out, Janice said, "Blake, we'll need some clean towels and blankets."

He turned back and winked at her. "Sure thing, Doc." He pushed a complaining Hoyt out the door and shut it behind them.

The blood pressure looked good, but her patient looked exhausted. Janice brushed a hand across the woman's damp forehead. "Try to tell me what you're experiencing."

"My water broke last night, so I took to bed, but the pains didn't come. They didn't start till this mornin'. They been real strong, but I've not been feeling like I need to push. Just hurtin' and the baby, well, I ain't feelin' no pressure down low like I did with the others. I just hurt so bad."

"Okay. Let me check and see how far you've dilated."

Sally nodded weakly. Janice pulled her hair back with a band and put on latex gloves. She didn't like what she saw. She wasn't effaced as a woman having her fourth child, and who had been in labor all day, should be.

Janice removed the gloves. "I'm going to examine your stomach to try and feel the baby's position."

Sally nodded again. Blake came back into the room then with a tall stack of towels and blankets.

"Where's Hoyt?" Sally asked.

"I put him to choppin' wood."

"How'd you do that? There's a pile out there a mile high."

"I told him we'd need it."

Sally laughed, then moaned as another contraction came. Janice squeezed her hand. "Okay, just breathe through it. In through your nose. Out through your mouth. That's it. Good."

When the contraction passed, she said, "Sally?"

The woman opened her eyes and looked at her. "What is it, Doc?"

"The baby's breach."

"Oh, God. Am I gonna lose her?"

"I'm going to do everything in my power to keep that from happening. First, I want to check the baby's heartbeat to make sure that it's strong, then," she hesitated for a moment, and continued, "then I'm going to turn it." Yes. Given the circumstances, it was the only thing she could do. "It will be pain-ful. If the baby's heartbeat is strong, I can give you something to help with that. If not —"

"I ain't worried about the pain. Just save my baby."

At Janice's words, Blake felt his knees go weak. He set the blankets and towels down and slowly backed toward the door.

"Blake, I need you to stay. Can you hand me a blanket?"

*Oh, God.* He took a deep breath and handed her the blanket. Janice took it and positioned it across Sally's legs. Then, she pulled Sally's nightgown back exposing her swollen belly. Blake set the towels and blankets on the dresser and grasped the bedpost for support.

"You okay?" Janice asked.

"Yeah. I'm good," he lied.

Janice squirted some kind of gel-like substance on Sally's belly, then rolled a triangular shaped devise across it. The sound of a strong heartbeat filled the room. Janice smiled.

"That's your baby's heartbeat, Sally. It's good and strong."

"Thank God," she said softly.

A tear rolled down Sally's face. Blake swallowed his queasiness and took a hand towel out of the stack. He blotted the moisture from Sally's face, and she smiled up at him.

"You're gonna be fine, Sally. Dr. Thornton is gonna take care of everything." He claimed the smile Janice gave him all for his own. God, she was an extraordinary woman. She wiped the gel off Sally's stomach, then got a syringe and a vial of medicine from her bag.

"What's that?" Sally asked.

"Something to help with the pain."

Sally shook her head. "I don't want to be drugged up. I want to have my wits about me when I welcome my baby into the world."

"This won't impair you. It'll just take the edge off the pain."

Sally considered that. Blake squeezed her hand. "It'll be okay," he said.

She chewed her lower lip, then moaned as another contraction hit. "Breathe through it," Janice said. "You're doing great. It's all going to be over soon."

After the contraction passed, Janice gave Sally the shot, then said, "We need to turn the baby now, Sally. Are you ready?"

Sally nodded.

"Squeeze Blake's hand."

Blake brushed the hair off Sally's forehead. She was a sturdy woman, but still, he hoped she'd be okay. She'd already been through so much. Janice grabbed a towel and bottle of something the color of iodine from her bag, then set them aside.

He refocused on Sally. "Go ahead. Squeeze. I can take it," he said.

But when Sally squeezed, he thought *he'd* need a doctor's attention before this was over. The woman had a killer grip. Sally moaned. She even cried out, then Janice said, "There. Oh, yeah. Here we go."

Hoyt burst into the room. "What's happenin' in here. I heard Sally hollerin' all the way outside. What are you doin' to my wife?"

"Oh . . . she's a comin', Hoyt. I can feel her. She's a comin'."

"She certainly is. She's crowning."

Blake moved back out of the way as Hoyt took his place at his wife's side. He should leave. This was a private moment, but he couldn't take his eyes away from what Janice was doing.

"Okay, Sally. This is it. With the next contraction, I want you to push. I don't have time to give you a local. Are you okay?"

*"Ohhh . . .* here it comes. *Mmm . . ."*

"Support her shoulders, Hoyt. Blake, dump my bag on the bed here next to me

241

and get a towel. Now!"

Blake did as she said.

"Okay, Sally. Stop pushing. Squeeze Hoyt's hand, scream, do whatever you need to, but don't push!"

Blake stopped, transfixed. It was the most amazing thing he'd ever seen. Still, something wasn't right. "What is that?" he asked.

"The cord's wrapped around her neck."

"Oh, Lordy. Is she okay?"

Janice cupped the baby's head and carefully unwound the cord. That done, she suctioned mucus out of its mouth and nose. Still, the baby wasn't moving. "You're doing great. One more push and she'll be here."

"She's okay then?"

"Sally, I need you to focus for me. Push with the next contraction. Let's get her here."

"I'm ready when you are."

"Okay. Push. That's it."

And then the baby was a squirming, round, red mound in Janice's hands. "That's good, Sally. You can relax now."

"Is she okay? Is my baby all right?"

"Everything looks fine. Blake, open up that packet for me please."

Sally laughed. She was actually laughing!

Janice indicated a sealed plastic package of surgical instruments. He opened it and held it for her.

"Sally, Hoyt, how would you feel about a son instead of daughter?"

"A boy? It's a boy?" Hoyt breathed in a hushed voice.

Sally just kept laughing and crying as Janice put clamps on the cord. She held the scissors out to Hoyt. "Would you like to cut the cord?"

He did as she asked. He looked at least three inches taller as he gazed at his son. When he'd finished, Janice rubbed the baby with the towel. It began to cry. A squeaky little noise that hardly qualified, but a cry all the same.

"Is he all right?" Sally asked again.

"Looks perfect," Janice confirmed as she handed the baby to his mother.

She cuddled the little bundle up close. "A boy." She looked up at her husband, love and tears shining in her eyes. "Hoyt, we have a son."

The huge man Blake had known most of his life melted. He tenderly kissed his wife, then his baby, tears shining in his eyes, too.

"Blake, I could use that warm water now and a large, clean bowl."

Blake retraced his steps to the kitchen and with the help of one of the girls, got the things Janice needed. Back in the bedroom,

Janice continued to work with Sally. When she'd finished, Hoyt took care of the soiled towels and the bowl.

As he was carrying them out, Sally said, "Hoyt, be sure and bury the afterbirth in the north end of the garden."

Janice frowned, but didn't comment. She turned her attention to the baby. She and Sally washed the tiny little boy together. When they'd finished, Janice took out her stethoscope and examined the baby.

When she'd finished, Sally asked, "How is he?"

"He's perfect, Sally. Absolutely perfect. You can breastfeed now if you'd like."

She turned to pick up the contents of her medical bag scattered across the bed while Sally settled the baby at her breast.

Blake watched. He couldn't help it. It was the most natural thing in the world. So amazing. That precious life nursing at his mother's breast would have died without Janice. He'd witnessed her saving a life. And he'd played a part. He got her here so she could do it, fetched things, and offered moral support. He couldn't process all that he'd seen here, but he knew it had changed him forever.

When everything had been cleaned up and put away, Sally's nightgown and the sheets changed, Janice held the baby while she sat beside Sally on the bed.

"Doc, we can't thank you enough for what you done," Sally said.

She elbowed Hoyt.

"Uh. Yeah. Thank ye, Doc. We're beholdin' to ya."

Janice smiled. "I'm so glad I could help. He's beautiful." She touched the baby's palm and he curled his tiny hand around her finger.

She snuggled him closer, her heart nearly bursting with emotion. He had a head full of dark, curly hair and huge blue eyes. "He's going to be a heartbreaker. What will you name him?"

"Well, we was gonna name him Charissa to go with Marissa, Larissa, and Clarissa. We just assumed it'd be another girl."

"I don't think that'll work." Blake laughed. He stood tall and handsome next to her, his arms folded across his chest. She didn't know how she could have gotten through this without him. She hadn't ever allowed herself to need anyone, but today, she'd needed Blake.

"Me and Hoyt talked while you was cleanin' up, Doc. If it's all right with you, we'd like to name him Thornton, because if it weren't for you, he wouldn't be here."

"And not only that. I mighta lost my Sally, too."

Janice blinked. She didn't know what to say.

"We'd call him Thorn," Sally went on to explain. "Doc?"

Blake touched her shoulder as she felt the tears fill her eyes. She clasped Sally's hand. "I'd be honored," she managed.

After a moment of pulling herself together, she handed the baby back to its mother and said, "This is your fourth child, so I'm sure you know how this works. With the complications you had, you're going to be more sore than you probably were with the other births. It'll be safe to take acetaminophen for the pain. I've left some on the nightstand for you. Anything stronger wouldn't be good for the baby since you're breastfeeding."

"I'll see that she don't overdo," Hoyt said.

"Is there anything else I can do for you before I go?"

"No. We'll be just fine, Doc," Sally said.

Janice stood and looked up at Hoyt. "I'd like you to bring them in to the office in about a week for a check-up."

She expected him to argue, but instead he agreed.

"I'll do it."

246

"Oh, Hoyt. Could we get a tree from the tall pines afterward?"

"Sure, darlin'. Anything you want."

She smiled up at her husband with love for him clearly displayed in her eyes, and all those old feelings stirred inside Janice. The intense desire to hold her own baby while a loving husband held her in his arms. A warm, welcoming home where they'd always be together to share and build a life together. To finally have and experience all the things she'd never known. Could it be possible? It seemed more than possible in this moment. It seemed so real with Blake standing next to her. Like a miracle on the same level as the birth of this precious child.

But she could never have this kind of family. The kind where the mother stayed home and took care of her husband and family. That's what Blake wanted, and she couldn't give it to him. With her, he'd have to stay with the children while she did rounds, saw patients, and went out on weekends and in the middle of the night to deal with emergencies like this. Did she really want her children to grow up like she had? Without a mother to care for them?

Janice stood. "See that she rests, Hoyt. She's had a long, hard day."

247

"I'll take care of her, Doc. Don't you worry."

She felt Blake's strong hand on her arm. "We'll see ourselves out."

"Thank you again, for everything," Sally said. "Will you send the girls in to meet their baby brother?"

"Of course," Blake said.

Janice was glad to let him take control. She was both mentally and physically drained. All she wanted to do was go back to her uncle's, go up to her room, close the door, shower, crawl into bed, and shut out the world. She couldn't deal with anything else today. In her world — her sterile, lonely world — she could work a twenty-hour day, handle case after case.

But this was different. She'd met these people in their homes, amid their loved ones. Her emotions had gotten all tangled up in the work she'd done since she arrived in Angel Ridge, with these people she'd grown to care for. The mother, whose family depended on her, dying of cancer. A precious little boy who would grow up without a mother to nurse him through his minor childhood illnesses. A woman with an absent husband who'd desperately wanted a child, but had lost it. And a perfect baby born into a family filled with love.

Janice rubbed her forehead with the back of her hand as they walked out to the car. It didn't help that she hadn't slept in nearly twenty-four hours.

"You all right?" Blake asked, his hand still on her arm.

He opened the door to his truck, but held her in front of him with a hand at her shoulder. She looked up at him and nearly broke down. It would be so easy to go into his arms, to let him comfort her, to let herself depend on him. Fall in love with him. He was everything a woman could want. But she wasn't a typical woman, and her life wasn't her own to give. For the first time, even with having delivered that incredible little boy, she regretted her choice of careers.

"You were amazing in there."

A shiver rocked her.

"You're freezing." He rubbed her arms. "Did you bring your coat?"

"I must have left it at your brother's house."

"Here." He settled his coat around her shoulders and said, "Let's get you inside, and the truck running."

He helped her up and went around to the driver's side. It was dark. No stars dotted the sky. She didn't even know what time it was. Blake started the truck and put it in motion.

He picked up the earlier conversation where he'd left off. "You were amazing back there. I've never seen anything like that. I would have been freaking out, but you were so calm. You calmed Sally, too. She didn't seem at all afraid. She just put her trust in you."

Janice closed her eyes and leaned back into the soft bucket seat.

"Janice?"

*"Hmm?"*

"You're awfully quiet."

He cranked up the fan and comforting warm heat filled the truck cab. Janice sighed. "I guess I'm just tried."

"And here I am, talkin' your ear off." He reached over and squeezed her hand. "I'm sorry. Sit back and relax. I'll have you home, safe and sound, in no time."

Home. With Blake . . . she closed her eyes and allowed the fantasy to come. After a long day at work, she'd come home. Blake would meet her at the door with a long, lingering kiss. They'd sit on the couch in front of the fire and talk about their days over a nice glass of wine. They'd prepare a meal together and talk some more. Then, they'd retire to the study to finish up with

250

work they'd brought home or just to read. When the hour grew late, Blake would take her book, set it aside, and pull her out of her chair. Hand in hand, they'd walk to their bedroom. They'd undress each other, make long, sweet love, and fall asleep in each other's arms.

"Wake up, sleepy head."

*"Mmm."* The dream seemed so real. Blake, she could smell his enticing cologne, reach out and touch his face, feel his lips on her wrist. She curled her hand around his neck and pulled his face to hers. His lips were warm and inviting, but she wasn't satisfied. Janice deepened the kiss, tilting her head for better access. Their tongues danced a heady tango that led to thoughts of a soft bed, tangled sheets. . . .

Blake lifted her off the couch and settled her across his lap. Janice blinked. She looked around. The couch sat in front of a crackling fire. A tall pine Christmas tree stood in a bay window. Blake supported her back with an arm while trailing hot kisses down her throat to her shirt collar.

Oh, Lord. This *was* real. Her brain must have short-circuited. Nothing was connecting. "Where am I?"

"My house."

Janice braced her hands against his chest

and broke contact with his lips. "I thought I was dreaming."

"Me, too. I think I've just been kissed by an angel."

"Oh, Blake. I'm sorry." She slid off his lap and backed up to the opposite end of the couch. "I wasn't fully awake."

"Don't go apologizin'. I'm not complaining. Well, I could complain because you stopped." His grin was wide and rakish.

She belatedly realized that not only was she not at her uncle's, but she was also not wearing her clothes. She looked down. She wore only the green flannel shirt she'd seen Blake in on Sunday when she'd brought the cat over. He'd looked sexy enough to pull her up short standing there casually leaning against the doorframe leading into his kitchen, fresh out of the shower, barefoot in jeans that were zipped only halfway up and, like his shirt, not buttoned.

She had to shake her head to clear the image. Back to the here and now. "Where are my clothes?"

"They were soiled, so I put them in the wash. They should be dry soon."

"Did you —" She made a wiggling motion with her finger. "I mean, I don't remember . . ."

"Don't worry. You disappeared into the

bathroom and came out properly covered carrying your clothes."

"Oh." Good. Or was it?

She leaned back into the corner of the couch, and tucked her feet under her. Blake traced the line of her jaw, his arm resting along the couch behind her, his body enticingly close.

"I made some vegetable soup and corn muffins. Are you hungry?"

It was all coming back to her. Their argument last night. The crazy scene with Blake in Heart's Desire. She'd hurried back to her uncle's office to treat Sammy Houston. Then Blake's sister-in-law had lost her baby. The long drive up to the Crawford's to deliver their son.

Janice looked over at Blake. "I don't remember the drive back or anything that happened after we got here. How long was I asleep?"

"About an hour and a half."

"How did I get inside?"

"I carried you."

That thought gave her pause. Her in Blake's arms and she didn't remember it? She really was out of it. She was still buzzing from the kiss they'd just shared, too. "Why didn't you take me back to my uncle's?"

Blake caressed her cheek with the back of his hand. "I wasn't ready to let you go. I was hopin' we could talk."

It would be so easy to get lost in his touch. Janice stood. "I should check in with my uncle. See how Susan is, and then call to check on your sister-in-law."

"Whoa." He took her hand as she passed by and looked up at her. "It's all taken care of. I called your uncle as soon as we got in. I didn't want him to worry. He had called Mable to let her know he stopped off at his cabin on the way back to town. He's spending the night there."

"Susan?"

He pulled her down to the couch with him. When he curved his arm around her shoulders and pulled her close to his side again, every nerve ending in her body rocketed back to high alert.

"That doctor you sent her to must be a miracle worker. He talked her into havin' some radiation treatments. Told her if it shrinks her tumors, it could make a real difference in the way she feels and in her prognosis. So, they're going to keep her for a couple of days."

"That's wonderful."

"You're wonderful."

Janice had to look away from the intensity

254

in his eyes. She tucked her hair behind her ear, then remembered she'd pulled it back into a ponytail. She must look a mess. She pulled the band out and combed her fingers through it. "What about your sister-in-law?"

"She's at home. She's having a rough time, but that's not surprising. She wanted that baby so bad."

"She's young. They can try again."

A muscle ticked in Blake's jaw. "Yeah. If my brother wasn't so worthless, they could."

Janice frowned. "What do you mean?"

"He doesn't want kids. Doesn't want to be saddled with them. But Bebe, havin' a baby is all she's thought about since they got married."

When Blake trailed a hand through her hair, Janice gave up and leaned into his touch. "That's too bad."

Blake pulled her closer and kissed her hair. "You didn't answer my question earlier. Are you hungry?"

"Starved. I skipped lunch." His arms felt so good around her. She suddenly found she didn't have the will to push him away.

"I'll fix a tray and bring it in here. We can eat in front of the fire."

He said the words, but didn't release her. Janice didn't care. The kitchen was too far away. "I'll go with you."

"No. Stay. Relax."

He slowly released her and stood. Janice grasped his hand and stood, too. "I want to come." She needed to be with him. To keep touching him.

"Okay."

They strolled back to the kitchen, hand in hand. Despite her misgivings, it felt right. Natural. And she was too exhausted to fight it.

While Janice watched, Blake ladled up bowls of steaming soup, poured iced tea, and filled a basket with corn muffins. He put everything on a tray and they returned to the parlor. They settled in front of the fireplace and ate.

"*Mmm.* This is delicious."

"Glad you like it."

"It was so nice of you to do this."

"I enjoyed doing it for you."

It was just like her dream, only better. Janice continued to eat, but she couldn't help asking, "Why?"

"Because I care about you."

She shook her head. "No," she waved a spoon back and forth between them. "This is just attraction."

Blake set his bowl aside and moved the tray from between them. "It's more than that for me."

"You hardly know me."

He took her hand in his. "I know plenty. I know that you are absolutely amazing. I watched you today. The way you calmly and confidently tackled every situation that was thrown at you."

"I must be a good actress. I was scared to death we were going to lose *two* babies today."

"But you dealt with each of those situations with such finesse. It got your patients through two very difficult situations. I still can't get over seeing that baby being born. Watching you bring that life into the world. Holding it in your hands. A perfect, precious little boy, alive, kicking and screaming, because of you."

"Some days, it's a good day. I'm able to take the things I've learned and use them to make a difference. Other days . . ."

"Other days, you still make a difference, because your patients know you've done everything you can for them."

It struck Janice again. This was so like the dream she'd had. She and Blake, in this house, sharing their days with each other. It would be so easy to believe the dream could become reality. Something she could claim for her own. But. . . .

Blake took her bowl. "What are you thinking?"

Janice welcomed his arms when they came around her. She put her hands around his waist and leaned her head against his shoulder. "You don't want to know."

"You're wrong. I want to know everything that's going on in that beautiful head of yours."

He kissed a spot near the top of her forehead. Janice chewed on her lower lip. She wanted to tell him everything in her heart and in her thoughts. Maybe if she said the words, it would all somehow make sense. Inside, it was just a jumbled mess of confusion.

He tipped her chin up with a finger until their gazes locked. "Janice, I don't know all the details of your life up until now. I know you pretty much raised yourself, and that you never had anyone you could count on. I'm tellin' you, if you give me the chance, I'll give you everything you never had. A home to come to every day after work. A husband who loves and cares for you. Children to fill your life with happiness and laughter."

"Blake . . . you may be willing to give me those things, but how can I give them to you? You'll spend most of your time here alone while I'm out treating patients."

He shrugged. "So it won't be a traditional family. Who has that anymore? We'll make it work just like everyone else."

She just shook her head.

He touched her face. "What's really holding you back?" A look of dread pulled at his handsome features. "Is this just attraction for you?"

She had to look away. She wanted what he was offering so much it hurt.

He hugged her tighter. "Tell me."

She chewed on her lower lip, still not looking at him. "I don't know what a real family is like." Her gaze collided with his then, and she felt tears fill her eyes. "How can I make a home for you when I've never had one?"

Could Blake be right? Had she been hiding behind her career all these years, keeping her personal life at bay because she was afraid of being proven inadequate in an area of her life where she desperately wanted to succeed?

"All I know about love is loneliness and disappointment. So —" her voice broke, "how can I love a person when I don't know how?"

# CHAPTER 11

"Oh, Janice," Blake touched her face. The fear and longing warring against each other in her eyes broke his heart. Her screwed up family had really done a number on her.

"Come here." He pulled her up against his chest and followed his heart. He kissed her, again and again until the feelings he knew they shared took over and the kisses became longer, deeper, hotter. She was so responsive to his touch. To his kisses. They were perfect for each other. Why couldn't she see that?

He broke the kiss and brushed her hair off her face. "Baby, I have no worries about your capacity to love. I've seen it in the way you care for your patients. In the way you obviously care for your uncle. Your heart's been so full for so long, it's got to be over-flowin'. Just let it come." He kissed her again. "Let it come. Don't hold back."

The fear in her eyes was winning the

battle. He could see it. "Don't be afraid." He cupped the back of her head and stared the fear down. "Tell me what you want. Let yourself say it."

"I don't want to be alone anymore." The words were barely more than a whisper. A tear fell from the corner of her eye.

Blake caught it with his thumb. "You're not alone here. You have an uncle who loves you and wants to get to know you. God, there's a whole town full of crazy people ready to accept and love you." He chuckled. "Maybe I shouldn't have mentioned that. I don't want you to run in the opposite direction."

"I don't want to run," she whispered, her gaze focused on the Christmas tree.

"Then stay." He tried to kiss her again, but she resisted.

"There's someone you're leaving out."

"What do you mean?" he said, confused by the mixed messages he was getting.

"You mentioned my uncle and the town, but . . ."

"But what?"

She looked up at him with those devastating green eyes and yanked his heart right out of his chest. "What about you?"

"Darlin', I've been yours since you found me in the front yard flat of my back."

"Blake . . ."

Janice worried her full, lower lip with her teeth, but didn't continue.

He kissed her. A quick, gentle pressure, then he squeezed her arms. "It's okay. Tell me what you're thinking. What you're feeling."

"When I was younger, I wanted a home and family. People who would love me and be there for me no matter what. That need was always met with disappointment. I was away at school. During breaks, I either went home with friends or to camps. Sometimes I studied abroad. I very rarely stayed to visit with my mother and father, which was fine with me, because when I did, I couldn't wait to leave."

Blake didn't speak. He just trailed his hands down to her hands and laced his fingers with hers, hoping she'd keep talking.

"After I began my own life, I insulated myself from those hurts. I created a world that I could control, with no one in it who could hurt me."

Blake brought her hand to his lips and kissed it. His heart broke for her. How incredibly alone she must feel. This strong, wonderful woman deserved so much more than an isolated existence.

"Since I came to Angel Ridge and met my

uncle and you and so many of the people here, things have changed. By stepping out of the safety of my life in the city, those old longings I used to get for a home and a family have resurfaced. I hate having those feelings again, because along with those old longings come the reality. I never had those things. I don't trust that I *can* have those things."

"But you can." Blake couldn't remain quiet any longer. "You can have all those things. We can have those things together."

"I know you want to believe that, but I don't know if I can let myself . . . hope."

He released her hands and pulled her up close to his side. He liked that she came willingly. "Tell me what you feel when we're together."

"I'm very attracted to you." She slid her hands across his chest. "I like being in your arms, kissing you, touching you. When you touch me, kiss me, I feel so much, I don't want it to end. But I know that's just attraction."

He shook his head and settled his arm around her waist. This was way more than attraction. "What do you feel when we're apart?"

"I think about you. Dream about you." She turned her head, focusing on the Christmas tree again.

"So, you can let yourself give in to the attraction, but when it goes too far, you pull away. Why?"

She abruptly stood and marched over to the tree, her arms crossed in front of her. "You were right. I pull away because I'm afraid I'll develop feelings for you beyond attraction."

Blake stood as well and followed using slow, measured steps. "And you don't trust that I can care about you. That I won't desert you."

She nodded.

This wouldn't be easy, but there was a simple answer. "There's only one way to resolve this."

She looked up at him. "How?"

He stood before her, reached out and touched her face. He loved the way she leaned into his hand. "Time."

"Time?"

"Spend time with me. Let me prove that I'm not going anywhere."

She considered that for a moment, but then caution blanketed her eyes. "I can't promise you anything beyond Christmas. I can't give up my life in the city. I can't just tell them I'm not coming back. I have obligations to my partners and my patients."

And she was safe there, she supplied silently.

"Fair enough. Give me till Christmas to prove to you that I won't betray what you're feeling for me. After that, if you still feel you can't relocate here, we'll discuss my moving to the city with you."

Shock registered on her face at his words.

"I love you, Janice." It felt so good to finally say it, he could barely restrain himself from shouting it. "If I have to move to the city with you to prove that, I will. I don't want to live a life here that doesn't include you."

"But your work, the house —"

"As a contractor, I can work from anywhere. I'll have to drive more, but I'm willing to make the sacrifice to be with you. As for the house, it'll still be here. When we're ready for it."

"How can you make promises to me when you don't even know if there's anything between us beyond attraction?"

Blake smiled. "I know there's more."

"How? How do you know?"

"What we have goes way beyond attraction. What's happening between us is rare." When he kissed her this time, she didn't pull away. That encouraged him to continue. Against her lips and interspersed with kisses, he said, "Just open yourself up to these incredible feelings we share. Let me prove to you that what we have is real. Something you can trust." He kissed her again. Longer. Deeper this time. "I love you, Janice." He whispered against her neck, "I love you. I'll do whatever it takes to make you believe that."

He sealed the promise with a hot, hungry kiss that left them both weak and breathless.

A heavy pounding on the door shocked them apart.

"What in the world?" Blake said.

"I don't know, but if you don't open it quick —"

"Blake Ferguson, open this door this instant or as God is my witness, I'll break it down!" Doc Prescott boomed.

"Uncle Charles!" Janice said in a shocked whisper, pulling at the hem of Blake's flannel shirt.

"Aw, hell."

The pounding started up again. That door was unlocked. He'd only have to try the knob to be inside, but the pounding was certainly more dramatic. Blake had taken one step toward the foyer when the old door banged open. In two angry strides, Doc Prescott was standing in the doorway to the parlor, and Blake found himself staring down the double barrel of a shotgun.

He held up his hands. "Whoa there, Doc. This isn't what you think."

"Uncle!"

Janice rushed to the older man's side and pulled at his arm. Not exactly what he would have done given the fact that the man was pointing a loaded gun at him.

"Easy there, Janice."

"What are you doing, Uncle? Put that gun away this instant," she insisted.

He shrugged her off. "I'll do no such thing." He swung his angry gaze to Janice. "Where are your clothes, young lady?"

"I delivered a baby today and soiled them. Blake gave me his shirt while he washed and dried them."

He raked her with an assessing gaze. "Couldn't he have given you some pants as well?" He refocused on Blake, wildly waving the shotgun at him.

Blake frowned, the doc knew better than to handle a gun like that.

"And why did you bring her here instead of to our home?" He took a step forward and continued, "I'll not have you sullying my grandniece's reputation, Ferguson. I demand satisfaction!"

"What?" Had he just been challenged? To a duel? Had the old doc finally lost it?

Like lightning, Janice grasped the barrel of the shotgun, tilted it to the ceiling, and then wrenched it to the side. Blake closed his eyes and prayed. When no shot discharged, he opened one eye a bit to find Janice holding the weapon. She stood there wearing nothing but his flannel shirt, looking regal and damned sexy. And incredibly angry.

"Uncle Charles, what has gotten into you? Coming over here, interfering in my affairs, and threatening Blake with a gun? You could have seriously injured him, yourself, or all three of us." She expertly opened the shotgun and gasped. "At least you had the good sense not to load it."

"Well," he blustered, "I wanted to scare the boy. Not kill him."

He'd certainly accomplished that.

She handed the weapon back to her uncle. "I am going to find my clothes. We can discuss what just happened here when I return. While I am gone, I expect the two of you to be civil to each other."

Doc Prescott grumbled something under his breath. Blake tried to refrain from patting himself down to reassure himself he wasn't bleeding from a bullet wound.

She pointed a finger at her uncle. "Promise me."

"Oh, very well."

"Blake?"

He held up his hands and took a step back. He wasn't about to further antagonize the man.

Janice turned and walked to the back of the house, toward the kitchen.

Doc Prescott didn't waste any time. He propped the shotgun by the door and marched into the room, pinning him with an angry glare. "How dare you, Blake Ferguson. I turn my back for one second, and you compromise my grandniece. This is not the behavior of a proper gentleman. I expected more of you."

"There was no compromisin' goin' on here, sir, I swear. My intentions toward Janice are honorable."

"I find nothing about this situation honorable. *And,* you haven't spoken to me. Not one word about your intentions, honorable or otherwise."

"I haven't had a chance. Me and Janice have been tryin' to sort it all out."

"Well?" he demanded.

"I'd like to court your grandniece, sir. I'd like your blessing, but I'll be seein' her with our without it."

"Insolent, ill-mannered —"

"Uncle!"

Janice hurried into the room and didn't stop until she stood between the two men. "What is the meaning of this? Why are you behaving this way?"

"I'm behaving as any responsible guardian would."

Janice laughed. "Uncle, I am well beyond the age of needing a guardian."

"Regardless —"

It was all Blake could do to keep from rolling his eyes. The older man swung his gaze to his as if expecting an explanation. "Janice was exhausted after the day she had, and I wasn't comfortable leaving her alone with you gone to your cabin. That's why I brought her here. Sir," he added.

Doc Prescott nodded. *Harrumph!* He took Janice's arm. "I'll speak to my grandniece regarding your request. If she is inclined toward you, I'll consider permitting you to see her."

He folded his hands in front of him. "Thank you, sir."

"Excuse me?" Janice said.

"Come, dear. Let me take you home. We'll discuss this on the way."

"Your medical bag and equipment are still in my truck."

"She won't be needing any of that tonight," Doc Prescott supplied. "Just bring it

270

by the clinic in the morning, Ferguson. Janice."

He ushered her out of the room. Janice looked back over her shoulder at him. Blake just smiled and thought, *Welcome to Angel Ridge.*

Out on the front porch, Janice wasted no time in questioning her uncle. "What was that about, Uncle?"

"Here now, my dear. Let me get you settled in the car. It's colder than a witch's — well, it's cold out here."

She hardly knew where to begin. She'd never experienced anything like that in her life. Once he had her settled in the roomy interior of his Cadillac and had gotten behind the wheel, she asked again, "What were you and Blake talking about when I came into the room?"

He put the car in motion. "Let's discuss this when we're safe and warm in front of the fireplace in our parlor, shall we."

"I'd prefer to discuss it now, if you don't mind. You were saying something about Blake having a request and me being inclined?"

"The Ferguson boy has asked my permission to court you."

"He did?"

"Albeit under duress, he did indeed. I dare

271

say that had I not forced the issue, he wouldn't have approached me at all." He shook his head. "Young people these days. There's a proper way to handle these things . . ."

Janice bit her lip to hold back a laugh. "So, what did you tell him?"

"I told him I would discuss it with you to see if you were inclined toward him."

"I see." She stared out the window, a feeling of pleasant warmth spreading through her limbs. Was this how it felt to be cared for? If so, she could get used to the feeling.

"Before tonight, I would have said the Ferguson boy was a proper young gentleman, suitable for you to spend time with. Now, I'm not so sure."

Janice was glad for the dark interior of the car that hid her blush. "Oh, Uncle. It was nothing, really. We just talked. He made me soup."

*"Harrumph!"*

"Honestly."

"I believe you were innocent in the matter, dear. However, I'm not so sure what might have happened had I not come back and, well, interrupted whatever was about the transpire."

The giggle slipped out before she could stop it.

"Young lady!"

She pressed her lips together. "I'm sorry."

He pulled into the drive. When he had placed the car in park and killed the ignition, he asked, "Janice, do you have a *tendre* for this young man?"

She pressed her hand to her uncle's cheek and said, "I like him very much."

His sigh was heavy. "Very well, then."

"You approve?"

"I admit, I had selfishly hoped to have you to myself for a bit longer, but if this is what you want, I'll not stand in your way." He held up a warning finger. "But I'll have my eye on that young buck. If he so much as —"

She grasped her uncle's hand and leaned forward to kiss his cheek. "I'm sure he'll be the proper gentleman."

"See that he is. Now let's get inside. I want to hear about your day."

Janice walked arm in arm with her uncle up to the house. Against all odds, she'd found an uncle willing to act as a father to her and a wildly sexy man willing to navigate old-fashioned social mores to date her. Could she be any more blessed? Could this be real? Could it last?

She had to admit, all these events combined to fill her heart near to bursting with hope for the future. A future where loneliness would become a distant memory.

Janice and her uncle spent the next day going through patient charts and just simply getting to know each other better. As the afternoon shadows began to lengthen, he said, "I think I'll head down to the diner for supper. Dixie's fixin' chicken fried steak. Would you like to join me?"

She could feel her arteries hardening just thinking about it. "No thanks, Uncle," Janice said. "I think I'll just make a salad and curl up with a book by the fire."

"You're sure?"

"Yes. You go and enjoy yourself."

"I hate leaving you alone."

"Don't worry about me. I'm used to being alone."

"Something that needs remedying."

Janice smiled, thinking how he hadn't liked her remedy of the night before, but linked arms with her uncle, and ushered him to the front of the house. "I'm in no danger of being lonely while you're at the diner having supper. Are you meeting Miss Estelee?"

"Not tonight."

At the front door, she asked, "So, tell me. Will we be hearing wedding bells soon?"

Her uncle chuckled. "Only if they're ringing for you."

Determined to get to the bottom of things, Janice pressed, "You spend so much time with Miss Estelee, I just thought —"

"Oh no, dear." He held up his hands and shook his head. "It's much too late for an old cuss like me to be contemplating marriage."

"Were you ever married?"

"No." He said the word immediately. Succinctly.

Janice helped him into his coat and held out his hat. "I don't understand."

"Nothing to understand." He smiled and patted her cheek, but the smile didn't reach his eyes. He took his hat and said, "Can I bring you anything? A piece of cake or pie?"

"No, but thanks for asking."

"Call the diner if you need me."

Janice watched as he walked away. Leaving the porch light on, she went back to the kitchen and removed salad fixings from the refrigerator. It was so quiet. That was the one thing she still hadn't gotten used to. She walked over to the parlor and put in a Christmas CD. With the volume up, she could hear it in the kitchen. Bing Crosby singing *White Christmas*. Much better.

As she tore lettuce and put it on a plate,

she sighed. She and her uncle had spent the day going through patient files so she could acquaint herself with each of the town's residents. It was as if her taking over as town doctor was a foregone conclusion. Despite the fact that she was far from committing, disappointing her uncle prevented her from saying as much. And besides, after the day she'd had yesterday, patient knowledge couldn't hurt.

*Meow.*

The kitten wove its way in a figure eight around her feet. "How do you keep getting in here, girl?" Janice picked up the cat and stroked her fur. She purred her pleasure. The mechanical whirring of the doorbell startled the kitten right out of her hands.

"Who could that be?"

Janice smoothed her hands down the legs of her jeans as she retraced her steps to the front door. Blake was silhouetted through the lace curtains, bathed in the soft porch light. She tucked her hair behind her ears and opened the door.

"Hi," he said.

"Hi." She rubbed her arms against the blast of cold air coming in through the front door.

He wore a heavy, tan suede coat that made his shoulders look impossibly wide. The collar was trimmed in worsted wool. He looked casually comfortable in dark jeans, boots and a black Stetson. Removing his hat, he smiled down at her, that sexy half smile that pulled at one corner of his mouth. Focusing on his mouth was a mistake. It reminded her of his kisses.

"This is a surprise."

"A pleasant one, I hope. What are you doing?"

"Freezing." She shivered. "Come inside."

"I have a better idea. Why don't you put on your coat, hat and gloves, and come out with me?" He stood aside giving her a clear view of a horse and buggy parked at the curb.

"Blake —"

"Don't ask questions. Just come. I want to acquaint you with some Angel Ridge holiday traditions."

She didn't need much convincing. The salad would keep. "Okay."

Blake helped her into the heavy coat hanging by the door. While she was putting on her mittens, he pulled a knit cap down over her ears and pressed a quick kiss to her lips while he wrapped her scarf around her neck. Janice leaned forward to continue the contact, but found herself being pulled by her scarf outside onto the porch then down the sidewalk toward a waiting antique carriage. The cold breeze took her breath away.

He jammed his hat back on his head. "I'll have you warmed up in no time."

"I can't believe you did this." The shiny red carriage was hitched to a beautiful white horse. "Where did you, I mean, how did you find a horse and carriage?"

"It's mine," he said as he helped her up. The seats had beautiful soft, white leather upholstery. "I store it out at my parents' farm. I keep my horses there, too."

"The horse is beautiful. What's its name?"

Blake had joined her in the carriage and was tucking layers of blankets around her. Warmth surrounded her, especially with Blake's side pressed so close to hers.

"This is Daisy."

"Oh, she should have daisies in her halter."

"We do that for the Fourth of July parade. The bell harness is more the style for winter. Snug and warm?"

"Very. It feels like there's heat in the floor."

"There are warm bricks under your feet. That's what folks used to do when they had to travel around in one of these in the dead of winter." He took up the reins and said, "Get up, girl."

They moved slowly down the street toward town. The cold hit her face making her cheeks and nose feel icy. She burrowed closer to Blake's side, wrapping an arm around his.

"I could get used to this."

She gazed up at him. "Me, too." She drank in the sight of him. The strong angular lines of his face, the way his long, dark lashes outlined his incredible eyes. He looked even better in a Stetson. He was definitely easy on the eyes. Looking at him for the rest of her life certainly wouldn't be a hardship. "Where are you taking me?"

"I thought we'd take a turn around Main Street. The town's real pretty at night with the gas streetlights burnin' and the tree lit up. The holiday window displays are nice, too."

"Sounds wonderful."

"So how was your day?"

"Uneventful."

"Guess that was a welcome change from yesterday."

"Yes. I slept in this morning. Can't remember the last time I did that."

"You earned it. Oh, I was out in the direction of the Crawfords today, so I swung by."

"How are Sally and the baby?"

"Don't you mean Sally and Thorn?" He chuckled. "Real good. They asked me to thank you again for them. Sally sent something for me to give you, too."

"Really? What?"

"It's in the boot. I'll give it to you later."

Janice turned and peered over the high leather seat back. "This thing has a trunk?"

"Yep."

He turned the carriage onto Main Street to slowly make the loop around both sides.

"Evenin' folks."

"Constable Harris," Blake acknowledged the welcome.

"Buggy's lookin' real fine, Blake."

"Thanks, Henry."

He tipped his hat. "Enjoy your evenin'."

Blake leveled a look on Janice that made her toes curl. "We will," he murmured.

They rolled down Main past Ferguson's, the Apothecary's and the bank. She looked at the buildings as if for the first time, taking in every detail. When they had started around the circle, they passed First Presbyterian. It was a tall, impressive church made of golden stone with a square bell tower and an elaborate round stained glass window. The double wooden doors weren't square, but bullet-shaped with wrought iron hardware.

"This church looks older than First Baptist."

"The congregation's older, but the building is actually the church's second. The first one burned down sometime in the late 1800s. They rebuilt shortly afterward. So, First Baptist has an older structure."

"Sounds like the source of debate on who has the oldest church."

Blake laughed. "You catch on quick."

Janice just shook her head and smiled. She knew nothing about the churches in her area. "It must be so nice to know the history of where you live. I can't tell you anything about my neighborhood."

"Livin' in the city's different. There's just no community feeling there. The pace is so much faster, I guess there's no time for such things."

"It's very impersonal," she agreed. Up until now, that had suited her. But since she'd stepped foot in Angel Ridge, she'd had an unsettled feeling about her life in the city. She looked up at Blake and was at least able to admit that he made her want something different for her life. He made it seem possible.

A spotlight illuminated the town library. A small tree out front was decorated and pine wreaths graced the oak door beneath an arched entryway. "That is such a beautiful building." She just couldn't get over it: a library that looked like a castle.

"Next to the churches, it's the finest structure in town. The McKays saw to that."

"They own the bank, right?"

"Yep. They own the library, too. The new computer wing I've been working on should be finished in a few more days."

"You've been working on it?" she teased.

"Well, I've been supervising the work," he corrected.

"I went by there at lunch and checked out some books. Everyone seemed proud and excited about the new addition."

"Yeah, well, it doesn't take much to get folks in a small town excited."

They admired a beautiful nativity scene that had been set out in the front lawn of the First Baptist Church. It was an equally impressive tall brick structure with round, white columns. Continuing down the other side of the street, he pulled to a stop at the angel monument and Christmas tree. The monument needed no ornamentation, but it had a thick velvet ribbon secured to its pedestal. The huge Christmas tree took her breath away. She'd never seen anything so beautiful. The robes of the golden angel adorning the top flowed in the gentle breeze, but the dark night obscured other details. It needed a spotlight.

He eased an arm around her shoulders

and pulled her close. "Kinda gets to you, doesn't it?"

She touched his wrist at her shoulder, liking the way she fit against him. "It feels like I stepped back in time." She turned toward him. "Do you think it looked like this a hundred years ago?"

"I'd say the storefronts have changed, but other than that, it's probably pretty close."

After a few moments had passed, he reluctantly released her and again set the buggy in motion by making a soft clicking sound. The horse's hooves beat a rhythmic sound on the cobbled street. Heart's Desire and DeFoe's Hardware made for a strange juxtaposition that only added to the town's ambiance.

Just as they completed the loop and passed by the diner again on their way out of town, Dixie stepped outside. "Blake? That you?"

He stopped the carriage. "Hey, Sis."

"Hey, yourself. Is that the doc you got buried under those blankets?"

"Hi, Dixie," Janice said.

Dixie rubbed her arms. "It feels about sixty below out here. Are y'all crazy or what?"

"It's not too bad," Janice said.

"*Mmm-hmm.* Let me get you a thermos of

hot chocolate."

"No need, Dix. We won't be out that long. I'll have her back at her uncle's in no time."

"No need arguin'. I'll have it out in a . . ."

She was inside and bustling behind the counter before she'd finished speaking. "Sorry," Blake said.

Janice snuggled against his side. "I'm not complaining."

"Keep that up, and we'll be back at your uncle's before I'd planned."

He lowered his head and swept cold lips across hers. They warmed instantly. Janice curled her hand around his neck and tipped her head to the side, encouraging him to deepen the kiss.

When he moved to do just that, Dixie said, "Oh! *Hel-lo*. Pretend I'm not here."

She held out the thermos with her back turned. Blake took it and said, "Thanks." Dixie hurried into the diner with a wave and without looking back.

"We better get on to the second half of our tour."

Janice swept her tongue across her lips. His kiss still lingered there, warm and intoxicating. Blake reluctantly looked away and said, "Get up." He slapped the reins on the horse's back and she moved forward.

"Maybe we should go to your place after

our tour. I don't think my uncle's going to be out all evening."

"Don't tempt me. Beyond not wanting to be on the wrong side of your uncle again, I have a plan, and it involves going back to your uncle's."

Janice frowned. "I don't understand."

"You will."

"I'm sorry about what happened with my uncle. He means well."

"I know. You mind tellin' me something?"

"Sure."

"Where'd you learn to handle a gun?"

"My father liked to go the club and shoot skeet every spare moment he had. He even had it set up on the yacht."

"You had a yacht?"

"My parents did. Anyway, in order to give the appearance of spending time with me, he would invite me along to the shooting range. It was also a good place to meet the kind of guys mother wanted me to date."

"I see."

"Uncle told me you asked permission to court me."

"Did he now?"

They were following a dirt road out of town that led up into the trees.

Janice nodded. "He approves, by the way. Thank you for indulging him."

285

"You're welcome, and I'm glad he approves, but I'm more interested in whether or not you approve."

She snuggled closer to his side. "I do."

He swung a heated glance in her direction. "Thank you."

"For what?"

He concentrated on driving the carriage again. "Giving me a chance."

She leaned her head against his shoulder. "Where are we going?"

"Up to the tall pines."

That had her sitting upright again. "Why, Blake Ferguson. Are you taking me up to Angel Ridge's version of Lover's Lane?"

"I'm taking you for another reason, but if you throw yourself at me while we're there . . . well, that's up to you."

"Are you saying you wouldn't be willing?"

He gave her that toe-curling look again. "I couldn't resist you if I tried, not that I would."

She laid her head back on his shoulder and sighed. If it weren't so cold, she'd think she was dreaming. They continued to go up, their progress slowed by the steep grade. The trees were so thick, overhanging the path, but not interfering, as if they expected visitors and welcomed them.

When at last they leveled off, they were in

a clearing. The pencil pines towered up to the heavens all around them, but a perfect oval, that mimicked the oval around Town Square, stood in the center of it all. He brought the carriage to a halt right in the middle of the clearing.

Neither of them spoke. A hush settled over the clearing. A feeling of welcome surrounded them. She glanced up at Blake and found him staring back at her. For some reason, it wasn't nearly as cold here as it had been in town and on the ride up. It made no sense. With the higher elevation, the opposite should be true.

Janice pushed the cap back off her head and removed her mittens. She wanted to touch Blake. For him to hold her in his arms and kiss her.

"This is amazing. It feels almost like a place out of time. Like it doesn't really exist anywhere other than inside our minds." She glanced away. "That sounds crazy. I'm a scientist. I'm not —"

He laid a finger on her lips. *"Shh."* When his lips touched hers, it felt perfect. Right in every way. She wanted the moment to never end. The idea of sharing her life with this man seemed not only possible, but clearly like the direction she should take. Would take.

When he broke the contact, she whispered, "Wow."

"You felt it, too."

Janice could only nod.

"Janice —"

It was her turn to lay a finger on his lips. Words could only spoil the moment. She rested her cheek against his heart and closed her eyes as he folded her into his arms.

As Blake held her close, his heart filled with such strong emotion that it felt like it would burst. "I love you." He whispered the words softly against her hair, but a warm, gentle breeze seemed to lift and carry them through the clearing in a never-ending circle that rose up to the sky. He'd heard all his life that this place was magical, but he wasn't sure he had ever believed it. In the past, he'd come up here alone and even with other girls. Then, it had seemed like nothing more that a clearing in the woods. He'd never think of it that way again.

She nestled her cheek more snuggly against his chest, but didn't tell him she loved him, too. That didn't bother him. He knew, in her own time, she'd come to him. A nagging voice at the back of his mind chose that moment to remind him that relationships with women never worked for him. They always left him in the end. Usually for someone else.

With Janice, he wasn't so sure that would be the problem. Even if he made the sacrifice and moved with her to the city, how much time would they have together? And if she decided to relocate to Angel Ridge, she'd be the town doctor. He wanted to make it work, but was she right? Could they?

He shook his head. He refused to let doubts ruin what was happening between them. This was their night. He'd promised to show her how much he loved her. He wouldn't be distracted from that purpose by anything. If he was lucky enough to win her, they would sort the rest out together. Other people did it. Surely they could, too.

He held her a little away so that he could look into her emerald green eyes. "I did bring you here for a reason."

"You mean other than to make-out?"

He wiggled his eyebrows. "That's just a bonus. I brought you here to get a tree for your room."

"A Christmas tree?" she breathed.

He nodded.

She looked around the clearing. "Is it okay to cut them?"

"It's actually encouraged. They grow so thick, it's as if one sprouts up full grown as soon as you take another down."

"I've never cut my own tree. I usually just pick one up at a nursery."

"Then this should be an experience for you." He stepped out of the carriage and offered his hand to help her down. "There's nothing like walking through the woods, picking the tree out yourself, and cutting it down." He got the hacksaw from the boot, and they headed for the edge of the clearing, hand in hand.

"Why is it so much warmer up here?" she asked as they entered the woods.

"This place sort of defies logic, so don't try to make sense of anything that happens here."

"Is this where the town angels reside?"

"Well, according to Miss Estelee, they make their rounds, but they're real partial to the tall pines."

"Really?"

"Yeah, but next time I see her, I'll have to ask her why I had to bring my own."

She shook her head, a wry grin tugging at the corner of her mouth. "You are a charmer, Blake Ferguson."

"I do my best, ma'am." She'd said the words as if she thought he were disingenuous, but the smile on her face showed the compliment had hit its mark. He'd take it for now. The words he wanted to hear her say would come later.

After a few minutes of looking around, Janice chose a tree and he handed her the saw. She seemed to enjoy sawing it down herself. Since it was such a small tree, it didn't take long. Blake picked it up and balanced it on his shoulder as they made their way back to the carriage.

After he'd secured it to the back, he settled Janice in and pointed Daisy back to town. When they reached the edge of the clearing, Janice touched his arm and said, "Wait."

He pulled in on the reins and glanced down at her. Her gaze swept the clearing one more time, then she tipped her face up to the sky. Bathed in silvery moonlight, her beauty struck him like a sucker punch to the gut. She took his breath away. Long, long silvery blonde hair that fell in a silky curtain around her shoulders and down her back. The curve of her cheek, the straight line of her nose, and full, kissable lips, all came together to form an utterly irresistible package.

When finally she looked back, she just stared at him. The heat in her eyes nearly scorched him. She pulled his hat off and brushed the hair back from his forehead, then trailed her fingertips down his cheek.

Blake closed his eyes and leaned into her touch. He clasped her wrist and pressed a kiss into her palm. Janice had other ideas. She turned his face and kissed him.

Intense feelings vibrated through him. When she teased the seam of his lips with the tip of her tongue, he willingly granted her access. After endless moments of allowing her to slowly drive him mad, he took control. He urged her back against the seat and unbuttoned her coat while she unbuttoned his. When he pulled her up against his chest, he felt feminine curves instead of bulky coat. The sensation fired his overwrought senses. He angled his mouth over hers and took them to the jagged edge of raw hunger. He wanted her — needed her in a way that defined the words.

He broke the kiss, but pressed the words in his heart across her face, down her neck, to her collar. "I love you."

"Oh, Blake."

He continued kissing and touching her.

"Blake."

The urgency of her words pierced the sensual fog of desire.

"Blake! We're moving. Fast!"

Blake turned and quickly grabbed the reins. "*Whoa*, Daisy. *Whoa*, girl."

She had taken them down the trail out of

the tall pines, and they were just entering town. Blake hadn't even noticed they were moving. They could have careened into a tree or worse. The cold hit him like a much needed slap in the face.

After he had the horse under control, he brought them to a halt. "I'm sorry, Janice."

She buttoned her coat and dove under the blankets. "Don't apologize." She laughed.

He jammed his hat on. "What?"

Her smile was contagious.

"That was some ride."

# CHAPTER 12

Back at her uncle's, Blake took the tree straight up to her room and laid it on the floor. Thank goodness her uncle had not been downstairs. After last night's fiasco, she was certain he wouldn't have approved her taking Blake up to her bedroom. She cleared off a table that sat next to a window and spread a folded sheet on it.

Blake entered the room carrying a large box.

"What's all this?" Janice asked as he shrugged out of his coat and removed his hat. She took his coat and hung it over the back of a desk chair, almost completely distracted by the way his sweater clung to his chest and flat stomach.

He tossed his hat onto her bed. "Let's see." He opened up the box. "Tree stand, lights, ornaments. Everything you need to trim the tree. I went by the hardware before I picked you up," he admitted. "I hope you don't mind me choosing everything."

She couldn't believe it. Looking into the box with him, she found everything she needed to decorate the tree. Janice put her hands in her back pockets and worked at pressing the emotion down.

Blake quickly moved to her side and lightly grasped her arm. "What is it?"

"I can't believe you . . ." She pressed her fingertips to her lips, then stood on her tiptoes and kissed his cheek. "I can't believe you did all this for me. Thank you."

He brushed off the gratitude. "Don't go thanking me yet. The night's still young."

"You mean there's more?"

"Maybe. Hey, there you are." Blake walked over to the bed and scooped the kitten up into his hands. "Has she been here all day?"

Janice nodded. "She keeps breaking in somehow."

"I'm beginning to think you don't like my company." He rubbed the kitten behind its ears.

Janice stood close, unable to imagine anyone not enjoying his company. "My uncle checked around and couldn't find who she belonged to."

"Guess we'll have to keep her then."

She petted the kitten he still held in his hands, not correcting him when he said *we*.

"Well, if you're going to keep her, don't you think you should name her?"

"I still say Houdini fits," he said, but seemed distracted. The look in his eyes nearly caused her to lose her train of thought.

"It's not a very good name for such a pretty girl."

"What do you suggest?"

"How about . . . Princess?"

He tipped his chin down, but said, "Whatever you want."

"You don't like it."

"I didn't say that."

"I can tell. What do you want to name her?"

"I'd like you to name her."

"How about Angel? Is that too trite considering where you live?"

"Maybe, but who cares. I like it." He cupped her cheek. "It reminds me of you."

"Angel it is then," she agreed softly.

He set the cat back on the bed and just stood there facing her, a hot, hungry look in his eyes. Janice was acutely aware of where they were. They'd only have to sit to be on her bed, wrapped in each other's arms, loving each —

Blake clapped his hands. "Let's get that tree decorated."

She took a step back toward the window. "The tree. Yes."

He grabbed the boxed lights, plugged them in, and they began stringing them around the tree. But he still had that smoldering look in his eyes that did crazy things to her pulse.

"You know, there's a legend about Christmas trees cut from the tall pines," Blake said.

"Really?" She had begun hanging the ornaments. He held the box, leaving her to place them the way she wanted. "There are legends about everything around here."

"*Mmm.* They say that if you put an angel at the top of the tree, you can make a wish and it will come true."

"Do you believe that?"

He shrugged. "I don't know. I'm not very superstitious."

She placed the last ornament and stood back to admire her handiwork. "I guess it doesn't matter. We don't have an angel."

"I wouldn't be so sure. There's this."

He lifted a parcel from the box wrapped in white tissue with glitter. "What is it?"

"I don't know. Sally Crawford gave it to me with strict instructions that I shouldn't peek. She wanted you to be the first to see it."

Glitter sparkled and fell around them as Janice carefully pealed the paper away. "Oh, Blake . . ." she breathed. Lying on the bed of tissue was a delicate, handmade angel. The dress and wings were made of hand-tatted white and gold lace. The doll's face was beautiful. She had long blonde hair with a ring of silk flowers around her head and ribbon streamers trailing down her back.

"She's stunning. Do you think Sally made her?"

"I'd say so. She's real handy with a needle and a crochet hook. Sells her goods down at the flea market from time to time."

"Can you put her on top?"

"Make you a deal. I will if you make a wish. That way if it comes true, we'll know it's not a superstition."

Janice nodded. "Okay." What should she wish?

Blake arranged the angel at the top of the tree, then stepped behind Janice and pulled her back against him. He wrapped his arms around her waist, and said against her ear, "What do you think?"

"It's the most beautiful tree I've ever seen," she whispered.

"Even more beautiful than the tree in town?"

Remembering she'd said the same thing

about that tree, she rationalized. "Well, it really doesn't compare. This one is much smaller."

"So, it's the most beautiful in its size class."

Janice playfully swatted at his arm.

*"Ow,"* he complained.

He pushed her hair out of the way and kissed her neck. "Did you make your wish?"

"No, not yet."

He kissed her again. "What are you waitin' on?"

"I have to think about it. I want to wish for the right thing." She didn't mention that thinking with his lips on her neck was out of the question. She closed her eyes and leaned into his touch.

"I see. You're not an impulsive wisher. Interesting."

She glanced back at him. "Are you making fun of me?"

He dropped a quick kiss on her lips. "Never."

She faced the tree again, and they both just stood there gazing at it. She closed her eyes and made her wish.

"Did you finally decide?" he said near her ear.

She nodded.

"Good, because I have something I want

to give you."

"Don't you want to know what I wished?"

"If you tell me, it won't come true."

Smiling, she said, "I thought you said you weren't superstitious."

He shrugged. "Why jinx it?" He reached down into the container he'd brought in earlier, retrieved a long thin box tied with a pretty red bow, and held it out to her.

"What's this?"

"Open it and see."

She untied the bow and lifted the top. Peeling back tissue, she found the dress she'd tried on at Heart's Desire. She glanced up at him, surprised.

"There's a dance Saturday night. I'd be honored if you'd go with me."

She lifted the dress out of the box, held it against her, and spun in a circle. "I'd love to. Thank you." She leaned across the box to give him a kiss, but stopped short when she saw it wasn't empty. "There's more?"

He looked, too. "There is?"

She pulled out a matching satin teddy with satin garters and silk stockings. His eyes widened, then his gaze heated. He turned away and set the box aside, but not before she saw his face redden.

"Oh, *um,* Candi got all that together for me. You hungry?"

Swinging the skimpy teddy back and forth on her index finger, she teased, "Not embarrassed are you?"

"Nope. Just tryin' to focus on something other than you wearin' that." He pointed at the lingerie in question.

"Such a gentleman."

He took a step forward, clasped the back of her neck, but didn't kiss her though he clearly wanted to. Instead, he seemed to struggle for control. "I'm hangin' on by a ragged thread, darlin'."

"Why?" she breathed.

"Because I'm trying to be a gentleman and at least feed you . . . first." Turning away, he dove back into the box and produced a small, insulated container. "So, you hungry or not?"

"Sure." After that exchange, the last thing on her mind was food, but she'd humor him. For now.

She put the dress and sexy undergarments back into the dress box while Blake spread a checked tablecloth on the floor. Next, he set out two plates, two wineglasses, and silverware with napkins.

"A picnic?"

"Yeah. Sorry we couldn't have it outside. Next spring, I'll take you down to Fort Loudoun and we'll have a proper picnic by the lake. But for now, this will have to do."

She didn't bother reminding him she wouldn't be here next spring because, in this moment, she wasn't too sure she wouldn't be.

He opened the container, and the smell of a savory chicken casserole filled the air. Next, he unwrapped a bottle of white wine and worked on removing the cork. She sat next to him on the floor and said, "Has anyone ever told you that you're amazing?"

He winked. "As long as you think so, that's enough for me." He poured the wine and lifted his glass. "Merry Christmas, Janice Thornton. May this be the best one yet."

Who needed luck or wishes or angels? She had everything she'd ever wanted right here, right now, right in front of her. "For you, too, Blake," she said softly as she touched her glass to his.

"With you here, it's a sure thing."

He always said exactly what her heart wanted to hear. She sipped her wine while Blake spooned casserole onto a plate and handed it to her. "What's that smile about?"

"Just wondering what will happen if Uncle Charles comes home and finds us picnicking in my bedroom."

He dropped the spoon in the container.

"*Aw,* man. Maybe we should move this downstairs."

He started to stand, but she delayed him by laying hand on his arm. "Why? Were you planning to compromise me?"

He wiggled his eyebrows. "Is that an invitation?"

She took another sip of wine. "I don't know." She glanced over at her bed with its frilly eyelet lace comforter and his black hat lying in the middle of it. "It's a twin." She let her gaze slowly travel from his head to his boots. "Pretty narrow for a man . . . your size."

He took her wine and set it aside. "You're playin' with fire, lady."

She trailed a lazy finger from his collar to his stomach. "I'll take my chances." She couldn't get the image of them standing in his kitchen in each other's arms . . . his shirt unbuttoned, out of her mind. He had a great chest sprinkled with dark hair that angled down a hard, flat, muscular stomach to a line before disappearing into his waistband . . . She'd like to get another look.

He cupped her elbow. "Where's your uncle?"

"He went to the diner just before you picked me up."

He checked his watch. "The diner prob-

303

ably closed fifteen minutes ago."

She pressed her lips to the hollow just behind his ear and eased her hand under his sweater. "Maybe he'll stop by Miss Estelee's before he comes home."

He sank his fingers into her hair and tipped his head to the side, giving her better access. "*Mmm . . .* if there's a God in heaven . . ."

"Janice, dear, I brought you some pie from the — diner. Ferguson."

"Or not," Blake mumbled as he leaned back, effectively breaking contact with her lips and hands. He glanced over his shoulder at her uncle and said, "Doc."

"What have we here?" he asked somewhat cautiously.

"Blake took me to the tall pines to get a tree. Isn't it lovely?"

"Oh, well, yes. Quite."

"And he packed us a picnic dinner. Wasn't that thoughtful, Uncle?"

Her uncle cleared his throat. "It was indeed." He still stood in the open doorway, so she said, "Come in and join us. Would you like a glass of wine?"

"Oh, no. Thank you. I'll just leave the pie and, *um,* if you're all right, I'll just retire to my study. Just downstairs, below your room." He pinned Blake with a look, driving his point home.

She stood and took the pie from him, kissing his cheek. "Thank you, Uncle. We'll be down in a bit."

"Of course. Ferguson."

"Doc."

After he'd turned and left, she rejoined Blake on the blanket. He sat there in a casually sexy pose, one leg outstretched, one leg bent with his arm draped over it while he leaned his weight on the other.

"Well, after last night, I'd call that progress," she said, sitting next to him, her legs tucked beneath her.

Blake pushed his hair back off his forehead. "I suppose."

"What's wrong?"

He smoothed a hand down her hair and said, "Nothing."

"That look on your face isn't saying *nothing*."

"I'm just being selfish."

"Tell me," she encouraged.

He took her hand and brought it to his lips. The slow slide of his mouth across her knuckles nearly short-circuited her brain. "I'd give anything for a few hours of your undivided attention. Without interruptions."

"That's not likely to ever happen."

"Not while you're living with your uncle,

anyway."

"I can always get called in on a case, as well."

"I know, but at least we could finish what we started before you left, and your uncle wouldn't walk in while I'm," he leaned close and whispered, "making love to you."

She felt his breath on her lips, soft and warm, but he didn't touch her. She moistened them with the tip of her tongue.

"Please. I'm dying a short death here." His voice was a hoarse whisper.

"Kiss me," she invited.

"Your uncle —"

"Is downstairs in his study." Touching her nose to his, she angled her head in anticipation.

"And at any moment, he could run up here to check on us."

She tested the texture of the dark stubble on his cheek with hers. "He wouldn't."

Blake held her at arm's length. "Baby, he's got my number and I'm not takin' any chances. He expects me to behave like a gentleman and you can be certain he'll make sure that I do in his own home."

She picked up her wineglass and took a long drink. The pale liquid burned her throat. Of course, he was right.

"I'm sorry," she said, and then she ruined

the apology by laughing. . .

"What's so funny?"

"You're being a gentleman, and I'm . . ."

"What?"

"Disappointed."

Standing, he pulled her up in front of him. "Don't be. I'm nothing if not resourceful. I'll find a way."

"Promise?"

His kiss was long, hard and hungry. "Promise. Now walk me down to my buggy. I need the cold air to cool me down."

For the remainder of the week, Blake did his best to make good on his promise to prove his love for her and find time alone for them. He told her many times that he loved her, and not just with words, but in his actions. After slow, sweet kisses. After hot, hungry kisses that made her feel like her insides were melting.

When at last he had her undivided attention, without interruptions, he told her he loved her as they snuggled under a blanket together on her grandmother's wicker porch swing with a million stars winking against a velvet expanse of sky. And again in front of the fireplace in his parlor, with the only light coming from the fire and the tall tree standing in the bay window and the Christmas lights hung outside.

She'd never felt so close to anyone. So loved. She trusted Blake completely and was even starting to believe that this time it would be different for her. She felt confident that he wasn't just going through the motions, and that he had meant it when he'd vowed he would be there for her no matter what.

With these new feelings of security, she'd come close to telling him she loved him, too. But when she tried, the words just wouldn't come. Tonight, she wouldn't let anything stand in her way. She'd share everything in her heart with him. It was time. Past time.

Tonight he would take her to the Snow Ball, but not if she didn't quit daydreaming. She had to get dressed. She'd been out with her uncle all day doing rounds of the "house to house" variety. Visiting with the patients beyond the examinations had chewed up a huge chunk of time.

When they'd finally headed home, they'd met a herd of cattle blocking the road. Apparently, the fencing holding them in their pasture had been cut. By the time their owner had gotten them out of the road and they'd arrived back at her uncle's. . . .

She checked her watch. She had just

under an hour to shower, change, do make-up and hair —

She jogged into the bathroom, throwing clothing in all directions as she went. After breaking the record for the quickest shower in history, she threw on a terry robe without drying.

*Meow.*

Janice nearly tripped over the kitten as she rushed into her bedroom. "Girl? How do you keep getting in here?"

*Meow.*

Janice scooped her up into her hand. "I don't have time to pet you now. Here. Lie on the bed. I'll take you downstairs for some milk after I'm dressed."

She was toweling her hair dry when she heard a knock at her bedroom door. "Yes?"

"It's me, honey," her uncle said. "May I come in?"

"Sure." She threw the towel aside and began combing her hair.

Her uncle entered the room, smartly dressed in a charcoal suit, a neatly starched white shirt and red bowtie. Janice swiveled to face him.

"Uncle Charles, you look so handsome."

"Thank you, dear. I just wanted to let you know I'm leaving to pick up my date."

"Miss Estelee?"

"Yes. She's prepared a meal for us. Would you like me to come back by afterward to take you to the ball?"

Janice smiled and straightened his bowtie. "Thank you, but no. Blake is picking me up."

"You're going with Ferguson?"

"Yes." Her uncle's lips were set in a hard line. She wondered where that was coming from. "Is something wrong?"

"No. No. I suppose I'm just being old-fashioned. I know that I agreed to your seeing Ferguson, and you have been spending quite a bit of time together. But, well . . . call me selfish." He patted her cheek. "I missed you all those nights you were gone this week. We lost so much time over the years."

Tears misted her eyes and clogged her throat. Her uncle hurriedly took her hand.

"Oh, there, there." He rubbed a hand in a circular motion on her back. "I didn't mean to distress you."

Janice sniffed. He handed her his handkerchief and she took it.

"What's upsetting you so, my dear?"

The fact of the matter was that no one had ever shown any concern over whom she dated. But she said, "I'm sorry. I'm not usually so emotional."

"Well, now." He cleared his throat. Taking the handkerchief from her hands, he dabbed her moist cheeks like he would a child. Another new experience for her. She'd always dried her own tears.

She sniffed. "Thank you . . . for caring about me."

"I'm going to care about you until I draw my last breath. That's a promise, Janice Annette Thornton. A promise I intend to keep. And if you'll allow me the privilege, I'll be a very active participant in your life."

She sniffed again. "I'd like that very much."

"Excellent."

His smile lit his face and eyes, and the hug they shared filled Janice's heart to overflowing with love for him. When he loosened his hold, he tapped her cheek with his index finger. "You've made an old man very happy."

"You make me happy, too, Uncle. More than you could know, but you'd better get going. You shouldn't keep Miss Estelee waiting."

He pulled his pocket watch from his vest. "Oh, my. Yes indeed. I should be on my way." He strode to the door, but turned back to her before he left. "You're sure you wouldn't like for me to stay until Ferguson arrives? I could call Estelee and explain."

"No. He should be here soon. You go on ahead. I'll see you at the ball."

"Yes, well . . . if you're certain."

Janice smiled. "Go."

He nodded and then was gone.

Janice retreated to the bathroom to dry and curl her hair. Then she stepped out of the robe and drenched her body in the wonderful smelling lotion she'd bought from the Naughty Boutique at Heart's Desire. Candi had guaranteed the scent was designed to drive a man wild.

Next, she stepped into the cinnamon-colored teddy that matched the dress Blake had given her earlier in the week. The same dress he'd seen her trying on the day they'd had that horrible argument. The teddy had a deep *V* that accommodated the low neckline of the dress. The satin felt totally decadent against her skin. Almost as decadent as the silk stockings that attached to its garters.

After she'd secured a lacy gold choker with sparkling rhinestones and matching drop earrings, she looked at herself in the mirror. It was like another woman stared back her. A woman in curlers who only had — she glanced at the bedside clock — no time to finish getting ready!

She pulled the hot rollers out of her hair and finger combed the long mass to give the style a sexy, tousled look. In the other room, she stripped the dress from its hanger and wrapped herself into it. Next, she stepped into the matching shoes. One more quick glance in the mirror to make sure everything was in place, then she grabbed the gold beaded clutch bag and rushed downstairs.

Fifteen minutes passed. Janice strode to the kitchen and poured herself a glass of wine.

*Meow.*

The little gray kitten stared up at her with big eyes, complaining loudly that she'd been left up in the bedroom when she'd been promised milk. "Okay, okay."

Janice poured milk in a saucer and set it in the floor for the kitten.

*Meow . . .*

"Give me a break."

Janice grabbed the saucer, nuked it in the microwave, and then put it back in the floor. The kitten happily lapped it up.

Janice carried her wine to the parlor and waited. She was halfway through the glass when the mantle clock chimed the half hour. This was very unlike Blake. He was always so punctual.

She picked up the phone and dialed his cell number. It went straight to his voice mail, and she hung up. Maybe he was still at home. She tried him there. Same as before. After four rings the answering machine picked up. Janice replaced the phone in its receiver. He must be on his way and had forgotten to turn on his cell. Or maybe he hadn't brought it along.

The kitten curled up in a wing chair and fell asleep. The minutes ticked by. The clock chimed the top of the hour. The dance would be beginning now. Still no Blake. No call of explanation either.

She began pacing back and forth on the Oriental rug. How could he do this to her? How could he stand her up after all they'd shared this week? Had he in the end lost patience and decided she wasn't worth the effort? Would he desert her like everyone else in her life had?

Maybe it was her fault. She hadn't given him any assurances. Hadn't told him once she loved him after he'd voiced the sentiment to her. Hadn't further dealt with the issue of whether or not she would relocate.

At the sound of a car outside, she set her wineglass aside and rushed to the front of the house. The sight of headlights in the drive lifted the heaviness in the region of her heart. She opened the door and hurried out onto the front porch to wait for him, unashamed of her relief that he'd finally arrived. She was certain he'd have an adequate explanation. She was just so glad —

The man coming up the walk was not Blake. Cory Ferguson stepped onto the porch. Even in the weak porch light, she could see he looked horrible. His dark hair stood out in all directions as if he'd been raking his hands through it. His shirt was wrinkled and partially untucked. The slacks weren't any better.

"Mr. Ferguson? Is something wrong?"

"Yes. May I come in?"

"Of course." She held the door open for him, and he preceded her inside. When they both stood in the foyer, he turned and took in her dress. Janice felt self-conscious for the first time since putting it on. She'd hoped Blake would be the first to see her in it, and that he would be there as a shield against other men who might look at her and get . . . ideas. She remembered her first meeting with Cory and how he'd come on to her. It didn't give her a good feeling now.

"I'm sorry, Janice. You must be going to the Snow Ball. I didn't think." He shot his hand through his hair. "I haven't been able to think clearly for awhile, now." He swung his troubled gaze back to her and said, "You look beautiful," almost as an afterthought.

"What is it, Mr. Ferguson?"

He paced the width of the foyer.

"I'm sorry. Would you like to sit?"

He stopped moving and stood before her. "No. It's Bebe. I'm worried about her."

"Has she experienced a complication from the D&C?"

"No. It's not that. She's won't leave her room. She's not eating. She doesn't sleep. Won't talk to me."

"It isn't unusual for women to go through a grieving period after losing a child, Mr. Ferguson."

"This isn't normal grieving. She's not coming out of it at all. I'm — I'm afraid for her."

"Did her doctor prescribe any medication?"

"Yes, an antidepressant. But Bebe refuses to take it. I tried to get her to see someone. A counselor. She refused that as well. I even had the pastor come by. She wouldn't talk to him either. I'm at my wits end, Janice. I hate to ask, especially since you have plans, but could you come and speak with her? Mom said she felt comfortable with you. You're a woman and a doctor." He ran a hand through his hair again. "I don't know if she would, but I'd like you to try, if you're willing."

Janice glanced at the clock. Blake was nearly an hour and a half late. He hadn't called. He wasn't coming.

So she turned to the only thing that had given her comfort in all the years of being alone. Her work.

She picked up her wrap and her purse and said, "Let's go."

Blake had just parallel parked at the curb across the street from Doc Prescott's, killed the engine, and shut off the headlights. He couldn't believe his eyes. His brother's Mercedes was parked in the drive. When he looked up at the porch, he saw him coming down the steps with Janice. Before he could react through the shock, Cory had settled Janice into his car, backed out of the drive, and was heading down the road in the direction of his house.

Blake fired the engine, wrenched the wheel hard to make a *U*-turn, and followed. He was an hour and a half late. His truck had broken down in the middle of nowhere. To complicate matters, his cell battery had died. With no way to call for help, no one for miles, all he could do was try and fix the car himself. It had taken forever, but he'd finally rigged the carburetor back together with not much more than a prayer. He hadn't even taken time to shower and change. Hell, he still had grease on his hands.

He'd come straight to Janice to explain, and what did he find for his trouble? His brother ushering the woman Blake loved into his car. Good Lord! How did his brother do it? Did he walk outside, smell trouble in the air, and move in for the kill? Blake had lost every girl he'd ever really cared about to his brother. He'd be damned if he'd allow it to happen with Janice.

He pulled up in front of Cory's house just as they were going inside. Blake didn't take time to think about what he would do or say. He stormed up the sidewalk and into the house.

"What the hell's going on here?"

"Blake!" Janice said, a surprised look on her face.

God, she looked incredible standing there in front of him. Like a model out of a fashion magazine in the dress he'd bought her. The material hugged her curves like a lover's caress. He felt rage wash over him in a white-hot tide because she was standing there with his brother's hand on her arm instead of his.

He advanced on them.

Cory held up a hand to warn him off, as if he could. "It's not what you think, Blake."

He didn't even feel his fist smashing into Cory's face. Blood squirted from his nose, but Blake wasn't satisfied. Before his brother hit the floor, Blake pulled him up and hit him again.

"Blake! Stop!" Janice tugged at his arm.

"Stay out of this," he bit out as he pounded at his brother's head and stomach.

"Oh, my God!" Bebe said from the top of the stairs.

"Blake, stop this now!"

He pulled back his arm to deliver another blow and found himself face to face with Janice. Her wide frightened eyes telegraphed a message to his brain to stop. Cory backed up until he found the wall and slumped to the floor. Blake looked down at his fist. His knuckles were cracked and bleeding, but he felt numb.

Janice backed away from him, disbelief and shock etching her features. She went to Cory. "I'm so sorry."

She began examining his brother as she had Blake that day he'd fallen from the ladder. The memory made him see red in light of the way she was touching him everywhere.

Cory moaned.

"Get up. Come on, I thought you were more man than me," Blake growled.

She turned to him, anger and hurt burning in her eyes. "You've done quite enough. What is wrong with you? Can't you see he's injured? He has a broken nose and broken ribs. His jaw may also be dislocated."

Bebe came to her husband's side, a towel and basin of water in her hands. "Oh, Cory."

He touched his wife's face, tried to speak, but passed out.

Janice checked the pulse at his wrist, then leaned her head close to his face. "His breathing is labored. Bebe, bring me your phone. I need to call my uncle."

Blake watched the scene unfold like a player in a *B* movie; still he couldn't stop himself. He wanted to inflict more of the pain he was feeling. If he couldn't do it with his hands, he'd use words. "Well, well. Isn't this cozy. The wife and the lover both distraught over their man."

"What?" Bebe breathed. She looked from Cory to Janice.

Janice swung her gaze back to him, hurt filling her expressive eyes.

She was a great actress. She transferred that look to Bebe. "Don't listen to him, Bebe. He doesn't know what he's saying. I came here to —"

The words broke off when Bebe stood, backed away, then rushed upstairs.

"Bebe!" Janice called after her. "How could you, Blake?"

Her voice even broke on the words. Nice touch.

"What's going on here, folks?"

Grady Wallace stepped into the foyer and took in the situation with a sweeping glance. He was wearing his dress uniform. He must have come straight over from the Snow Ball. Word traveled fast.

"I'm glad you're here, Sheriff," Janice said. "I need your help. First, this man needs medical attention right away, and I have to get my uncle over here to assist in stabilizing him. Do you have a cell phone? Can you call him?"

"Sure." He handed her the phone. "Why don't you make the call while I have a talk with Blake, here."

He handed Janice the phone, and she made the call while she continued to monitor Cory closely. Grady turned and looked Blake up and down.

"What brings you by, Sheriff?" Blake asked.

The man rotated his hat in his hand as he spoke. "Well, now, funny you should ask. I got dragged away from the social event of the season *and* my date to come out here and investigate a crime. You see, Bebe Ferguson called dispatch. Said you was down here beatin' the hell outta your brother, and that if I didn't get here quick to break it up, you were gonna kill him. Guess somebody beat me to it — the breakin' it up part. From the look in your eyes, I'd say you'd a still been at it if they hadn't."

He looked from Blake to Janice who was still tending to Cory, ignoring the exchange between him and Grady.

"I think you better come down to the station with me," the sheriff was saying.

"That won't be necessary."

"Well, I'll be the one who decides what's necessary, and I think you need to cool down. So, let's go."

Grady gripped his arm. Blake shook him off, his eyes locked on Janice's back. He flexed his hands.

"We can do this the hard way, if you want, Ferguson." He removed the cuffs from his belt. "Makes no difference to me."

Janice's uncle chose that moment to join the circus. Mable trailed in after him.

"What in the world?" He went to Janice's side and looked Cory over. "Was he robbed? Did somebody break in here and do this?"

Janice looked up at her uncle, back to Blake, then at Cory again, but didn't speak.

"What's your assessment, Doctor?"

"Broken nose. Two, maybe three broken ribs. His jaw may be dislocated, and he has a possible punctured lung. He needs immediate transport to the hospital."

Her uncle nodded. "Let's get Carl over here, then." He took the cell phone from her hand and punched in the number. "How long's he been out?"

"About five minutes. I think he passed out from the pain."

"Did you administer anything for that?"

"No. I don't have my bag."

"Where's Bebe?"

"Upstairs. I need to go speak with her. Make sure she's okay."

"She witnessed this?"

Janice nodded.

"That's the last thing she needed after what she's been through. Go then."

Janice stood and walked up the stairs without so much as giving him a glance.

"Ferguson?"

Grady grasped Blake's arm again, shifting his attention from Janice and her uncle. "Yeah. All right. I'll go with you."

He needed to get out of here. He didn't ever want to see his brother again.

323

# CHAPTER 13

"What is the meaning of this, Blake Ferguson?"

Dixie walked into lock-up dressed out in her Snow Ball formal: a floor length red plaid skirt with a fuzzy green sweater and a choker with a poinsettia on it.

"You look great, Sis." He squinted at her. Had she tipped the ends of her dark red hair — green?

"Flattery will get you nowhere, mister. I cannot believe I am standin' in lock-up havin' to bail my brother out of jail. Grady said he picked you up for assault at Cory's, and that Cory had to be taken to the hospital. I said he must have someone who looks like your twin, because my brothers would never beat each other into bloody pulps. Tell me Grady is yankin' my chain because he didn't want to show the town what an excellent dancer he is and ruin his tough cop image."

Grady came in behind Dixie with the keys and unlocked Blake's cell. He stood and faced the sheriff.

"Blake, I'll have to bring you back down here and book you if your brother decides to press charges."

Dixie's mouth gaped open. "I am dreamin'. This is all a bad dream."

Blake watched as Grady reached down and squeezed his sister's hand. "I'm sorry about this, Dixie. I was really lookin' forward to tonight."

"Wait a second," Blake said. "Are you saying you took my sister to the dance?"

"Well, I wouldn't call it that since he got called away to deal with an emergency, that apparently was you, almost before it began."

"Why didn't I know about this?"

"I don't need your permission — or anyone else's, for that matter — to go out on a date, Blake Ferguson. However, that didn't stop Grady from asking for permission from Daddy." Dixie shook her head. "Now," she looked up at Grady, "tell me why you had to haul him down here. I trust you to give me the straight of it."

Blake really didn't want to rehash this.

"Bebe called dispatch and said Blake was at the house beatin' the — *um* — beatin' up Cory. Bebe sounded so scared, Clara called and asked me to handle it personally."

Dixie swung her accusatory gaze to him. "Now why, pray tell, would you go over to Cory's and beat him to the point that he has to be taken to the hospital?"

"Do we have —"

Dixie held up a finger to delay his words as an electronic version of *Jingle Bells* echoed through the corridor. Dixie dug into her sequined Santa purse and pulled out her cell phone. "Hello? Oh, Mother. Hi."

She pierced him with a lethal look. Blake moaned when he heard who was on the line. Her calm tone belied her anger.

"Yes, I heard. How is he? *Uh-huh . . .* oh, that's good. Yes, I'll take care of it." She looked back at Blake. "He said what to Bebe?" She crossed her arms and turned away then, clearly furious. "If I see him before you do, I'll tell him. Right. Bye."

She ended the call and returned the phone to her purse. "Your brother is being released from the hospital. I need to get over to his house and clean up any remnants of blood so Cory's distraught wife — who just suffered a miscarriage — won't freak out when she returns home and is reminded of what happened."

"If you expect me to feel guilty —"

"I expect many things, the first of which

is an apology for making your sister come to a jail to pick you up when she should be dancing the night away, showing off her fabulous new ensemble." She swept her hand down her side, indicating her dress.

"You look great, Dix," Grady said.

"I'm sorry, Dixie," Blake said, and he was. He hated dragging her into this mess.

"Next, you can apologize to me, Mother and Daddy, Cory and Bebe — and not necessarily in that order — for forgetting that fighting is not how Fergusons resolve their problems. And when they're finished with you, Doc Prescott wants a word."

Blake looked away. "If you'd like to lay blame somewhere, talk to Cory."

"Well, I'd love to, but it would seem that his broken jaw had to be wired shut. So, you'll be doing the talking, and you *will* be forthcoming with a properly contrite apology."

"I can't do that."

"You can and you will, but I refuse to argue the point in the middle of a jail cell." Her voice had gotten incrementally louder as she finished the sentence. She took a breath and a moment to regain her composure. "Do I have to sign anything to take him out of here, Grady?"

"No. You're free to go. Will you be okay

with him? I'd be happy to take him home in the department's Jeep."

"I've been standin' up to my brothers since I was a baby, Grady. He knows better than to start somethin' with me." To Blake she said, "Let's go. We both have a mess to clean up."

She started in on him as soon as he folded himself into her cherry-red Volkswagen Beetle. The same one she'd saved up for from waitin' tables at the diner in high school. "What is your problem? Have you completely taken leave of your senses? How could you storm into that house and accuse Cory of infidelity? Has that family not been through enough? They just lost a baby. Bebe has been in terrible shape since she came home from the hospital — something you'd know if you'd come by to check on her."

"I sent flowers."

Ignoring that, she continued. "Well, I've been taking food over. She doesn't eat. She doesn't sleep —"

Blake interrupted the flow of words. "I know what I saw."

"Oh, this should be good. What was that? And while I'm askin', why are you dressed like that with filthy, bloody hands. Weren't you takin' Janice to the dance?"

"I broke down out in Coon Hollow."

"Coon-Godforsaken-in-the-Middle-of-Nowhere-Hollow? What in the world were you doin' up there?"

"Looking over a piece of property where a client wants to build. By the time I got the truck running again, I was late pickin' up Janice."

"Did you call her?"

"My cell phone died."

"Oh, this just keeps gettin' better. Do continue."

"I got to her house just in time to see her leaving with Cory. They drove straight to his house."

"And?"

"And you know the rest."

"Oh, no. You went off just like that? Did it occur to you that Bebe might have been sick? That he got Janice and took her to his house because Bebe needed a doctor?"

Oh God. His breath clogged in his chest. That thought hadn't entered his mind. Nausea churned his gut. That's what happened when the anger took over. How could he have let that happen?

"Are you tellin' me that you went off on Cory, half-cocked, because of something that happened between you two when you were teenagers? What was her name? Ellen?"

"Ellen. Tracy. Dawn. Tammy."

Dixie mumbled. "Men. Never grow up. Stupid, adolescent —"

"He stole Tammy from me when I was twenty-six."

"Good point. Any woman who can be *stolen,* as you so eloquently put it, is not worth having in the first place, but I digress. Back to your misspent youth.

"When Mother and Daddy sent you off with that preacher to build houses in Louisiana, you know, after you got expelled for punching that teacher in the face? I thought we'd never see you again. You were angry at everything and everybody. I didn't know you any other way." Her knuckles turned white against the wheel. "But when you came home, you were the Blake that I've come to know and love. In fact, I can't remember you losin' your temper since then — until now."

Blake raked a hand through his hair. "I really don't want to talk about any of this with you."

"Well, you're sittin' in my car and I'm driving you away from the jail. That gives me the right to say anything I want, and since you have nowhere else to go, you will listen.

"I don't have to tell you that you have a wicked temper. You have to keep control of it, Blake."

Blake chanced a look at his sister when she fell silent. To his utter amazement, he saw tears welling up in her eyes. He couldn't ever remember seeing his sister cry.

"I don't want to lose you, Blake. I can't stand the thought of things going back to way they were before Mother and Daddy sent you away."

She was right. He knew it. She knew it. He felt awful for hurting his strong, seemingly unflappable sister. He closed his eyes and dropped his chin to his chest. What was wrong with him? He'd completely lost control, and he made sure he never lost control. He had to.

Dixie sniffed. "You know what? You don't deserve a woman like Janice. For some reason, unknown to woman, she fell for you, and this is how you treat her?" Shaking her head, she pulled into Cory's driveway and killed the engine.

"What are we doing here?" he asked.

"I told you, we have to clean up the foyer."

Blake opened his door. "I'm going home."

He got out of the car and walked over to his truck. "You can run, but you can't hide, Blake Ferguson," his sister called after him.

Ignoring that, he put the key in the ignition and turned it. Nothing happened. It didn't even crank. Great. He'd have to walk. He turned the collar up on his coat and made his way down the sidewalk.

Dixie was right. He couldn't hide from the doubts she'd planted where Janice's motives in this were concerned. He felt terrible for not trusting her. But his brother, that was another matter. He didn't trust Cory further than he could throw him.

Still, if Bebe had been in a bad way since the miscarriage, he supposed it was possible that Cory had come for Janice because his wife had needed a doctor. Not likely given the fact he'd never played the attentive husband before. But possible.

Could he have made a mistake? Could old hurts and jealousy have stolen what little good sense he had and the most incredible thing that had ever happened to him?

"Who's there? That you, Blake Ferguson?"

Blake peered into the darkness toward Miss Estelee's house. What was she doing out on her porch on a cold night like this? "Yes, ma'am. It's me."

"Well, come closer. Don't make an old lady holler."

Blake sighed. "Yes, ma'am." There was no denying a request from Miss Estelee. He walked up her sidewalk to stand before the porch.

"Come on up," she said.

He walked up the steps. "Why are you sittin' out in the cold, Miss Estelee?"

She rocked a steady rhythm in her rocking chair. "Good for the circulation. So, you got yourself in some trouble tonight."

"Word travels fast."

"Doc told me."

He should have known. They'd probably been at the Snow Ball when Doc got the call to come to Cory's.

"Well, what do you have to say for yourself?"

Blake was taken aback. "Meanin' no disrespect, Miss Estelee, but I'm not sure we should be discussing this."

"That's where you're wrong, Blake Ferguson." She rocked forward and shook a short, crooked finger at him. "And twice you've been wrong in an evenin'." Her chair squeaked when she rocked back and said, "I've took a likin' to that young lady doc. She's from good people. You got no right to be sullyin' her name."

Blake rested his hands on his hips. The last thing he needed right now was a dressing down from Miss Estelee.

"She didn't do them things you said."

Hell, he knew that now, but . . . . "How do you know?"

"I know."

*Here we go,* he thought. *She's about to launch into a discourse on the latest antics of the Ridge's supposed resident angels.*

"Pride comes before a fall. That's what the Good Book says. I reckon you fell good and hard. *Mmm-hmm.*"

He took a step back. "If that's all, Miss Estelee, I should be gettin' home."

"Oh, that ain't all. Trust is a precious thing. Once it's broken, it takes a heap of fixin' to get it back. That is, if a body cares to get it back."

Blake puzzled over her words, trying to decipher their meaning. "Are you talking about my trust being restored?"

"Yours was never broke."

She said the words that only confirmed what he already knew. Dread filled his heart at hearing it out loud. "I have to go."

He walked down Miss Estelee's sidewalk out onto the one that ran parallel to Ridge Road. He looked to the left. Another two blocks and he'd be home. He could shut himself away there and nurse his wounded ego. Maybe not show his face in town for a few weeks until everything blew over. He looked right, back toward the lights of town, his brother's house, and Janice.

334

His sigh was heavy. He turned right and retraced his steps to his brother's.

# CHAPTER 14

Janice was gone. She'd apparently left town immediately following the fiasco the night of the Snow Ball. When she hadn't returned by Christmas Eve, Blake took himself to Doc Prescott's and faced the music.

"I don't know where she is and if I did, I wouldn't tell you."

"Sir, I know what I did was unforgivable, but I want — I mean, I *have* to try to make it right."

"I'm sorry, but you lost that right when you broke my grandniece's heart."

Blake sat in the chair situated in front of Doc Prescott's desk. He leaned forward, his elbows on his knees, so that he could look into the older man's eyes. "Doc, I love Janice."

"Is that so? Do you treat all the women you love with mistrust? I shouldn't have to tell you trust is not something that comes easily to Janice. If you'd taken the time to get to know her as you should, you'd know that."

The doctor wasn't saying anything Blake hadn't repeatedly beaten himself up over in the past week. "Can you at least tell me when she left?"

"When I returned from taking your brother to the hospital, she'd packed her bags and was gone. Although why I'm telling you even that much is a mystery, because it was your actions that took her away from me. I think you should leave, and take that cat with you. She complains incessantly. Nothing I do consoles her. She found a home with Janice and is lost without her." He ended with a sneeze.

Blake looked around the office and found Angel lounging on a stack of files. As if aware of the attention, she meowed. He knew how she felt. He was lost without Janice, too.

Walking over to where she sat, he scooped her up into his hand. At the door, he turned back to Doc Prescott. "I have no right to ask anything of you, but if she calls, will you tell her I desperately need to speak with her?"

"She won't call."

"What makes you say that?"

"She sent me a postcard from the airport

saying she was taking a trip and that I shouldn't worry. She also said she wouldn't contact me until she returned."

"Where did she go?"

"As I said, I don't know."

Think, Blake. Think. In the time they spent together, had she mentioned a trip she'd planned? Where did she say she was going before she'd decided to spend the holidays in Angel Ridge?

"Was there something else?" Doc Prescott prompted.

"Skiing." Blake re-entered the office and began pacing. "She said she'd planned to go skiing before she decided to spend her vacation here."

"Yes, well, that certainly narrows the field."

"Oh! I didn't know you had company."

Both men turned to see Miss Estelee standing in the doorway. The doctor rose. "Come in, my dear." He jerked a thumb in Blake's direction. "*He* was just leaving. What brings you by?"

"I thought I'd be here for the call."

"Call?" both men said at once.

"Your grandniece is about to call."

Blake looked from Miss Estelee to Doc Prescott, staying with the latter. "You knew she was going to call all along," he accused.

"I knew no such thing."

The phone rang. The two men just stared at it. No one moved to answer it.

After three rings, Miss Estelee said, "Well, shouldn't someone get that? She might not call back."

Doc Prescott held up a hand to warn Blake off and beat him to the phone. "Hello? Oh, my dear, I'm so glad you called. *Um* — just a moment, Janice. I need to clear some riff-raff out of my office."

Glaring at Blake, he pointed at the door. Miss Estelee stood and took his arm. "Drive me home, would you Blake? My old bones are a achin' somthin' fierce today."

Miss Estelee ushered a resisting Blake out the door, and Uncle Charles continued the conversation.

"I'm so sorry about that."

"Is something wrong, Uncle?"

"No, dear. Everything is fine now that you've called."

She hesitated, as if weighing her words. "I won't keep you. I just wanted to wish you Merry Christmas."

"Christmas is tomorrow, dear."

"I know, but I thought you might spend the day with Miss Estelee, and I don't know her number."

"Well, I had planned to spend the day with

my grandniece."

She sniffed. "I'm sorry, but I had to leave. I just couldn't stay any longer."

"Dear, I know everything. I know you're hurt, and I wish you'd come home so I can help you through this."

Surprise laced her words. "You know?"

He sat heavily. His chair creaked with the effort. "Yes."

There was a long pause of silence on the other end of the line before she said, "Do you believe what Blake said about me and his brother?"

"Of course not! How could you think I would?"

"I don't know. I guess I'm not sure of anything anymore." Her sadness weighted the words into silence.

He leaned forward and braced his arms on his desk. "Well, I'm sure of one thing. Running away solves nothing."

"What else could I do?"

"Stay here with me, as you promised."

She sighed, sounding like all the spirit had been drained right out of her. That wouldn't do.

He cleared his throat. "I have something to say to you, Janice, and I'm afraid it won't be easy for you to hear."

He paused. When she kept silent, he

continued. "I know your parents did not set a good example, but I expected more from you. Running away from family at the first sign of difficulty is something your parents would do. I had convinced myself you were nothing like them, but you've proven me wrong."

"That's unfair, Uncle."

"Is it?" From the tone of her voice, he guessed that had gotten her hackles up. Good. "You promised you'd go to Christmas Eve services with me tonight."

"You have Miss Estelee."

"She insists on going to services alone on Christmas Eve. Always has. I had hoped this year would be different with you here, but once again, I will be there by myself wishing I had family with me."

"Oh, Uncle Charles," she pleaded, "I can't face the people in Angel Ridge knowing what they must think of me."

"Poppycock! You mean you can't face Blake. He hurt you, Janice. Look him in the eye and tell him as much, then get on with your life."

"It isn't that simple."

"Of course it is. If you go to the airport now, you can make it to midnight services. Turkey's in the oven for brunch afterward."

"Uncle —"

"Come home for Christmas, Janice. This is where you belong. Come home."

After hanging up the phone, he whispered a prayer to the wind. He'd have to leave the rest up to Miss Estelee's angels.

"Are you plannin' to sit around this monstrosity of a house and sulk indefinitely? I don't know who looks more miserable. You or that poor kitten."

Blake gave his sister a look. She'd been over every day for the past week, bringing food, checking up on him. She was like a mother hen. He wished she'd just go away and leave him alone, but he didn't say it. He was in deep enough with his family without digging in deeper.

"They're saying we might have a white Christmas."

Blake still didn't speak. He stared into the empty hearth while absently stroking Angel's fur. Unfortunately, Dixie didn't need a partner to carry on a conversation.

"You are coming to Mother's and Daddy's before midnight church services tonight, aren't you? Everyone's expecting you."

"No one would care if I didn't show."

"Mother would care, and I will care if you disappoint her."

"I'll make an appearance," he conceded, "but don't expect me to stay the whole time."

"What's the big deal? You and Cory made up, right?"

Blake shrugged. "I didn't deserve his forgiveness."

"Yeah, well, I could almost agree with you, but after all he put you through in the years previous, he had it coming."

Blake shook his head, still not believing that all those years Cory had acted the way he had because he was jealous of him. Jealous because he was tall and Cory was short, Blake could build things and he couldn't. He'd always felt inadequate presenting their parents with homemade gifts. By the same token, Cory had hated that the things he gave them were store-bought and soon forgotten.

"You went a little overboard with all the damage you inflicted," Dixie continued, "but what's done is done. Still, you did the right thing, apologizing. But I digress. Before you come over, be sure to shave that scruff off your face and put on fresh clothes." She leaned forward, sniffed, and made a face. "Smells like you haven't been out of those in a few days."

"Anything else?"

"Yes. It's cold in here. Why don't you light a fire?"

He hadn't lit a fire since Janice left. It brought back too many memories of the nights they'd shared in front of the fireplace.

"Fine. I'll do it."

Blake grabbed Dixie's arm before she could get up from the couch.

"If I wanted a fire, I'd light one," he said in even, measured tones.

"Sheez. You are like a bear with a thorn in his paw. Reminds of when Cole Craig messed things up with Josie Allen. Fortunately, I am not easily dissuaded from my purpose, and my purpose is to make sure that you don't throw your chance for happily ever after in the garbage."

"There's no such thing as happily ever after. My long list of failed relationships is proof."

"Okay. That's it." Dixie stood so she could tower over him, then lean down to poke his shoulder as she made each point. "You will quit wallowing in self-pity this instant. I'm here to see that you go to her, tell her you're sixty kinds of an idiot, and beg her forgiveness."

Blake moved out of the line of fire. Cuddling the frightened kitten against his chest, he rubbed his injured shoulder. "In case you haven't noticed, she's gone. She won't be coming back."

"Get real. She has to come back. She may not come back to Angel Ridge, but she most certainly will return to her medical practice in the city. Instead of sitting around here feeling sorry yourself, you'd be better served coming up with a plan for sweeping her off her feet when she gets back."

"How am I supposed to know when that'll be?"

Dixie raised her eyes heavenward. "Men. How would you survive without the help of females? Call her office and make an appointment."

"I don't need to see a doctor, Dix."

She threw up her hands. "Oh, dear Lord." She leaned in close, made eye contact, and spoke slowly. "You won't be going to the appointment. You'll simply *make* the appointment in order to ascertain *when* she will be back in town."

He nodded slowly. "Okay. Say she does come back. How am I supposed to get her to talk to me?"

"That's your problem." Dixie grabbed her purse and headed for the door.

Blake followed. "Dix!"

"Gotta fly. I'm catering the Allen-Craig wedding tonight. Things to do, *et cetera, et*

345

*cetera.* Be at Mother's around nine. Or better yet, be at First Baptist around eight-thirty to help me carry out boxes."

And with that she was gone.

He'd forgotten about Josie and Cole's wedding. He and Cole were old friends as well as colleagues. He should be there, but the thought of watching Josie and Cole begin their lives together made him even more miserable.

He returned to his spot on the sofa, again facing the cold hearth. Angel curled up in his lap.

*Meow.*

She stared up at him. Dixie was right. She looked miserable, too.

"I know you miss her." Blake stroked the fur beneath the kitten's chin. She settled down and fell asleep. "I miss her, too," he whispered.

Christmas Eve. He pulled the jewelry box out of his shirt pocket and opened it to reveal a diamond engagement ring. The one he'd planned to give Janice tonight.

He leaned his head back against the couch. He'd made such a mess of things. His deep-seated jealousy had superseded his better judgment and cost him the only woman he'd ever loved.

He looked up at the Christmas tree, the

one he'd brought down from the tall pines the day before he'd met Janice. He remembered again what people said about the trees from up there. That they were magical, and if you topped them with an angel, any wish you made on the trees would come true. He'd told Janice about the legend when they'd placed her tree in her room. He'd heard it all his life, but had never given it much credence.

It would take a miracle to win Janice back. Dixie was right; he had to take action. He set Angel aside and walked over to stand before the tree, closed his eyes, and for the first time in his life, made a wish.

"Please," he whispered, "bring her home to me."

A sharp wind rattled the windows and shook the tree so that the ornaments and bells on it jangled. Blake opened his eyes. He smiled. Miss Estelee would say it was *them angels a workin' their magic.* The agitated cat was weaving around his feet. She gazed up at him with an expectant look in her eyes. Could tonight be the night he'd finally claim his very own Christmas miracle? For some reason, suddenly, anything seemed possible.

He wasn't wasting any more time sitting in his house alone, waiting for it to come to him. He took the stairs two at a time, Janice's engagement ring clutched in his hand.

Janice drove by the church at twenty minutes to midnight. There were no spaces in the parking lot, so she continued down Main Street looking for a vacant space. After she'd parked the car, she watched families file by as they walked together to church.

Janice continued to watch people pass, but she didn't get out of her car. All she could think was that she'd never had a family to attend Christmas Eve services with at midnight, but now she did. Her uncle would be waiting inside the church, probably saving her a seat. Still she couldn't get out of the car. Worry, fear and hurt kept her stationary.

What would people think when they saw her come in? What would they whisper behind their hands as she walked by? Would Blake be there with his family? Could she endure seeing him again, or would the hurt come along with the tears, forcing her to leave and embarrass herself further in front of the town she'd grown to love?

Janice gripped the wheel and rested her forehead against her hands. She didn't want to disappoint her uncle, but she didn't think she could go through with this. She wasn't ready to face Blake and the town again. The hurt was too fresh. Just the thought of their last encounter brought tears stinging her eyes. As much as she'd cried in the past week, she would have thought there'd be a point when they would simply dry up. Sniffing, she pulled a couple of tissues from her purse.

She jumped when she heard a tapping at her window. An elderly lady in a red velvet dress, with matching coat and hat, stood outside the car. After she'd rolled down the window, the lady bent and peered in at her. Janice recognized the woman now. It was Miss Estelee.

"Well, bless me. I knew you'd come." She tapped her cane on the cobbled street and cackled. "Yes, indeedy. Them angels is a dancin' around this town tonight, havin' a high old time."

"Merry Christmas, Miss Estelee."

"Yes, yes. Don't just sit there. Step out and let me have a look at you."

"Oh, I wouldn't want to make you late for the services."

"Here, now. Don't you know it's impolite to argue with an old lady?"

Janice reluctantly did as Miss Estelee requested.

"Oh, look at you." Miss Estelee made a clicking sound with her tongue. "Your pretty eyes are all red." She gently tapped Janice's cheek with bent fingers encased in white gloves. "Poor dear, don't you know it's Christmas Eve?"

Janice frowned, unable to follow what Miss Estelee was saying. She pressed a tissue to her nose. Of course she knew it was Christmas Eve. It was why she'd just spent eight hours on planes and in airports trying to get back to her uncle.

"Miracles happen in Angel Ridge on Christmas Eve. Why, here comes one now."

Miss Estelee nodded at a group of people approaching. Janice turned to see Patrick and Susan Houston walking down the sidewalk with Abby and little Sammy in tow.

"Doc Prescott, Doc Prescott!"

Sammy, who insisted on calling her by her uncle's name, came running up and flung his arms around her legs.

"Well, my goodness," Janice said as she smoothed his unruly red curls.

"Looky, looky. My Mommy is feelin' better."

"I see that. I'm so glad."

"I come to the Doc's to bring you a card I made, but he told me you wasn't there."

He looked up at her with huge, serious eyes.

She stooped and grasped his hands. "You made me a card?"

He nodded. "To thank you for makin' me and my Mommy feel better."

There were the tears again. She swallowed hard. "I'm sorry I didn't get to see it."

"That's okay. I left it with the other doc. He told me he'd make sure you got it."

Susan and Patrick both said, "Merry Christmas, Doc," then told their son, "Let's go, Sammy. We don't want to be late."

Sammy hugged Janice again, and then ran to catch up with his family. Tears misted Janice's eyes again. The wish she'd made on the Christmas tree she and Blake had gotten from the tall pines and placed in her room had come true. She'd wished Susan would be able to celebrate another Christmas with her family.

"It's not too late for you to claim a Christmas Eve miracle for your own, but if you want the true love miracle, you'd better hurry. It's nearly midnight."

"Oh, Miss Estelee. True love's not for me."

"Time will tell." She tapped the watch she wore on a chain around her neck and then stepped back up on the sidewalk as she continued on her way to the church.

Janice stood alone in the street, now, with

a clear view of the angel monument in Town Square. A tall, dark-haired man stood there looking back at her . . . Blake.

Janice sucked in a ragged breath. He looked devastatingly handsome bathed in the weak light of the old-fashioned street lamps. Dressed in dark pants, a dark turtleneck sweater, and his black leather blazer, the only color came from a red scarf hanging down the front of the jacket. A soft breeze blew that lock of hair across his forehead. He didn't bother to push it back into place.

Their gazes locked and something told her to go to him. Her feet began to move as if they had a mind of their own. The closer she got, the stronger her determination became. Her uncle was right. He had hurt her. She should tell him as much and get on with her life. She couldn't continue in this horrible melancholy that had pressed in on her the past week. She had a life to return to. People who depended on her. A medical practice that needed her focus.

When she stood only a few feet away from him, her resolve nearly crumbled. He reached out and touched her cheek, but quickly pulled his hand back. "I'm sorry. I wasn't sure if you were real. I can't believe you're here."

"Neither can I," she confessed.

On closer inspection, she noticed that dark smudges stained the skin below his eyes. The angles of his handsome face seemed more defined. Starker. "What brought you back?"

She read the look in his eyes, and it said he was almost afraid of her answer. Still, he waited for her response.

"My uncle. I promised I'd come to Christmas Eve services with him. He reminded me of that today."

"You promised me Christmas, too."

"You said you loved me, but at the first test of that love, you betrayed my trust."

He squeezed his eyes shut and glanced up at the angel monument. "I know."

The whispered words sounded like they'd been torn from him.

"How could you have accused me of such a horrible thing? What did I ever do to make you mistrust me so?"

"Nothing." He glanced back at her. The hopelessness in his eyes spoke to her soul. "I let old hurts make me doubt I could have a love of my own."

"What are you talking about?"

He shoved his hands in his pockets and brushed his foot across the dead grass. "Cory spoiled most of my past relationships.

He made it his mission to steal away every woman I ever cared for. Not because he wanted them, but because he could."

"I see. So, you're saying you thought I was the type of person whose head could be turned by an attractive, married man."

"No, I didn't believe that of you, but I didn't trust Cory."

She continued as if he hadn't spoken. "Not to mention you thought me the kind of woman who could be, how did you put it? Stolen away?"

"I know it's no excuse, but at the time, I let anger get hold of me. Thinking straight wasn't on my list of priorities."

"You should have trusted me."

"I know. I've gone over it a hundred times in my head, and every time, I feel like such a fool. You were the best thing that ever happened to me, and I let my insecurities where Cory was concerned ruin everything."

He took her hand in his. Squeezed it. When she looked up into his eyes and saw the raw pain there, naked and exposed, she knew she was lost.

"I'm so sorry, Janice. I don't expect you to forgive me, but still, I'm praying you will. I love you." He put his hand over his heart. "I love you so much it hurts. I swear, if you give me a second chance, I'll spend the rest of my life proving it to you."

She wanted to believe him, but the agony she'd lived in the past few days held her forgiveness in its grasp. "Blake, I'm a doctor. That isn't going to change. I interact with a lot of people. Male and female. I can be out until all hours of the night, and there will be times when you won't know where I am, who I'm with, or what I'm doing. Trust is crucial."

"I know what you do is important. I'm willing to do whatever it takes to make this work. I'm not saying things will always be perfect. I'm human enough to want you all to myself every now and then, but I understand that won't always be possible. I may not like you having to go out in the middle of the night —"

"But I'll still go," she interjected.

"I know."

Strain pulled at the hard angles of his handsome face. He loved her. He really loved her. In a thousand lifetimes, she'd never find another man like Blake.

She chewed on her lower lip. "You know, you could come with me some of the time." She saw the hope flair in his eyes. "You did make a pretty good assistant."

He managed a weak smile. "Who knows, with practice, I could be first-rate."

Janice stepped forward and framed his face with her hands. She smoothed away the tension around his eyes and mouth with her thumbs, then pressed her lips to his. Blake's arms came around her so tightly she struggled to breathe.

After a moment, Blake asked, "Can you forgive me for actin' like a fool?"

"If you can forgive me for making you work so hard to prove yourself to me."

Blake just laughed. As they kissed again, the church bells chimed midnight. When the sound of the last bell echoed and settled into the stillness of the quiet town, they broke the kiss. Snowflakes fell from the sky, enveloping them in the soft hush of the first snow, blanketing the moment in magic.

"You're my Christmas wish come true, Janice Thornton."

"You're my one and only love, Blake Ferguson."

His smile at her profession warmed the heart she thought had shriveled and died a week ago. She wondered how it was possible to feel so much without shattering into a million glittering pieces.

"I have something for you."

He took a step back and dropped to one knee in the snow. Janice pressed her fingertips to her lips, but was helpless to keep the tears at bay when he pulled a small, velvet box from his coat pocket. He opened it, and a perfect emerald cut diamond sparkled from a beautiful, simple platinum setting.

"Janice Thornton, will you make me the happiest man in Angel Ridge by becoming my wife?"

"Yes," she whispered through the tears. "Oh, yes."

He removed the ring from the box and slipped it on her finger. It was a perfect fit. He took her hand in both of his and kissed the ring.

Janice tugged at his hands until he stood before her again. She laced her fingers behind his neck, smiling her happiness up at him.

"How soon will you marry me?" he asked.

"I'd marry you now if it were possible, but I guess New Year's Eve will have to do."

He kissed her again. "I can't think of a better way to start the year."

After another breathtaking kiss, he asked, "Where will we live?"

Janice smiled. She'd dreamed all her life of having a home like the one her grandparents had lived and loved in, but looking up into Blake's eyes and seeing the love shining back at her, she said the only thing she could. "Now and forever, my home will be wherever you are."

As they kissed, the angel sitting atop the tree in Town Square lit up much like the glow of love shining in their hearts. Janice didn't even question it. Like Miss Estelee had said, Christmas in Angel Ridge is a time of miracles.

I'm sorry. Pardon me while I blow. I cry every time I hear that story. It took those two so long to find love that when they finally did, I think the angels on high sang *The Hallelujah Chorus*.

Breathe in.

Breathe out.

Okay. I think I can continue now.

Janice and my brother, Blake, married early in the morning on New Year's Eve. It was a beautiful outdoor wedding up in the tall pines with Christmas snow still on the ground. The bride wore a stunning white cashmere pantsuit and a white, full-length fur that belonged to her grandmother. The Doc gave it to her for Christmas. Blake stood tall and handsome beside her with Cory at his side as best man and me standin' up for Janice as maid of honor. Doc Prescott gave the bride away. They drove away in a sleigh led by two of the finest white horses you ever saw. Yep, drove straight to the diner for the wedding reception to end all wedding receptions, with me doin' all the cooking, of course.

I got everything I wanted for Christmas this year. My best friend, Susan? Her cancer is in remission. The doctors won't say she's cured, but I say miracles happen every day, and no one's arguing with me. And then there's Blake. He found the woman of his dreams, and after an extended honeymoon to the Caribbean, the couple is living in the old Prescott place that Blake so lovingly restored.

The bride is Angel Ridge's new town doctor, but Doc Prescott still comes in two days a week to give her more time for her family. And, of course, he'll be back in the saddle while she's out on maternity leave.

That's right. Sometime next fall, the population of Angel Ridge will increase by two new Fergusons. Janice and Bebe are both expecting about the same time.

We'd all do well to remember this wise saying. *A fool loves where he lives, but a wise man simply loves.* That's the gospel according to Dixie.

I hope you enjoyed the holidays in Angel Ridge. I know we sure enjoyed havin' you. Come back any time now, hear?

# My Christmas Angel
## A STORY OF ANGEL RIDGE

### Angel Ridge, Tennessee
### Christmas Eve, 1883

I smoothed my hands over the soft, red velvet dress Grandma had made me, admiring my reflection in the dresser mirror. It fit perfectly and had transformed a school girl into a poised young woman.

"Mary! Let's go. We're late!"

"Coming, Mama." I took a deep breath, trying desperately to slow my pounding heart.

Moments later, wrapped in our warmest coats, we all climbed into the wagon and settled in for the short ride to the church. My mind raced with possibilities as snow flakes swirled about my head. Would he be there? Seated with his parents in the back pew just like he had been every year since I could remember? *Please God,* I prayed, *I have to find a way to meet him this year.*

Christmas Eve was the only time he and

his family ever came to church. I didn't know who they were and didn't dare ask. He was too special to even speak of. I secretly called him my Christmas angel. Sometimes I wondered if I hadn't conjured him up every year, right out of my imagination . . . my hopes . . . my dreams.

Because we always sat in the third pew from the front, one good look at him was all I ever got. Last year, while the preacher was going on with one of his typical long prayers, I turned around to steal a look at my angel. All I caught was Mama's sharp elbow in my ribs. I swear, that woman has eyes clear around her head. Even on her eyelids!

When our wagon at last rolled to a halt in front of the church, winking candles in the windows invited us to come worship. But I had other things on my mind. My hands began to shake when my brother helped me down, and I nearly fainted as a cold breeze stole my breath. Somehow, I made it all the way to the front porch. Papa held the door as Mama walked inside, but my feet seemed frozen in place when I heard the organ music filter out into the crisp, winter night air.

"Mary?"

"I . . . I . . ."

"Close the door," Mama said sternly. "You're letting all the warm air out."

I had to do something quick. I didn't want this Christmas Eve to be like all the rest. "I . . . left my Bible . . . in the wagon."

"I'll get it, honey." Papa patted my gloved hand. "You come on inside where it's warm."

"No! I mean, I'll get it." I dashed off before Papa had a chance to argue. Of course, my Bible wasn't in the wagon. I had to go in by myself, or I'd be doomed to only another brief glimpse of my angel as Mama ushered me to her pew.

Had he ever paid me any mind as I made my way up the aisle with my parents each year? Probably not. I must have seemed like a child to his older eyes. But tonight would be different. I was a woman now, almost eighteen, and nearly finished with school. He'd notice me in my new red velvet dress that Grandma said brought out the color of my hair and eyes like never before.

Leaving my coat in the wagon, I hurried back to the church. I hid from Mama's searching eyes just outside the sanctuary doors. The choir softly hummed *Silent Night* as Miss Ruth made her way to the front of the stage for her solo. Miss Ruth had the best voice of anybody, and I knew when she

363

started singing, no one would see me slip in. I'd have scant time to put my plan in motion, which was good. That way, I wouldn't have time to change my mind.

I slid into the little space at the end of the pew, right beside my Christmas angel. He seemed surprised, then scooted over to make room. I shivered, not from cold, mind you, but from at last catching his attention.

The heavenly chorus surely was smiling on Miss Ruth, for her voice reached every corner of the candle-lit room, filling it with that special glow only a Christmas carol can bring. Or maybe it was my angel, so close that I could feel his warmth, smell his clean scent. I chanced another look at him then, and stopped breathing. He had the unearthly beauty of an archangel who'd just left the presence of the Almighty. His long golden hair hung in silken waves to his shoulders. And when his clear blue eyes met mine, the tender look he gave me went straight to my heart.

For an endless moment we stared at each other, then he smiled hesitantly and shifted his gaze back to the cap crushed between his hands. I trained my eyes on Miss Ruth and took a shaky breath. Two things registered: he'd smiled at me; and he was alone. In fact, there wasn't a single person nearby.

The church was always filled to capacity on Christmas Eve. But tonight, it was as if God had dropped two empty pews between the Joneses' six squirming kids and the last row where we sat.

As Miss Ruth began another verse, he leaned toward me and whispered, "Why aren't you sitting with your parents?"

Unable to come up with a proper answer, I asked a question of my own. "Why aren't you?"

His focus returned to the cap, which he had wrung into a mangled line. "They died . . . back in the summer."

"I'm sorry." Without thought, I reached out and covered his hand with mine.

His cap fell to the floor as he enfolded my fingers in a warm, tight grip. "Will you come out with me, Mary?" he asked softly as Miss Ruth launched into the third verse.

"Now?" Lordy, Mama surely would see the two of us sneaking out the back like a couple of thieves. I looked up to where she sat with Papa, my brothers and my sister. They seemed to be in some kind of trance. As did everyone else, I realized suddenly as I looked around. Even the Jones children had ceased their fidgeting. Except for Miss Ruth, the entire congregation remained perfectly still.

He stood, and I did as well. We moved soundlessly through the doors into the still night. Strange, I thought, it wasn't nearly as cold now as it had been earlier. I didn't even feel the need to fetch my coat from the wagon.

He took my hand and placed it in the bend of his arm as we walked toward the deserted town square. Though a layer of snow crunched beneath our feet, the flakes had stopped falling. I looked up to a sky filled with more stars than I had ever seen in my life, and thanked God for suspending the snow and replacing the dark, gray cold with an ideal night.

"How did you know my name?" I asked at last.

He gave me a shy, sideways look. "Everyone knows the name of the prettiest girl in Angel Ridge."

I blushed at his compliment. My heart beat so loudly, I feared he must surely hear it. "Thank you," I managed. "What's your name?"

"John."

John. Such a common name. *His name should be Michael or Gabriel,* I thought. For this man was far from common.

When we reached the center of town square, he invited me to sit on the park bench near the bronze angel monument. I did and spread out the skirt of my dress. He watched me and smiled. "You look very fetching tonight, Mary. Your grandma is the best seamstress in Angel Ridge."

I frowned. "How'd you know my grammy made this?"

He shrugged. "All the folks who can afford it hire her to make their dresses at Christmas and Easter, don't they?"

"Yes. That's how she manages to give all her twenty-seven grandchildren Christmas presents."

"She's a good woman. You're blessed with a fine family, Mary."

I thought he must be missing his parents somethin' fierce tonight. "Would you like to come back to my house for dinner? Mama always puts out a big spread on Christmas Eve." One more would hardly even be noticed.

"Thank you, but I'll have to be gettin' on."

"Where do you live, John?"

"Up in the tall pines." He nodded to the hills just north of town.

"You know, it's strange. I've lived here all my life, but the only time I've ever seen you and your family was on Christmas Eve."

John smiled sadly. He slid his arm around behind me, resting it against the bench. "My pa didn't like comin' into town or goin' to church. But my ma, she always said that as long as we were alive and able, we ought to honor the Creator at least one day a year." He turned away then, but not before I saw the wistful look in his pale eyes. "Christmas was her favorite time of the year. She so loved seein' the town all gussied up. It was nice livin' with them these past years."

He made it sound as if he wasn't really a part of their family. "Were you adopted?" I asked.

"I guess you could say they took me in," he said evasively. "Come on. There's somethin' I'd like to show you."

I thought I should be getting back, but couldn't bring myself to leave him. Not yet, anyway. He drew me close. I couldn't take my eyes off him. He seemed to radiate an inner light that made me all warm inside. Made me want to stay with him now, and always.

I stood and placed my hand in his. It was soft and warm, his fingers long and well-shaped, like a musician's. I felt safe with John, despite the fact that I knew next to nothing about him, and instinctively knew I could trust him with my very life.

We entered the woods and followed a well-worn path to a clearing, where we stopped and gazed up at the starry night sky. Tall trees surrounded us on all sides, creating an opening that looked like it could take a body straight to Heaven.

"It's beautiful," I said reverently.

"Close your eyes."

With my hand still in his, and my head tipped back, I did as he asked.

"Listen."

I tried, but heard nothing more than the sound of my own heart beating. He moved around behind me and wrapped his arms about my waist. I rested my head on his shoulder, my eyes still closed.

"Now, breathe in . . . deep and slow. Then breathe out."

I placed my arms atop his and moved my fingers along the back of his hands. His cheek felt like the smoothest silk against mine. A sense of contentment came over me such as I had never known. Absolute serenity. Perfect peace.

"Do you hear it now?" I felt his lips brush against my ear when he spoke.

It was when I felt his breath on my face that I heard it . . . A chorus of perfectly blended voices singing praises. It floated down on us in a charmed moment suspended in time.

I wanted to open my eyes, to look into his

and tell him of the joy I felt, but a pleasant lethargy that dictated I keep them closed overcame me.

The voices lifted to a distant hum almost like the sound of crickets in summertime. John's warm, soft lips caressed my cheek, murmuring words of love that he wrote on my heart. His beautiful hand trailed up the curve of my neck to tilt my head slightly until his lips hovered above mine. When our lips at last touched, our souls eternally intertwined. In that moment, I knew I belonged to John. Then, and forevermore.

Wanting to share my feelings with him, I at last opened my eyes. To my profound dismay, I found myself alone in the woods, my hands holding nothing more substantial than a bough of mistletoe.

"John?" I called out, as I looked all about the clearing. The cold of the chill December night pressed in on me, making me shiver uncontrollably. "John!" I called again, but the sound of my voice echoed and fell into the oppressive silence that surrounded me.

*Next year . . .* the wind seemed to whisper the words from the tall pines. *On Christmas Eve . . . always on Christmas Eve.*

As I made my way back to the church on legs numbed by the cold, I puzzled over what had just happened. I should have been desolate, having found my one true love, only to lose him. But instead, the contentment and peace I had experienced while in the clearing with John, remained with me.

When I re-entered the church, I walked to the third pew and sat next to my father.

"Where's your Bible, sweetie?" he asked just as Miss Ruth finished singing her carol.

I looked about the church and frowned. The Jones children squirmed as their mother scolded and their father just looked tired. The two pews behind them were filled. The back pew was filled as well, save the one spot at the end where John and I had sat.

"Did you leave it at home?" Papa pressed me when I didn't respond.

I looked back to him and said, "Yes. I must have."

He squeezed my cold hand and said, "That's all right. You can look at mine. Where'd you get the mistletoe?"

"What? Oh." I looked down at the rich green sprig I held in my hand. "Outside." I smiled a secret smile and touched my fingertips to my lips as I remembered the kiss I'd shared with John just before . . .

The preacher stood and began to read the Christmas story. The sermon about God's gift of love at Christmastime held a new meaning for me. I thank God for showing the world His love, and for giving me John's.

He came to me again the next Christmas Eve, and every Christmas Eve since. The gift of John's love has sustained me all the days of my long life. Although I only have him with me one day a year, he's never far away. When I need him, his presence surrounds me like a comforting hug. When I long to see him, I catch a glimpse of him as he disappears around a corner. When I ache for him, he comes to me in my dreams.

He promises that someday we'll be together for eternity. Oh, how I long for that time to come when, at last, our love will be complete. But until then, we'll have Christmas Eve.

# DIXIE'S READING GROUP DISCUSSION QUESTIONS FOR A HOME FOR CHRISTMAS

1. In *A Home for Christmas,* Janice Thornton wants something so badly, she's afraid to even hope for it, much less seriously consider it a possibility: a home and a family. Have you ever wanted something that much? How did you overcome the fear and go after it?

2. Blake Ferguson has dreams, too. Dreams of a home filled with a large, loving, traditional family. Discuss his methods for going after Janice and winning her heart despite the reality that a traditional family with her would not likely be possible.

3. Miss Estelee sure is an interesting character with a lot of unanswered questions surrounding her like how old is she really? Where did she come from? Why did she never marry? Who broke her heart, or did she do the breaking? And what about her

373

and Doc Prescott? What do you think that's about?

4. Blake and his brother, Cory, have a sibling rivalry. Have you experienced this or do you know someone who has? How do you deal with sibling rivalry? Is it possible to avoid sibling rivalry in a large family?

5. Blake has anger management issues. Why do you think he has anger issues?

6. Having grown up together, Dixie is long-time friends with the town sheriff, Grady Wallace. What do you think the future holds for these two characters? Will Dixie find love with Grady?

7. What Christmas traditions did you enjoy as a child that hold warm memories for you? Are there any in *A Home for Christmas* that you'd like to adopt for your Christmas celebrations?

8. Do you believe that Christmas is a time for miracles? Have you ever experienced a Christmas miracle?

9. Which do you prefer at the top of your

tree and why? An angel or a star or maybe a ribbon. If you have an angel this year, will you make a wish on it?

10. Discuss storylines and characters you would like to see in the Angel Ridge Novels. Designate a person in your group to write them up, send them to Deborah Grace Staley, P.O. Box 672, Vonore, TN 37885. If your idea is chosen to appear in a book, you reader's group will receive an acknowledgement in the novel!

Please follow the Angel Ridge Blog
www.angelridgenovels.blogspot.com

# MEET THE AUTHOR

A life-long resident of East Tennessee, **Deborah Grace Staley** is the youngest of four children. Since there were not a lot of neighborhood children to play with and no siblings close in age, she learned to amuse herself by creating stories that played out in her head. For some reason, she never gave a thought to committing them to paper.

Her love of romance novels was born between high school and college by reading as many as one per day. After earning her degree, she tried out a couple of careers before settling into the legal field. Meanwhile, she kept reading romance while her own stories kept spinning around in her head, but now were demanding to be written. So she took a couple of novel writing courses, joined Romance Writers of America, and began attending conferences for romance writers.

It took nine years before Deborah's dream

of being a published romance novelist became a reality. Still, she never doubted that it would happen when the time was right. "To every thing there is a season, and a time to every purpose under the heaven." Ecclesiastes 3:1.

Today, Deborah has retired from the life of a paralegal and works in higher education. Married to her college sweetheart, they make their home on five acres in Maryville, Tennessee in a circa 1867 farmhouse with gingerbread trim that has Angel's Wings. She has one son whom she loves to watch play baseball.

Now that her stories are out of her head and on paper, she's so thankful for the opportunity to share them! She loves to hear from readers via e-mail at dgracestaley@aol.com or via snail mail at P.O. Box 672, Vonore, Tennessee, 37885. Visit her website at www.deborahgracestaley.com

The employees of Thorndike Press hope you have enjoyed this Large Print book. All our Thorndike, Wheeler, and Kennebec Large Print titles are designed for easy reading, and all our books are made to last. Other Thorndike Press Large Print books are available at your library, through selected bookstores, or directly from us.

For information about titles, please call:
(800) 223-1244

or visit our Web site at:
http://gale.cengage.com/thorndike

To share your comments, please write:
Publisher
Thorndike Press
295 Kennedy Memorial Drive
Waterville, ME 04901